PAY THE PRICE

SAMANTHA GAIL

DSTAR PUBLISHING

For Kathleen Workman;
Thank you for believing in me even when I couldn't believe in myself

CONTENT WARNINGS

This book contains graphically explicit material that is not suitable for readers under 18 years of age. Please know that reader discretion is advised. Content includes, but is not limited to:

- -(on page) sexual assault
- -(on page) sexual assault of a child
- -repeated acts of torture and body mutilation
- -(on page) rape
- -degradation
- -references to suicide
- -knife violence
- -gun violence
- -religious abuse and manipulation
- -physical, mental, and psychological abuse
- -slut shaming
- -murder

Please read with your mental health in mind.

PREFACE

"Revenge is an act of passion; vengeance of justice. Injuries are revenged; crimes are avenged."
    -English writer, Samuel Johnson

CHAPTER
ONE

1990

He watched her closely from above the newspaper clutched in his hand and periodically sipped from the black coffee on the table. She continued to greet customers as they entered the coffee shop, upselling the new cinnamon bread they could sample with their morning joes. Her laughter filled the room when one of her regulars cracked a joke about the "spring breeze" blowing outside during what was one of the worst storms of the season.

This was exactly why Duke was intoxicated with her. Even a stuffy joke from a middle-aged man in a cheap suit elicited a spark that only she could provide. No one was too small for her to notice while everyone deserved a bright grin and kind word. She took the job requirement of making every customer feel special and welcomed to heart, which had resulted in Duke's presence in the coffee bar every day for the past seven weeks. No matter how long he lingered, no matter how many refills he requested, Alessa's cheerful reply, "Coming right up!" caused an animalistic ache in the pit of his stomach. He didn't know how long he could wait to possess her.

Watching her had become his sole obsession, and he lived for the moments when he could steal her attention away from the other guests.

If he knew how to manage it, Duke would lock the doors and prevent anyone else from entering the shop. He longed to see Alessa alone and away from the prying eyes of the world. She was meant for him—that certainty was as strong as his instinct to breathe. Alessa would forever change his life.

"You're not gonna hurt my feelings by turning down a sample of this cinnamon bread, are you?" Alessa's hazel eyes had a mischievous twinkle in them as she extended a basket across the table to Duke. He was so lost in his thoughts he didn't see her approach. He silently chided himself on his carelessness. He didn't like to ever be caught by surprise.

"Just the coffee, as always," Duke replied softly. He stared intensely at her face, trying to memorize every freckle, every crease that created her beautiful glow. Truly, with her light blonde hair surrounding her thin face, Duke wondered if others could see the halo hovering just above her. He had never ordered anything other than coffee, yet every morning she attempted to entice him to eat one of their many pastries or sandwiches. He found it endearing that she continued to offer despite his multitude of refusals. It was yet another reason Alessa captivated his attention, for no one else had ever displayed that kind of fortitude with him.

She smiled even brighter at his rejection. "One of these days I'll find out what you like!" She offered a quick wink and then returned to her place behind the counter to restock the muffins on display. Duke absent-mindedly turned another page on the newspaper, not bothering to read a single word. Her words echoed in his head.

He intended to show her exactly what he liked.

2011

"You're assigned the patients in Room 212, 214, and 216 today," Mary, the charge nurse, instructed. "And don't let me catch you out back smoking again all day!"

Stella rolled her eyes and grabbed the charts Mary placed on the counter in front of her. Mary was just being a bitch because her husband said she had to stop smoking. Stella would love to tell Mary where she could shove it, but jobs that paid this well to be a glorified babysitter didn't come around very often in this town. Instead, she headed down the hall to check on the patients in her assigned rooms.

The man in Room 212 was sitting up in bed and eating what looked like oatmeal a cat vomited up. Stella tried hard not to pucker her nose at the smell, but he seemed to like it, so who was she to argue? She doublechecked his chart and informed him that they would be in to transport him down to dialysis in an hour. The man nodded without really looking at her, staring blankly out the window and chewing on the vomit/oatmeal mess in his bowl. Hopefully all the patients would be this easy today.

Room 214 proved to be an even easier case as his charts indicated that nearly every hour of every day was filled with some kind of therapy.

"I can handle this," Stella muttered to herself. Her fingers itched along the outside of her back pocket where her cigarettes were waiting for her first break of the day. Sixteen-hour shifts were far too long for a nurse aid to be much good to anyone, but in a state facility like this, there were never enough employees for the number of patients hospitalized.

Rounding the corner, Stella found Room 216 in an alcove that looked as if it was originally intended to be a janitor's closet. The room itself was small enough that she momentarily questioned if it *was* a closet that had simply been mislabeled with a room number. However, a small hospital bed was pushed against the far wall, with a rectangular window at the top illuminating the tiny room with dismal gray light. Stella could see the peeling roof of the hospital from where she stood in the doorway, but nothing more than that. She approached the patient's bed with caution as the room was eerily quiet. Although the man in the bed was connected to several different machines attached to the wall behind him, not a single one produced a sound of any kind. The man's dark brown eyes darted to her face, questioning her appearance. They widened slightly as she stepped closer to his bedside, and an involuntary shudder slid down her spine. There was something eerie about him, some kind of warped familiarity that she couldn't quite put her finger on.

"What's your name?" Stella asked. The man's eyes glanced down to the chart at the end of his bed and back to her.

"What, cat got your tongue?" she said. Silence continued to envelop them until she rolled her eyes again with impatience. Snatching his chart, Stella saw that the man was in fact a quadriplegic and completely unable to move.

"No one knows if he can actually speak or not," Mary suddenly said from behind, causing Stella to jump and drop the man's chart on the ground. "Never made a peep since they brought him in."

"So what am I supposed to do with him all day?" Stella asked with irritation.

Mary shrugged. "Try to get him to talk. Keep him alive, I guess. He's not really one we worry about here." She turned on her heel and left.

Probably to go antagonize another poor soul, Stella thought bitterly.

Turning around the room, Mary's words sunk in as Stella observed the dust gathered on the solitary chair next to the door and the cobwebs stretching across the corners of the room. Clearly housekeeping didn't even bother with this patient anymore. Stella picked up the chart and read the man's name aloud, "Avery Winslow." The man had no reaction but continued to gaze at her with an unwavering stare that made Stella feel uncomfortable.

"Doesn't your family ever come to visit you and raise hell about this shit?" Stella asked. She couldn't imagine a complaint of this magnitude going unnoticed with upper management.

Further inspection of his chart revealed that there were no family members listed. "So you're a loner, like me," Stella said. "It's much easier that way, believe me. Although hell, you already know that by now."

The chart didn't contain much more information. For all Stella knew, the man had every known ailment medicine could identify. Avery might as well not even be in the hospital.

Stella grabbed a pillowcase from the bottom drawer of a small cabinet in the opposite corner and wiped off the chair. She pulled the chair closer to Avery and plopped herself down, propping her non-work approved black combat boots on the bed. A quick glance out the door revealed the interior of the room could not be seen from the hospital hallway beyond. Stella whipped out a cigarette, turning on the air vent as she did so. "You don't mind if I smoke, right? Not gonna rat me out?"

Avery's eyes bored into her face and Stella interpreted this as acquiescence. She lit the cigarette and inhaled a slow drag, enjoying the burning feeling traveling through her lungs.

How did I wind up like this? she wondered.

Life sure had a funny way of beating her down. While working at the hospital could never be called dull, it certainly wasn't where she imagined she would be at this point. Having to sneak cigarette breaks like she was back in high school made her back teeth grind in irritation.

Still, a nurse's assistant was a lot better than a felon, sex worker, or bitter baby mama like all of the other girls she grew up with. Stella would take her independence any day of the week over being in their shoes. Despite how much she slacked off at work, she really did work hard to get herself out of the gutter.

But as she looked around the drab gray room, adamantly ignoring the intense stare of the patient in the hospital, Stella failed to see how her current location looked much different.

1990

Another week had gone by with Alessa's kindness radiating to his soul. She had never noticed, but Duke began to follow her outside of work, too. He knew about her roommate and their two-bedroom apartment near the university, Alessa's daily morning run through campus, and her preference for Chinese takeout from the restaurant at the end of her block. She was a creature of habit, blissfully oblivious to the man stalking her every move. He even managed to watch her through her bedroom window one night when she forgot to pull the blinds all the way down.

The way he felt watching her undress and massage lotion into her body caused Duke to touch himself right there in the middle of the sidewalk. His need to possess her nearly overwhelmed him and he couldn't believe his own recklessness. Mother had never explained the physical manifestations of love and Duke's thoughts ran wild with images of Alessa's naked body under his own.

His poor mother was home alone, but that was a guilt trip for another time. He couldn't allow thoughts of her condition to permeate his limited time with Alessa. Seeing her from a distance, never being allowed to touch her, to love her in the ways in which she deserved, already served as a special kind of torment. Mother would use other methods to punish him for his disobedience, though he wanted to make the argument that dark magic was already at work.

Mother had warned him for as far back as he could remember about the evil that dictated the world outside their home. It was why they remained together in the farmhouse he grew up in despite his ventures into town—he was too scared to leave the safety of Mother's arms. She taught him about dark magic, the hateful, sinful power that infiltrated others and let them do wicked things. But Mother assured him that she would always protect him as long as he obeyed her. He believed it and had never had a reason to question her.

Duke's muscles tensed as a young man with tanned skin and gelled blonde hair walked into the coffee shop. Alessa's smile could light up the room when she saw him. A small squeal escaped her lips and she rushed around the counter to throw her arms around him.

Who the fuck was this?!

"You told me you wouldn't be back until next week!" she gushed to the man, her hands roaming through his hair and down his neck. His cream-colored shirt stretched tightly across his back and Duke could see the faint line of a black tattoo through the thin material. Mother always said tattoos were a mark of the Devil. Only those living in sin marred the perfect canvas God created of their flesh.

The man pulled Alessa in tighter so her entire body was pressed against his. Duke's vision began to darken around the edges.

The man smiled. "The project finished early, so I hopped on the first plane I could get." He leaned in to kiss her and Duke's fist slammed into the mug on the table, knocking it to the floor. Alessa immediately pulled from the man's embrace to clean up the spill.

Duke glared at him while she wiped the coffee off the floor with a rag hastily grabbed from the kitchen. It felt as though the rage building inside him would set off an atomic bomb. The man did not seem to notice, watching Alessa intently as she threw away broken pieces of the ceramic mug. "Let me get you a fresh cup," she told Duke.

Returning back behind the counter, the man stepped forward. "I hate that you work here, sweetheart. Now that my project is over, please just stay home. This is beneath you." The pompous tone to his voice set Duke's teeth on edge. This man had no clue what Alessa was capable of, the warmth and light she radiated, and how, like a moth to a flame, Duke could not stay away if he tried.

She merely gave him a patient smile and said, "We'll talk about this later." She returned to Duke's table, a new mug filled with steaming hot coffee in hand. "Are you okay over here? Did any of that coffee spill on you?" It took Duke a moment to register it was he to whom she spoke.

"No," he shook his head and sent another glare in the man's direction. "Who is that?"

Alessa giggled as she glanced back. "Oh, him? He's my fiancé, Harrison. He won't bother you, I promise." She brushed her hair behind her ears and her face flushed slightly as she met Duke's eyes. He wondered if he had anything to do with this reaction or if it was all Harrison's doing. She returned to the counter and engaged Harrison in conversation, fully bending over to lean towards his words. Although Duke could not see from his angle in the shop, he was certain that Alessa's voluptuous breasts were on full display for this intruder. Duke gripped the newspaper in his hand so tightly that the pages began to tear.

Although he could not hear their whispered conversation, Duke glared at the pair through slitted eyes. He had watched Alessa nearly every day for two months and never once had he seen a ring on any finger. She had never gone anywhere with this man, and never once indicated she was in any kind of relationship, let alone one committed to marriage. This revelation had him seething and greatly complicated Duke's plans.

Upon further examination, Harrison's profile began to look vaguely familiar. Duke could not quite place where he had seen him before, but there was something recognizable in his features. No matter the level of familiarity, Harrison was a bug that must be squashed. An interference of this kind would not prevent Duke from uniting with Alessa. Of that, he was certain.

2011

"So what did you do to wind up in here?" Stella asked the silent patient. She had smoked through half a pack of cigarettes and scoured his room for anything interesting with which she might entertain herself. Every surface was covered with a heavy layer of dust. There was not so much as a change of clothing in any of the drawers. Her other patients had long gone onto their various appointments, but in a room without a view or even a book, there was little to occupy her time. Sheer boredom had led her to inquisitively pepper him with questions, though Avery's mouth never opened in an attempt to respond. He continued to watch her, rarely blinking, in a way that unsettled her.

The cloudy gray light filtering through the window reminded Stella of one of her foster homes, the third home she was placed in, but the home that probably had the most lasting impact. It was the only one that stuck out clearly in her memory, a small farmhouse in rural Ohio, which was often shrouded in cloudy gray days the same as the weather currently outside the window. There were five foster children there at the time, including Stella, as well as Mr. and Mrs. Barton and their three children. Their biological children were treated far better than the foster kids; by that time, Stella had spent long enough in the system to know that is always how families operated. Foster kids were dispensable, a dime a dozen, constantly rotating through homes and hands. The Bartons were no different, using foster kids as a free labor force to care for their farm animals and clean their barn. The days were long, filled with cow shit and arduous work, and for the other children, each night led to an exhausted sleep from working in the fields all day. This was never the case for Stella.

Even now Stella could smell the faint wisp of whiskey and tobacco from Mr. Barton's stale breath as he hovered his body over her in the tool shed. She shook her head as the fear gripped her heart again, refusing to allow the memory to consume her in the present.

Stella grabbed Avery's chart again, though she had read through it more than eight times so far. Other than the obvious limitations of his paralysis, he actually had few health issues listed. It was hard to determine ailments when the patient never communicated them. All the other patients in the hospital would complain if they got so much as a papercut because it meant a visit to the doctor rather than sitting in their bed. She had been surprised to discover Avery had been in the same room for nearly 20 years.

I would rather scratch my own eyes out, she thought.

Although Stella had not worked at the hospital for very long, she had only been in this particular unit for a few short weeks. The reassignment was meant to "temper her rebellious spirit," according to the memo on file with Human Resources. Apparently working with terminal patients was supposed to reduce the number of complaints Stella received while simultaneously allowing the hospital to retain an employee, a rarity at the moment. She had no desire to kiss up to anyone in this unit either, and so far everyone was exactly the same: inflated egos that demanded reverence. Stella longed to be the one holding the pin that made them all pop.

Still, it wasn't a bad gig, all things considered. She had been emancipated from the foster care system at 16-years-old after rushing through her GED and a state tested nurse aid program. The judge agreed it was in everyone's best interest for Stella to finally be on her own and responsible for herself. They meant it as reality check, but the lesson had been for them: Stella thrived on her own and succeeded in supporting herself legally without any further run ins with law enforcement. She would rather jump off the Golden Gate Bridge than to ever risk going back to jail. One of the only things she ever fought for in her life was to have her juvenile record remain sealed. She had not had a single incident since.

Even Stella had limits. This job presented a nearly unlimited earning potential since they were always so short staffed. So while she was not going to make friends any time soon, she knew it was better for her in the long run to play their game. Besides, terminal patients did not really bother her. Death was inevitable and most people deserved to die far earlier than they did, in her opinion. "The road to Judgment Day was packed" was always the running joke in her last group home.

Suddenly one of the machines above the man's head began a low beep. Stella hit the acknowledgement button to turn off the sound and followed the tube down to the side of the bed. Avery's colostomy bag had filled with urine and feces, but the crusty remnants at the top indicated how long it had been since a clean bag was provided. She suspected the previous STNA would simply empty out the bag in the toilet and reattach it since colostomy bags were expensive and often scarce in a poorly funded state hospital.

Unable to restrain herself, she lifted Avery's sheet and dressing gown to follow the tubes to his penis. While there was some redness, there were no signs of infection. Stella shrugged and left the bag alone. There was still some room for additional urine and perhaps if he got a little uncomfortable from a urinary tract infection, he would start talking. Clearly no one else was going to come in the room and check him anyway.

She imagined the look on Mary's face if she, Stella, got to announce that the mute patient finally spoke. There would finally be a real reason for the stale "celebration" cake in the break room every other day. Stell might actually be deemed good enough to be off the Human Resources' naughty list and have her disciplinary probation end.

Inspiration setting in, she sat back down with a manic glee in her eyes. "Avery," she stated, "I think I'm gonna be the one to make you talk."

CHAPTER
FIVE

1990

Duke's hands began to numb from the cold as he stood across the street from the law office Harrison entered an hour ago. Although he was confident he concealed himself well behind the dumpster in the alleyway, Duke knew that if someone were to come upon him there was no reasonable explanation for his presence there. Duke had never been one to operate without a plan, but the need to learn more about this Harrison person and determine if he would derail his future with Alessa was too great. He had come too far and was too close to give up.

Without warning, Harrison strode briskly out of the office and entered a black BMW parked in front of the building. He was now carrying a briefcase, but his face displayed an arrogance that only wealth could instill. Duke's brain suddenly connected the dots and recognized where he had seen Harrison before. This was none other than Harrison Pierce, the rich socialite known for his distaste of his status and wealth. Duke had read about him in the newspaper while sitting at the coffee shop.

Although Harrison did not actually work or run a business of any kind, his wealth and reputation only seemed to be growing. There had been several articles describing Harrison as an eccentric who refused to associate with anyone.

How could that be Alessa's fiancé?

Since Duke's vehicle was still parked near the coffee shop, he abandoned Harrison and headed back to pick up the van. Alessa should be getting off work soon and as it was Thursday, she would have two classes back to back at the university. Without a campus permit or ID, Duke had little access to her there. Thursday was his least favorite day of the week.

It was pure kismet that led Duke into that coffee shop in the first place. He had never been allowed to drink the stuff because Mother claimed it stunted people's growth. She wanted him to be a big man because Mother felt "big men get the job done." Duke never quite learned what job that was, but he grew up with the idea that he needed to reach a certain size to be a real man. One fateful morning on a walk to the post office, a sudden freezing rain drove him to seek shelter inside the coffee house.

As Duke stepped inside, a strong gust of wind hurled the door wide open. He yanked on the handle and felt another set of arms joined him. The wind and rain sprayed into their faces, but with a fourth and final tug, the door closed with a snap. His companion began to laugh next to him, a lilting symphony that caused something to stir in Duke's chest. His eyes lit upon Alessa, her golden hair damp and plastered to her face and a wide smile brightening the room. Duke's mind completely blanked as to where he was or why he was there as time stood still. Her beauty overwhelmed his senses.

Her rich laughter continued to ring out through the shop. "Who says you can't have an adventure as a barista?" she cried. The merriment dancing in her eyes was so foreign to Duke; he had never seen eyes with such mirth before.

She went to the counter and grabbed some napkins that she handed to Duke. "See if these will help wipe you up while I grab a clean towel from the back!"

Moving on autopilot, Duke blotted a few spots on his face. What was happening? Why did he feel this way? The woman quickly returned, carrying two raggedy towels and handed the larger one to Duke.

"I'm Alessa," she said. "Let me get you a cup of coffee, on the house."

Suddenly Duke knew what Mother was talking about when she explained the concept of soulmates to him. Alessa was an angel who was waiting for him this whole time. He was struck by love at first sight, and Cupid's arrow aimed dead center to his heart. She was his real purpose in the world. He only had to prove it to her.

In the two months since that day, Duke stalked Alessa like a hunter after his prey. She consumed his every thought, determined his every action, and he wasted away hours upon hours imagining their future together. He did not know how to approach her, or even what to say if he mustered the courage, but for the time being simply gazing at her was enough. He learned so much by merely observing her interactions with her co-workers and the customers at the coffee place. Duke never had any friends before, nor had he ever really associated with anyone other than his mother, so the grace with which Alessa managed her relationships both shocked and enthralled him. She was so kind, so considerate, in a way that warmed his heart and made him yearn for a life outside his farm. Mother always cautioned him against "townies" because of their dark magic and sinful ways, but how could Alessa be evil when her laugh caused Duke's chest to flutter? How could someone so positive be so horrible?

Mother was wrong. Alessa was pure and true, a woman worthy of joining their family. Now that Harrison Pierce had arrived, clearly full of dark magic that could destroy Duke's happiness, it was time for Duke to claim Alessa once and for all.

CHAPTER
SIX

2011

Stella felt triumphant. She managed to pilfer a couple scalpels, several needles, and a small bottle of rubbing alcohol from the surgery supply room without Mary or any of the other staff noticing. It wasn't really stealing, Stella figured, if it meant the patient in Room 216 began to speak. Her methods might raise a few eyebrows from the powers that be, but if no one had voiced a concern over the care of this patient yet, she doubted anyone would notice if he had a couple small marks.

Back in Avery's room, it was as if no time has passed. The man laid as stoically in his bed as he did before, his eyes never wavering from her face. As Stella wheeled a patient table next to him and placed her tools down, there was no trace of fear or question. For some reason, this irritated her.

"Do you not even care what this means, dude?" she huffed. She held a razor sharp 23 scalpel in front of his face. "I can gut you like a fish and you aren't gonna do shit about it, are you?"

He continued to gaze into her eyes without so much as glancing at the scalpel. There was no indication he even understood, which only drove Stella's irritation further. Weaknesses were the worst trait a person could have. Being weak at the group home would get you beaten up after the case workers left. Being weak would mean all your belongings were stolen and you were bullied by all the other kids who sensed your inferiority. Stella learned very quickly that she could not allow herself to show any weakness. She often took it upon herself to shove the crybabies into walls or throw their shoes into the dumpster to help toughen them up. The world was gonna shit on them no matter what, so it was really an act of mercy for her to make them understand that sooner rather than later. Avery Winslow was just another poor sap who needed to be broken and Stella would be the one to do it.

Stella grabbed Avery's right hand, closest to the opposite wall. Using the scalpel gingerly, Stella carved around his pinky nail, drawing a small pool of blood that trickled down his finger. The movement felt odd to her since she had never held an instrument like that before. She eagerly watched his face for any sign of pain, however. Although he did not utter a sound, Stella felt sure his eyes looked tearful. At least they were finally off her face and giving his awful stare to the ceiling.

She tried again on the ring finger on his right hand. This time she plunged the scalpel in a little deeper as her hand grew more familiar with the movements. There was far more blood, enough to create a stain on the sheets as it dripped down between his fingers. She eagerly moved on to the middle finger, slicing around the fingernail so deeply she felt the hard jolt as the scalpel hit bone. As she glanced up at Avery, Stella was elated to see a single tear roll down his cheek, his eyes never wavering from the ceiling.

"Guess you do feel pain, eh?" Stella taunted him. "You can't keep playing dumb with me, dude." She jerked his chin roughly to face her. His eyes did not betray any sign of pain, but another tear slipped down his cheek. "I'm gonna make you talk, one way or another."

Stella glanced quickly at her watch and realized she needed to go pick up one of her other charges soon. She roughly yanked the white blanket with the blood stains off and rolled it up into a ball. As long as she dropped it off in the laundry herself rather than letting a housekeeper pick it up, no one would realize it came from Room 216.

She grabbed some cotton and the rubbing alcohol to briskly wipe around his fingers. Unless a doctor came in to examine his fingernails, from the doorway the hand would look the same. Just in case, Stella threw the new blanket over his entire body, leaving only his head and neck exposed. She wrapped a rag around the scalpel and other utensils and slid those into her pocket. She would take them home rather than risk getting caught in the Sterilization Lab again.

Outside the room, Stella felt her elation return. The power racing through her made her feel immortal. She had managed to cut that man and not get caught! And he proved that he did have some feeling left if he was able to feel those cuts to his fingernails! Not all quadriplegics do, according to one of the medical journals lying in the staff room. Although he had not uttered a sound, he showed emotion, which was more than any of his records indicated Avery Winslow was capable of.

He probably deserved to have his hand hurt, Stella reasoned, if he did something to end up there at the state facility. She was doing a public service, really. And as long as she didn't get caught, there was no reason she shouldn't continue.

CHAPTER
SEVEN

1990

The time had come for Duke to put his desires into action. Harrison had been at the coffee shop daily, dominating all of Alessa's time and attention, though he wore crude disguises like ratty baseball caps and large, square sunglasses. Duke could tell who he was simply by the arrogant swagger in all his movements. Alessa seemed immune to Harrison's condescension and frequently laughed off the man's barbed comments about how filthy the shop was or how lowly it appeared for Alessa to work as a barista. She would smile at Harrison whenever he said something too harsh, cupping his cheek with one of her delicate hands, and remind him that she was exactly where she wanted to be so that ought to be good enough for him. Duke silently cheered her on every time she put the asshole in his place.

For that was most assuredly the kind of person Harrison Pierce was. Duke had continued to follow him to various banks, restaurants, and once even to an art gallery over the past week. It infuriated him to lose time in any capacity with Alessa, but there was no alternative if he was going to get rid of Harrison Pierce for good. At every location Duke observed the man to be pompous and rude, especially to anyone in the service industry. He could not fathom how someone as beautiful and kind as Alessa could be drawn to a demon like Harrison, but it had to be some sort of evil spell like Mother always talked about. If Duke was ever going to have a future with Alessa, he needed to act fast and protect her.

In all of the times when Duke followed them, never once did he see Harrison and Alessa go anywhere in public together. It was rather odd, even to Duke's limited knowledge of relationships, that they never had any kind interaction outside of visits to the coffee bar. In the novels he had read as a teenager, courtship involved dancing, romantic gestures, and physical intimacy. If he had been engaged to Alessa, Duke reasoned to himself, he would have trouble stopping himself from shouting it on every rooftop in the area. He would need to place it on a billboard along the county highway near his home. Alessa was not the type of woman you hide, she was the kind of woman who deserved monuments to the sky declaring worship at her feet.

Duke knew Alessa arrived at work around 5 a.m. every morning. She was the only employee present for several hours because business did not pick up until more students were heading on campus for the day. Most of the other businesses along the road did not open until much later in the morning, making traffic nearly nonexistent at this time of day. There would not be anyone to see what Duke was about to do.

The sky was still an inky black, stars as the only bright pinpoints in the monotony. Even the air was still in the hush of the early morning. A sense of purpose radiated down to the depths of his soul, making his adrenaline pump that much harder with anticipation. He pulled his mother's old van into the alleyway behind the coffee bar and turned off the ignition. It was approximately ten minutes until five, plenty of time for him to lie in wait for her.

What Duke was not anticipating was Harrison's presence that morning. The interloper's arm possessively encircled Alessa's waist as they aimlessly milled to the back door together. Alessa's eyes were gleaming and happy even in the darkness of the alley, and Duke felt a surge of jealousy so strong it made bile rise in his throat. It should be his arm wrapped around Alessa as he escorted her to work, not Harrison's.

Blinding, jealous rage was the only explanation for Duke's outburst.

He reached into the back seat of the van and pulled out a metal snow shovel he had recently purchased for the next winter and slowly exited the vehicle. He did not close the door and ignored the ringing in his ears as he approached the pair, shovel raised behind his head. Alessa gave a startled cry a second too late as Duke brought the shovel down hard, bladed side down, against Harrison Pierce's forehead. Blood seeped out from the blow to the man's head and he crumpled in a heap at Duke's feet. Alessa opened her mouth in horror and swallowed a gulp of air in preparation to scream, but Duke dropped the shovel and seized her, firmly gripping her mouth closed.

"You will do exactly as I say, Alessa," he whispered to her. A dull ache formed in his stomach at the terror in her beautiful hazel eyes as she cowered back from his touch. He did not want to frighten her. "I will save you from him and everything will be fine."

Confusion furrowed her eyebrows together and she shook her head violently. It sounded as though she was trying to repeat the word "no" over and over again from beneath his hand.

Duke sighed heavily. This is what he had been afraid of when he realized Harrison had her under a dark spell.

"I'm sorry, my love," he murmured, the smell of her hair intoxicating him. He pulled her closer to him so his entire body felt her warmth. "This is for your own good." He quickly cracked the back of her head into the concrete wall behind her and leaned down to catch her as her body slumped forward. She was out cold.

Gingerly, he scooped up her legs and carried her to the back of the van. He already had a blanket and small pillow forming a makeshift bed. Just in case, he tied a thick rope around her wrists behind her back as well as her ankles. That would have to do until they returned home and he could use the chains. There was no telling what the dark magic would make her do in order to return to Harrison.

Duke turned back to Harrison's body. The man was beginning to rouse, turning his head to the side and tenderly pressing a hand over his open wound. Duke picked up the shovel and struck him again, this time with the flat side rather than the edge, and the man immediately quieted once more. It would only lead to more problems if Duke left him behind, so Harrison would need to come with them.

At least then I will have the joy of killing him, Duke thought.

He hastily tossed the shovel onto the passenger seat and began dragging Harrison's body around to the back of the van. Duke pulled Harrison by the ankles and felt a small thrill of satisfaction as Harrison's head bumped along a small pothole in the road. After stuffing the unconscious man tightly into the space behind the third row, Duke realized he had not brought anything else to tie the man's wrists and ankles together. He had not anticipated needing more than what Alessa would require.

Duke felt a nasty grin spread across his face. There was one thing in the van he could use. He retreated to the sliding door where Alessa had been deposited and pulled a small toolbox from underneath the driver's seat. He withdrew a pair of workman's heavy duty gloves from the back pocket of his jeans, a habitual placement when one lived in the country, and extracted a thick cord of barbed wire from the box, saying a silent prayer of thanks that he had not returned it as Mother had instructed. She had punished him severely when he came home with the thick coil of barbed wire rather than the chicken wire she requested, not that she had explained the difference prior to his purchase. Now it would serve a far better purpose.

He made quick work of the makeshift cuffs around Harrison's extremities, pulling down his socks to ensure the barbs stuck into his flesh. If he awoke during the car ride and tried to fight his bonds, it would decimate the arteries around his wrists. Duke nodded in satisfaction and returned the remaining wire to the toolbox. A shaft of moonlight illuminated Alessa's face and he paused, lovingly brushing the hair back from her forehead. Her radiant beauty still took his breath away. Too happy to contain his joy, Duke kissed her temple.

"Nothing will keep us apart now, my love," he promised before slamming the door shut.

CHAPTER
EIGHT

1990

Detective Edwin Greene sighed as he crumpled yet another sheet of paper at his desk. The weight of defeat was still something he struggled with after more than 30 years on the job. He closed his eyes and pinched the bridge of his nose as he allowed his mind to go blank in order to better collect his thoughts.

The Harrison Pierce case had no leads. For a trust fund brat with more money than God, he kept relatively few friends and a low profile. Outside of a housekeeper at the family estate, no one could recall relevant information as to his daily activities. Mr. Pierce apparently had a habit of confirming attendance at galas and benefits, then never showing up. In fact, Edwin suspected the timeline of when the man went missing was actually different than the day he was reported. It was hard to find a man who rarely appeared, but no one seemed to know where he was actually going. He answered to no one, and in that respect, Edwin had to admire him a bit. However, after two weeks of no contact with anyone, even an eccentric socialite was bound to be reported as missing.

"You got a minute?" The distinguished Deputy Police Chief Harry Millhouse entered Edwin's office without waiting for a response. Edwin noted the formal uniform, with numerous badges and crests pinned to

Millhouse's chest. The two men went through the Academy together, with Millhouse's ambition determining his rising star through the police force. While there was never an unfriendly word between them, Edwin found Millhouse's company to be exhausting. His focus never seemed to be so much on solving crimes, but on the notoriety and influence it could bring him to be associated with high profile cases. Since Edwin had been assigned the Harrison Pierce case, Millhouse had frequently stopped by the office to check in and offer sage tidbits like interviewing the staff again to see if they remembered anything else or checking the three other properties Pierce owned. Things that were all standard procedure anyway.

Edwin stood up to pour Millhouse a cup of coffee from the table in the back of the office. "What can I do for you, Harry?"

"I just finished a meeting with the Chief and Commissioner to finalize our upcoming budget. We've gotta prepare for the new recruits now that our funding grant was approved. We'll be hiring six new officers," Millhouse said proudly as though the funding was strictly his accomplishment and not something designated by the city council. "However, we all realized that hiring new officers doesn't mean much when there's no room for growth."

"So are you announcing your retirement?" Edwin teased. He felt a tightening in his chest of apprehension. He had a pretty good idea of where this conversation was headed.

Instead Millhouse laughed. "I haven't fully made my way up in the world just yet." His wry smile indicated how close he felt he was to achieving such. "No, actually your name sort of came up because we were thinking of officers who may be hitting the end of their service."

Edwin let out a slow breath. This is what he had been expecting as soon as Millhouse mentioned the budget, a budget Millhouse had actively campaigned for to gain recognition with the city council as the white knight of the police force. "I have no intentions of leaving the department any time soon, Harry," he stated firmly through clenched teeth. There had been pointed barbs directed his way for months about his supposedly imminent retirement and rumors circulated throughout the precinct. Edwin slammed the coffee mug down on the desk with enough force to slosh some over the side.

Millhouse held up his hands. "Whoa, whoa, just hear me out. It's not that you're not an asset to the department, you are! You've solved some of the worst crimes our city has faced." Edwin detected a hint of jealousy in Millhouse's tone at these words. "But you've been here in the same crime unit for most of your career. You're not moving up. You're not giving others a chance to tackle the big issues."

This caught Edwin by surprise. This meeting had nothing to do with money or pushing Edwin into retirement. This was purely motivated by Millhouse's disdain for Edwin's lack of promotion. As if Edwin had never been offered promotions and accolades throughout the years. Edwin chose to stay where he was because he liked the thrill of solving crimes and could not bear to ride out his days behind a desk. He had no interest in becoming another puppet for the Chief.

"So what are you trying to tell me?" Edwin finally sputtered. His skin felt hot and he acutely registered how much he needed a glass of stiff whiskey in his hand rather than a coffee mug. While he was grateful to know where the rumor mill started, it was unnerving to hear someone so cavalierly discuss his career—a career that had consumed his entire adult life.

Millhouse smiled again. "We are just having a discussion, Ed. There's no need to be testy. Nothing has been decided at the moment."

Edwin suspected this was false. Millhouse didn't tend to discuss things he did not already possess the power to change. Yet another reason Edwin avoided him when he could.

"I'm working the Harrison Pierce case right now. You know we can't trust something that high profile to just anybody. My record speaks for itself on that one."

Millhouse nodded in agreement. "But we could give you a partner to mentor so that he can take your place as soon as you decide to retire. Which can't be far off after 30 years," he pointedly added.

Edwin involuntarily shivered. He had a partner for his first couple years in the crime unit, a man everyone called Shelley. They were inseparable and moved so in tuned an observer would have thought they were mirror images. Edwin had never been so close to someone before and the sting of losing Shelley still hung around him in an immense, dark cloud. Losing Shelley was akin to losing a limb, not just a brother. Edwin had refused to work with anyone else since. He didn't think he could survive another loss and there was no good way to work these kinds of investigations without forming an airtight bond. To face these monsters, partners needed an infrangible trust, to know without hesitation that the person next to you would risk their life to save yours. It wasn't something you could develop with just anyone.

"Then what are you asking of me?" Edwin repeated.

"Oh no, I am telling you," Millhouse corrected him. "Your new partner will report tomorrow."

The indignation Edwin felt caused his otherwise calm demeanor to snap. "Like hell he will! You know I won't work with a partner!"

Millhouse shrugged and walked to the door. From the doorway, he turned back and said simply, "You don't have a choice, Edwin."

CHAPTER
NINE

1990

Duke dragged Harrison's limp body across the threshold and onto the floor in front of Alessa. He had not been able to contain himself upon arrival at the seclusion of his home and had quickly plunged a buck knife he used for hunting into the side of Harrison Pierce's head as soon as he parked the van. Harrison never woke from the last strike of the shovel, and now he never would. Minimizing the threat felt exhilarating.

Alessa screamed loudly into the rag wrapped across her mouth, choking on her sobs. The blood pooled around her feet from Harrison's head and she stood on the tips of her toes in a vain attempt to avoid the crimson puddle. Yet again she yanked her hands as if she had the strength to break the metal chain binding them to a support beam overhead.

Duke could see her eyes were bloodshot from crying, but this yielded only fury. How dare she cry for Harrison? He never loved her like Duke did. She didn't even realize how much better things would be now that she was here with him and Harrison was gone.

"I have to show you," Duke suddenly muttered. The comprehension sparked inspiration. He must woo Alessa properly; show her that he could be romantic, the true man of her dreams. In the books he read, Duke knew love was often sparked by grand gestures and soft words. Men planned dates, gave presents, and wrote poetry. Therefore Duke had to do the same. Without another glance at Harrison's body, Duke raced up the stairs on the far side of the room.

A few minutes later, a loud crack made Alessa jump. Duke pulled a small, round table down the stairs, one of its wooden legs wobbling dangerously. He placed the table underneath the lantern hanging from a post near the door and withdrew two stools from the darkness beyond. From his back pocket he revealed a soiled tablecloth that he draped over the top. After another trip up the stairs with another resounding crack, a plate with a few pieces of cheese and bread was placed on the table.

Standing back to admire his handiwork, Duke made a satisfied nod and advanced towards Alessa. "We're going to eat now, like a proper date," he told her. With one swift tug, the metal chain was pulled from its hook and Alessa crumpled into his arms. She immediately began to swing at Duke's face, but he merely pulled his head back without comment. Dropping her to the ground, he used the chain around her wrists to slog her thrashing body through Harrison's blood to the makeshift dinner table. Alessa continued to whip her limbs in any direction she could, but it was no match for Duke's strength. He sat her on a stool and took his place on the stool opposite her, with only enough room for the plate on the table between them. His eyes were burning with a passion and intensity that would frighten anyone when he said, "I'll remove the rag, but you cannot fight me."

The moment Duke's hand withdrew from her mouth, Alessa bit down with all the strength she could muster. With a bellow of rage, Duke backhanded her across the face. The force of the blow knocked her head back and she blinked rapidly as if to regain her vision.

"It's rude to turn down food, my love," Duke stated flatly.

"I'm not your love," Alessa spit venomously. "And I won't eat anything you've touched!"

This time the power behind his hand sent Alessa's body sprawling to the ground. Her head cracked against the stone floor and blood pooled on her scalp. Shivering, she glared at Duke's domineering form and whimpered.

His eyes burned into hers. "You will love me, and you will never leave me."

As he bent down to pick up the chain binding her wrists, Alessa made one last feeble attempt to fight him off by punching both fists against his jawline. While Duke did not even seem to register the blow, his facial expression hardened into one that elicited pure terror. His eyes went black and the muscles tensed across his entire body. Gruffly, he yanked her chin down and stuffed the rag back inside her mouth, further than before to where she was choking and gasping for air. Her hands automatically reached towards her mouth to pull the rag far enough out to breathe and Duke stopped them. With one violent tug, he pulled her arms forward by the chain binding her wrists and the *pop!* sound from Alessa's shoulders dislocating from her body echoed throughout the room. No rag was enough to cover the horrific screams Alessa shrieked. Her whole body went limp as Duke clamped the chain around her wrists back on the hook hanging from the support beam in the middle of the room.

CHAPTER
TEN

2011

The soda in Stella's bottle fizzed as she poured it into a paper cup. Bottles, even plastic ones, could be used as weapons by unruly patients and when launched as a projectile, they hurt. Stella had even learned the hard way once when a patient stole the bottle cap and tried to swallow it whole in order to make himself choke: boredom led people to do very stupid things. It had therefore become a force of habit to deposit her drinks into a paper cup while at work to avoid the chances of it being used against her. Although Avery Winslow did not necessarily pose a threat, she was used to the paper option by now.

Room 216 remained as silent as it had earlier; Avery appeared to be sleeping. Stella mused at whatever dream the man must be having because his sleep seemed fitful. His head turned sharply from side to side and a few beads of sweat worked their way down his nose. She fought the urge to wipe his brow and instead sat down to withdraw another cigarette from her pocket.

The man did not wake, but Stella enjoyed the peaceful solitude. The hospital was always so loud and there was always someone coding, most of the time on purpose. While the job was far from glamorous and not what she set out to do with her life, it wasn't the worst place she had ever worked. Most of the kids who were emancipated from the foster system around the same time as her had turned to selling drugs, selling their bodies, or wound up in jail. She was grateful to have gone another route, but the constant parade of people grated on her nerves. Stella preferred being alone and craved silence above all else. Sometimes it was agony to go into the hospital and be surrounded by people, tuning in and out of conversations, and having her every move watched by prying eyes. It was sensory overload and Stella was not equipped to manage it most days. Coping skills weren't her strong suit.

The cigarette ashes fell to the floor as she used her boot to smudge them into the drab tile. Like everything else in the hospital, the rooms were bland and about forty years out of date. Most of the patients in this location were terminal in some form or another, and the budget never managed to stretch far enough to update any of their facilities like their sister hospital did an hour away. That was where the high-profile patients were held. Hospital systems, like most other organizations, wanted the shiny and new dedicated to whatever earned them the most attention. It had little to do with helping people and everything to do with lining the pockets of already rich men.

Stella quickly pulled down Avery's blanket and smashed the burning cigarette butt into his chest. His eyes popped open and his jaw clenched, but still he said nothing. Stella had done the same thing with all of her cigarettes that morning and was becoming accustomed to the faint smell of burning flesh. She had removed his hospital gown entirely as there was no need for an additional barrier between his body and her.

He glared at her as she flashed a quick grin in his direction. "Good morning, sunshine!" she said. She pushed her thumb down hard into the fresh blister from his most recent cigarette burn, causing him to wince. "I get bored when you sleep, so I need you to stay awake for me."

Reproachful eyes burned into her soul as she pressed harder into his flesh. Blood seeped from underneath her thumb, which she wiped away with another finger. She considered tearing open the other partially scabbed blisters just to make them sting a little longer when she heard footsteps coming closer. Stella whipped the blanket back up to his chin and mimed placing a hand along his forehead right as Mary walked in.

"There you are!" Mary exclaimed. "There's a huge mess down in one of the other rooms and we are trying to get it cleaned up until the house-keeper arrives. The guy managed to slice open a wrist or something. Come help!"

Mary paused slightly, ready to turn on her heel. She stared suspiciously at Stella for a moment.

Stella realized she still had a hand on Avery's forehead. "I was just checking him. He seemed to be having a bad dream or something," she explained lamely. It was a feeble excuse, one that did not make sense since protocol was to check patients' temperatures with the thermometer that swiped across the forehead, but it was the first thought that came to mind.

For some reason Mary did not question her. She simply nodded and barked at Stella to hurry up before exiting the room hastily herself.

Stella exhaled slowly and thanked whatever gods were guarding her. Even if the guy had no family to complain, she could not fathom the amount of trouble she would be in if she got caught. At least enough to fire her, but more likely than not she would leave the building in handcuffs.

"You better not let anyone else see what's on your chest." She hovered over him, only a few inches from his face. "I will kill you, make no mistake about that!"

The man didn't nod, but his eyes widened in a way that let Stella know he believed her. He couldn't do much if another nurse or someone came into the room, she realized, but it made her feel better to impart the warning to him. Room 216 was her new playground and she would make sure everyone knew to stay away.

1990

When Alessa came to, Duke was prepared. He agonized over her actions while she was unconscious, confused as to why she rebutted his advances. Had he not shown her what sacrifices he was willing to make for their love? How could she not see that theirs was a true love? It had to be some sort of magic of Harrison's; he had bewitched her in some manner and now there was no way for her to see any face other than his. Mother had always warned him about what the devil was capable of, and now he was seeing it firsthand. But Duke knew how to counter that magic.

In *The Tell-Tale Heart*, one of the stories Duke snuck out to the barn to read as a kid, the main character was driven to madness by what he had done, yet Duke felt no guilt with his creation. That had to be a sign that his actions were right, that his instincts were driving him to perform miracles. His love for Alessa was blessed and Mother's God wanted him to succeed. Duke would not succumb to paranoia over his actions like the man in the story, an idea he had never questioned until now. Perhaps there was a reason Mother did not want him to read fiction; perhaps nothing in novels was ever true.

He had spent the time Alessa was incapacitated using a freshly sharpened Victorinex blade and now had the perfect solution. As Alessa began to stir, Duke excitedly grabbed his completed project from the table and bent down low over a stool.

Alessa's eyes slowly blinked open and fell on the horrifying sight at her feet. Harrison's body was still spread out on the floor, but where his face should be now revealed an amalgamation of blood, muscle, and bone. Harrison's eyeballs were exposed, his eyelids having been removed, and his teeth bared without any visible lips. Alessa choked on the vomit trapped by the rag in her mouth.

Yet this was nothing compared to the horror by the table. For there stood Duke, his broad shoulders heaving with adrenaline, and a grotesque mask of some kind on his face. He took a step towards Alessa, further into the light, and revealed that the mask was actually Harrison's face peeled off his body. Duke was wearing Harrison's skin, blood dripping down his neck and into the collar of his blue shirt.

"Now you can love me." Duke barely breathed the words. It sent an electric current of fear through Alessa's body. She was paralyzed, barely even drawing a breath as her jaw dropped open at the sight before her. The vision of Harrison's flesh stretched taut across Duke's face rendered her mute, tears silently streaming down her cheeks.

The tears moved Duke to triumph. His plan was working! Alessa could now see their love and Harrison's spell was breaking. The joy coursing through him invigorated life he didn't know he possessed. His overwhelming need to own her, to inhale her heavenly scent, to feel the heat of her bare skin returned and before he knew what he was doing, Duke's hands pulled her breasts from the top of her shirt. Eagerly, he cupped them with his hands and pinched her round nipples with reckless abandon. The whimper escaping her mouth urged him onward, for clearly they must be the sound of desire referenced in his books. Using Harrison's lips, Duke kissed the base of Alessa's throat, committing the taste of her skin to memory. He felt his erection growing in his jeans and yanked the zipper down with such force, it snapped off.

"My love," he whispered in Alessa's ear.

Her eyes were glassed over in a way that reminded Duke of the

Renaissance paintings from a history museum, so besotted was she with him now that he used Harrison's face to break through the witchcraft binding her. Duke was her savior and he could barely contain his bliss at the thought. He pulled her leggings down to her ankles and cupped his length in his hand as he finally saw her sex. She was even more beautiful than he imagined…flawless skin, with a feathery light down of hair drawing an arrow to the apex of her thighs.

Alessa began to sob, clamping her legs together tightly. Duke, having never been with a woman intimately before, assumed she, too, was so overcome with emotion and desire for the love they were about to consummate that she could not contain herself either. "I know, my love," he cooed. "We will do this together. Shhh…don't cry."

Duke could not deny her any longer. He grabbed both her hips in his hands, pulling her to his erect member. With her hands bound above her head still, the stretch caused her arms to further pull away from her shoulder sockets. Alessa wailed in pain. Realizing the distance was too much to fully engulf her, Duke yanked the chain off the hook, allowing Alessa's body to topple to the floor. Fat tears flowed freely down her face and into her hands as she tried to cover her eyes from Harrison's blood on the floor. Duke pushed her to lay flat, her ass exposed to him like a luminescent trophy. Alessa tried to cross her legs and deny him access, but it only took one shove for his cock to enter her.

Euphoria was not enough of an explanation for the way Duke felt. She was so tight, so perfect. Surely this was proof that they belong together when he fit inside her the way puzzle pieces connect together.

Suddenly an acidic smell filled the air and Duke felt himself grow wet. Alessa was urinating! He yanked her head up by her blonde hair and saw nothing but revulsion in her eyes. So Harrison still had a hold over her? Duke would fix that!

He roughly slammed her head back to the ground, pinning her face down to look at what should be Harrison's eyes, and thrust his erection deeper inside her. Pressing his other arm against her back to hold her in place, Duke penetrated her five more times before releasing himself in her. Utterly spent, he withdrew his cock and watched in awe at the mix of white and red that flowed from her sex. She was his now, body and soul. He simply had to remind her of that as often as possible.

With an eager, maniacal laugh, Duke flipped her over on her back to face him. Sticky blood mottled her cheeks and matted her hair. Her nostrils flared and she defiantly stared everywhere but at the man astride her. Gathering her shirt around her waist in one hand, Duke used the other to hold the chain binding her wrists above her head. "Shall we go again, my love?" His knee spread her legs wider as his erect length shoved inside her…again…and again…and again…

CHAPTER
TWELVE

2011

S tella deposited another patient in his room and headed down to the staff lounge for her lunch break. Normally she didn't have any time to eat as her 20-minute break was spent outside chain smoking and avoiding Mary's constant nagging. However, since her pack of cigarettes was already gone, she headed into the breakroom to grab another soda from the machine.

Mary sat with a chart and a salad in front of her, surrounded by two of the Barbie nurses. Stella referred to all of the nurses as Barbies because they all possessed the same blonde hair and wax-like quality as the doll. Most of them only worked there as part of a scholarship requirement with the nursing school a few hours away; upon graduation, you worked at the hospital of the state's choosing for three years in order to "pay back" the loans from nursing school. However, the nurses sent to this facility tended to be the ones with the poorest grades and the worst attitudes. Most of them only went into nursing in hopes of meeting a rich doctor to snare into marriage, which weren't the sort of doctors you would find at a facility like this one. Stella hated the lot of them.

She crossed the room to the vending machine, hoping to get in and out without catching Mary's attention.

"Have you managed not to kill anyone today, Stella?" sneered Veronica, the head of the Barbie nurses. Her French manicured nails clacked on the side of her water bottle as she spoke.

Veronica seemed to take Stella's attitude as a personal insult. She had intentionally hid paperwork or left out medications in rooms Stella was assigned to get her in trouble since the day she transferred into the unit. Veronica also seemed to relish in bullying her, something Stella assumed most women outgrew in grade school. These types of comments were common if Stella and Veronica worked the same shift.

"My Satanic ritual won't be complete until the full moon, so you've got time to fix your spray tan," Stella quipped. "You're no good to me unless you're nice and orange for the Dark One." She fed a dollar bill into the vending machine and didn't bother looking at them.

Veronica gasped. "Is that a threat? Mary, did you hear her threaten me?" She pushed herself away from the table, as if the extra two feet of distance might protect her from an attack. The other Barbie nurse rubbed Veronica's shoulder and glared at Stella.

Mary sighed. "Stella, we've talked about this. Do I need to send you down to HR again?"

Stella put her hands on her hips. "She's the one who started it!"

"She asked you a perfectly reasonable question in our line of work," Mary corrected. "People are dying around here left and right. Do not keep taking things so personally!" She stood up and huffed as she gathered all her paperwork together.

Veronica smirked. "Mary, please email me the form to file a formal complaint. I think Stella should go see HR to realize how seriously we take threats."

"And references to Satan!" piped up the other Barbie nurse. Stella realized the girl was clutching a silver cross hanging from her neck and it was all she could do to stop herself from rolling her eyes.

A Bible thumper at a state hospital? Really?

Another heavy sigh escaped Mary's lips. She didn't even bother looking at Stella to say, "You'll be called down once the complaint is filed, Stella. You know the drill by now." She hurried out the door, clutching the papers to her chest.

Stella was so incensed she threw her unopened bottle of soda down towards the Barbie nurses. Coke shot out everywhere, dousing the two of them. "Make sure you mention that in your report, bitch," Stella muttered.

1990

A sharp knock on the door snapped Edwin out of his reverie. He had been up half the night, tossing and turning over the Harrison Pierce case and the prospect of a new, unwanted partner. By five in the morning, he had given up on sleep and thrown on his sneakers for his daily run. It was going to be a long day.

"Come in," he barked at his door.

A young man with tan skin and a face full of freckles, around 24-years-old, walked in. His curly brown hair had globs of gel in it, unwilling to yield control. He had on a suit that looked starched to a crisp; it did not move as the man stepped across the threshold, making him walk in a manner that reminded Edwin of the Tinman in the Wizard of Oz. He stifled a laugh.

"Sir, I am Detective Kevin Gaines, reporting for duty," the young man said. He drew himself up tall and squared his shoulders as if preparing for a fight.

Edwin snorted. "At ease, Gaines. I'm not gonna hurt you. Have a seat." He gestured to the chair across from his desk. He stood up and helped himself to another cup of coffee, offering it first to Gaines.

Now that Edwin had given the boy some direction, Gaines split into a wide grin. "Thank you so much, sir! Everyone warned me that you would be scary!" Seeming to realize the rudeness of his comment, the poor boy's face reddened. He averted his gaze down to his coffee mug.

Edwin, on the other hand, was intrigued. Someone had already told his new partner to watch him…that could only be Millhouse's doing. "And why would someone warn you about me?"

The young man's face burned a deeper shade of crimson. "I'm not sure, sir." He set his coffee mug down on the desk and seemed to gather courage. "I believe I can be an asset to your investigation on Harrison Pierce. I've already begun familiarizing myself with the case and I'm really good with cyber investigations."

This surprised Edwin. He had read about so-called "cybercrimes" and the kinds of advances computer technology had made with investigation, but he had never seen anything firsthand. He didn't even know how to navigate computer software and avoided using one at all costs. However, with Harrison Pierce's interest in technology and his recent venture into robotic research, perhaps the kid could be useful to the case after all. As long as he didn't let Gaines get too close to him on a personal level, maybe he could help Edwin locate the missing millionaire.

Edwin nodded. "I'll take that into consideration. Show me what you got, kid."

Gaines looked relieved. He twisted around his seat, surveying the room before asking, "Where is your computer?"

"Don't have one."

Gaines swallowed awkwardly and asked, "And where am I expected to work?"

"Maintenance is going to rearrange the furniture so we can squeeze another desk in here, but they won't get to it until this weekend. Come on, we need to head out and talk to a business associate of Pierce's. He just came back from Shanghai." Edwin grabbed his coat. "Oh, and in the future, always keep paper copies of your information. You never know when you might need it."

The two detectives clambered into Edwin's car and soon entered the highway. Gaines talked incessantly on the drive, filling Edwin in on his parents, two younger sisters, and his proudest moment as the head of his class at the police academy. Edwin tuned in and out of the conversation, navigating heavy traffic as they headed into the city. Gaines launched into an energetic dialogue about the ways in which crime could be reduced in their town, with particular emphasis on the petty theft and vandalism near the university. He didn't seem to notice Edwin's lack of participation and happily continued the one sided conversation.

Edwin sensed that Gaines was not only eager to prove himself, but also to earn Edwin's approval. Gaines reminded him of a bit of himself at that age in that they both were positive to a fault. Edwin started out on the force with rose colored glasses, too, until Shelley broke the truth to him. The thought unsettled Edwin and he shook it from his mind.

"What do you know about Harrison Pierce?" Edwin interjected.

Gaines didn't comment on the sudden subject change. "I know he is worth an estimated ten million dollars and has started expanding his fortune into research ventures. He likes to fund projects, but hasn't created a company of his own to utilize the information they give him." Gaines' tone as he said this had a hint of disapproval, which Edwin inquired about.

"I think he is hiding something and typically millionaires hide things for the wrong reasons," Gaines admitted. Edwin nodded at the insight, but did not comment.

As they veered off the highway, Edwin explained who they were going to see. Franklin McElroy was a real estate tycoon turned private investment firm broker who had been seen with Pierce at a bank in Rio de Janeiro a few times in the past year. It was not much to go on, but Edwin hardly had any viable leads at this point. He couldn't leave any stone unturned. McElroy was often seen in the gossip columns with multiple women on his arms, typically around half his age, and had the reputation of being a bit of a philanderer. Edwin doubted McElroy would be very forthcoming with information. Men in power knew that knowledge is often the best way to keep that power.

Franklin McElroy's gate loomed at the end of long driveway. It was an ornate, iron monstrosity, wide enough to allow three cars to pass through when both sides were open. A tall brick wall stretched as far as the eye could see surrounding the property on either direction, with enormous trees bowing overhead as if to block out the sun. Despite the earliness of the day, the area was dark and still. Edwin had the ridiculous feeling that he was entering a dungeon. He buzzed on an intercom and identified himself and Gaines. A curt voice declared, "Proceed. Park in front of the garage," in a vaguely European accent.

As one side swung backward to allow the vehicle entry, Edwin reminded Gaines, "Let me do most of the talking. Take notes, all right?"

Gaines nodded and asked, "What do I do for notes without a computer?"

Edwin rolled his eyes. "Ever heard of a paper and pen? Didn't they teach you that at the Academy?"

Gaines flushed a deep shade of red. "Guess I forgot," he mumbled.

"There's an extra notepad in the glove compartment," Edwin said curtly. "Always come prepared."

A three-story estate came into view as the driveway curved. It reminded Edwin of a French chateau. More ornate ironwork decorated the windows and a large, circular fountain spurted water out of several angels' horns in the middle of the drive. A massive six car garage stood to the left of the house; Edwin backed his car at an angle on the side of the building. The house was surrounded by the same massive trees that guarded the driveway, creating a dark overcast above.

"Preparing for a quick getaway?" Gaines commented playfully.

"You never know, kid. Keep your eyes and ears open," Edwin said, scanning the upper windows for signs of movement. His years as a veteran investigator would not allow him to stop scanning the perimeter. It was simply second nature. He continued to search the area surrounding the home as the partners approached the door. Before they could knock, a small man in a plain black suit opened the door and welcomed them inside to a two-story foyer, complete with a curving grand staircase. Edwin suspected McElroy enjoyed displays of his wealth.

The man spoke in the same faintly European accent as the intercom.

"Mr. McElroy has been detained on an important phone call. I will show you to the library. He will join you shortly. May I offer you a beverage?"

Both officers declined. Gaines glanced briefly at Edwin before asking, "What is your name, sir?"

The man offered a small smile. "I serve Mr. McElroy. I am of no consequence. This way, please." He strode quickly down a hallway to the right and led them into a library fit for a palace. Floor to ceiling bookshelves ran two stories, with an open galley surrounding the top floor. Despite the spring heat, a fire blazed in a fireplace at the far side of the room, behind a massive oak desk. Centered were four cozy armchairs surrounding a round coffee table. Hints of gold and more angels like the ones from the fountain decorated the corners of the room, the corners of the desk, and outlined the three large windows opposite them.

Oh, the things money can buy, Edwin thought wryly.

McElroy's butler invited the men to have a seat and make themselves comfortable. He reminded them that Mr. McElroy would arrive momentarily, then excused himself, shutting the door behind him.

Gaines emitted a low whistle. "Would you look at all this?" He gazed wistfully around the room. "The guy must be doing something right, eh?"

Edwin shrugged. "Or something very wrong." Rather than sit down, he began to pace around the room. The desk was completely bare, showing no signs of use. Although everything was clean, there was an air of emptiness about the room, as if no one had stepped foot inside for a long time. It even smelled as though the room had been stagnant and vacant for some time. There was nothing personal anywhere to be seen.

Gaines walked to the nearest bookshelf and attempted to read the titles. Most of the books looked to be old, leather volumes. However, upon pulling one off the shelf, Gaines held it up for Edwin to see. "It's blank," he said quietly. "These aren't real books."

Edwin nodded. "Just the show of having a library in an old estate," he agreed. "We were brought here on purpose."

Suddenly the large door creaked as Franklin McElroy entered the room. Faster than Edwin could have imagined, Gaines slid the empty book back onto the shelf and stood with his hands casually in his pockets. McElroy smiled in an indulgent sort of way at the detectives, holding his hand out to Edwin. His long, dark hair was pulled back halfway to stay out of his face, but he had several days' worth of scruff along his round jawline. His shirt was unbuttoned in the top three buttons, revealing a black swather of chest hair. Dark eyes raked Edwin up and down, sizing him up. Edwin pulled himself a little straighter to accentuate the several inches in height he had on McElroy and stared at him dead in the eye. This seemed to amuse McElroy.

"Gentlemen, welcome to my home. Please sit down." McElroy sat down in one of the large armchairs and gestured for them to do the same. Edwin sat immediately across from McElroy, maintaining the eye contact, and introduced himself.

"We are not here to take up much of your time, Mr. McElroy," Edwin began. "We are hoping you can tell us a little bit about Harrison Pierce."

McElroy sighed loudly. "I am afraid there is not much for me to tell. I don't know much about Harrison beyond our brief business dealings. I have invested some money in a few of his projects, that's all." He leaned back in his chair, folding his hands over his large belly before eyeing them expectantly.

"What kind of business dealings?" Edwin asked.

"A few research projects for sustainable housing in Brazil," McElroy said smoothly.

Edwin's eyebrows went up. "You have an interest for sustainable housing in Brazil?" That didn't sound like something a former real estate tycoon would support.

"I have an interest in making money, Detective Greene," McElroy replied. "If we can find a sustainable housing option near the rainforest, I could launch the housing market with the first community of its kind in that area. Foreign investments tend to be more…lucrative." He gleamed maliciously. Edwin knew he was referring to the many loopholes in foreign tax law.

Gaines scribbled quickly on his notepad. "Was Mr. Pierce close to an answer of sustainable housing?" He glanced at Edwin out of the corner of his eye, no doubt remembering his agreement to leave the questions to his partner.

McElroy nodded. "When you have the right motivation, it is easy to find the answers."

Edwin and Gaines exchanged a furtive look. "What kind of motivation?" Edwin asked.

A deep belly laugh escaped their host. "Gentleman," he chuckled, "what sort of motivation ever makes a man determined to succeed?" When neither of them answered, he shook his head and smiled widely, clearly entertaining himself with their naivety. "Only a woman can do that."

CHAPTER
FOURTEEN

Stella wound a loose thread from her scrub top round and round her finger as she waited for the Human Resources representative to call her name. Anger still flared at being called in, but Stella had lots of complaints before that all led to slaps on the wrist. The hospital was too short staffed to do much of anything, especially for STNA's who were not contractually obligated to stay. She assumed this would be a similar sort of meeting.

A man she didn't recognize opened the office door to her left and called out, "Stella Andover?"

She stood up and walked in. The door clicked loudly as he snapped it shut behind her. "Have a seat," he instructed, walking around the large desk piled with papers. Stella perched herself on the edge of the hard, black office chair across from him. The room was void of windows or decoration, with only a solo fluorescent light above them. A second desk with a hutch and an outdated desktop computer sat behind him.

"Who are you?" she asked.

He shuffled some papers on his desk as if looking for the right file. "My name is Malcolm Glasswell, and I am the new HR director at this facility." He picked up a large manila folder and flipped it to the second page. "Stella Andover, 20-years-old, employed with us for six months, complaints on file-seventeen. Good lord, seventeen?" This seemed to get his attention because he looked at Stella for the first time. "Someone's been busy, I see."

Stella rolled her eyes. The condescension in his voice was grating her nerves. "Yeah, I'm good at making friends. So what are we doing about this? Another verbal warning?" She crossed her legs and began swinging her foot with impatience, daring him to say something about her unapproved black boots.

He sat back in his chair and thoughtfully rubbed his chin, as if assessing her for the first time. "Seems to me that after what is now your eighteenth strike, you should be out," he commented lightly.

Without meaning to, Stella laughed. "Please. You need me far more than I need you. Just give me the 'play nice' lecture and let me get on with my day." She folded her arms across her chest and glared at him.

"That's not the way I see it," he countered. He read aloud from her file, "Complaints for threatening employees, stealing, inappropriate language…I am well within reason to fire you for those." Glasswell's eyes brightened as he read further. "There's a reprimand here after you were caught having sexual relations with a janitor in a closet."

Stella fixed her gaze on the floor. "He and I were coming to an arrangement," was all she offered as explanation. She tried hard not to blush or reveal her embarrassment over that incident. It was not her finest hour, exchanging a few weak humps and sloppy kisses in a dingy closet just so the janitor kept his mouth shut when he found her smoking in an empty patient room. She hadn't meant to get caught.

Malcolm stood up unexpectedly and came around behind her. She stiffened as he towered over her, much closer than anticipated. His sandy brown hair fell in his eyes as he leaned down, with one hand on the desk and one hand on the back of her chair. His face was only inches away from her. "That's not how I run things," he said softly. He cocked his head as if he were assessing her again, her natural defiance keeping her eyes on his in a challenge.

This is a match he won't win, she thought.

Suddenly his eyes dropped down to her breasts, her scrub top tight against her large chest. Stella was used to this reaction; it had been like that since puberty. Although she was rather on the short side, her body always maintained voluptuous curves and full lips. While she had never been what one would consider a traditional beauty, she was often called "sexy" and "alluring." She always received attention, whether she wanted it or not. All her foster homes had been proof enough of that.

"I see no reason why I shouldn't fire you on the spot for threatening another employee," Malcolm whispered. The hand on the back of the chair began to lightly trace her shoulder and down her arm. "I could even press charges against you," he warned as his hand continued grazing.

The hair on the back of Stella's neck stood up. Despite how tough she tried to portray herself, she had always tried to avoid legal troubles. She knew firsthand that once the courts were involved in your life, they would never leave. Her juvenile record was over an inch tall. The last thing she wanted was to face criminal charges as an adult; those could ruin your life permanently, a black cloud that would follow you to the ends of the earth.

Stella instinctively realized where the director's thoughts were headed and she swung her long waves over her shoulder. "And what can I do to make you reconsider?" she asked. She looked up at him provocatively through her lashes.

A wicked grin crossed Malcolm's face. "I was hoping you would be agreeable," he said. "Show me how sorry you are and I will find an alternative for firing you."

Stella swallowed the bile that had gathered in the back of her throat. Through gritted teeth, she mumbled, "I am sorry and I am willing to show you."

The human resource director nodded and leaned over. Stella heard the distinct click as the door locked. His hands gripped her shoulders from behind and pulled her to her feet. With a quick swipe, the desk chair was pushed out of the way and Stella felt his erection press into her lower back. His hands slid down so they were fondling her breasts, pinning her arms to her sides. His stale breath came hot in her ear as he whispered, "Pull down your pants and don't make a sound." She glared at him over her shoulder but unzipped her jeans and shoved them down.

His left hand wrapped her hair around his fist and tugged her head back as his right hand pulled her scrub top up, exposing her breasts. He exhaled harshly through his teeth at the sight of her lacy purple bra. "I knew you'd be a dirty girl."

Forcefully, he bent her over the desk, using his left hand to press her face against the papers. She heard a zipper and felt his dress slacks slide down. His right hand eagerly guided his erection into her folds, pausing only to spit on his hand and wrap it around himself before shoving into her once more.

Stella braced herself on tiptoe as he thrust several times into her, each thrust more aggressive than the one before. Her head began to ache from the pressure of his fist pinning her upper body to the desk. He let out a ragged breath and shook, withdrawing his cock to finish over her ass. He smacked her right cheek before using a tissue to wipe some of the cum off her. She grimaced as she felt his stickiness press into her back when her pants came up. She would need to change after this.

Disgusted, she threw up an arm to push him away from her and yanked her shirt back down over her breasts. She could feel the heat in her face as she glared at him.

Malcolm, however, seemed quite undaunted. He zipped his pants back and straightened his checkered tie before sitting calmly in his chair on the other side of the desk. He pulled her file in front of him again and said, "Yes, well, since you showed some remorse for your actions, I will arrange for a committee hearing to consider retaining you as an employee. I will schedule it for…three months out?" He looked at a calendar at the bottom of the paperwork.

Stella was stunned. "You'll 'consider retaining' me?" she asked incredulously. Fire practically erupted under her skin, her anger was so swift and potent.

He smirked at her. "Yes. You will check in regularly with me for coachings and as long as you continue to show me how sorry you are, I will vouch for you at the committee." His message hit her loud and clear. As long as she continued to let him use her for his pleasure, she could keep her job.

"And what if I tell anyone what your 'coachings' entail?" Her eyebrow rose as she challenged him.

That made him laugh. "Good luck with that," Malcolm snorted. "With your track record, who in the world would believe you?"

1990

Duke tested the chain around Alessa's wrist once more. Her eyes stared off vacantly into the distance in a way that continued to unsettle him. No matter how many times he had made love to her or tried to fan the sparks he felt between them, she had never reacted or responded. She would not meet his eyes or look at him in any way. She lost the glow that drew him to her, and he couldn't find a way to ignite it again.

Quietly he peeled off the face mask he had created from Pierce's skin. He continued to wear it whenever he sought release in her, hoping it would break through to whatever was plaguing Alessa and reveal the passion he sensed lurking under the surface. Duke constantly murmured sentiments of his love, reminding her how luscious he found her body as he stroked her, whispering plans of their future in her ear as he laid beside her—all to no avail. Alessa as he knew her remained a distant memory.

Duke stepped over Harrison Pierce's body as he made his way up the stairs. He didn't intend to hold onto it for so long, but until he found a proper disposal site, it served a better purpose to prevent Alessa from attempting to run up behind him. This had happened once when Duke thought he was making progress in their love affair and he left her unchained. He had only reached the second step when he suddenly felt her lunge on his back, and although momentarily stunned, he still regretted how hard he threw her body against the wall as he ripped her off. She had latched onto his t-shirt so tightly that when he grabbed her over his shoulder and wrenched Alessa's body off, his t-shirt had torn clear in half and remained clutched in her hand as she went airborne. It hadn't been Duke's finest moment, but his rage at her having dared to attack him served as a warning for how fiercely Pierce's spell still consumed her.

Since he had placed the body there, Alessa avoided the stairs at all costs. Duke had even been forced to move the table to the other side of the basement because she refused to eat in such close proximity to Pierce. That had been the only word she had uttered in two weeks, "No." It was more of a growl than anything else.

Plus, it really was starting to stink. Even Duke had his limits.

Entering his kitchen, he briefly narrowed his eyes at the bright light filling the room. It was a sharp contrast to the dark in the basement, however, he preferred the soft glow of the lamplight below. He hoped it helped with the romantic ambience, but at this point, he doubted every-thing. Nothing Mother told him had led to Alessa's love.

He slammed a fist on the wooden island in the center of the room. Duke was not used to feeling such frustration; he had never wanted for anything in his life before.

Mother was tucked into her bed upstairs, sleeping heavily with all the pain killers Duke continued to supply her. She had not left her room in months, and for once, Duke was grateful to be left alone. Her punish-ment would be swift and severe if she saw how badly he was ruining things with Alessa. He was failing both of them, and he did not know why.

Glancing in the corner, Duke remembered that he needed to chop more wood if he was going to cook anything on the stove for dinner tonight. He exhaled heavily as he exited through the back door and grabbed the hatchet leaning against the wall.

Trekking a mile into the woods behind the house did nothing to resolve Duke's nerves. Hiking normally served as an activity that cleared his head and helped him relax, but Duke felt so many conflicting emotions right now that his brain buzzed. He had never had a reason to question his mother before—had she not guided him through his entire life all on her own? But yet her counsel on courtship, on how to be a strong man a woman deserved to love, now fell flat. She had lectured him relentlessly on taking control, being the one to make decisions in a relationship, taking sexual pleasure that was owed to him as the head of a household, and all other manner of fundamental relations between a man and woman.

His mother had been a force of nature when he was younger, teaching him how to live off the grid, completely independent of anyone else, yet she had also taught him the importance of family, the importance of their airtight bond as mother and son. Duke could not remember his father and his mother's only explanation had been that his father simply had "gone on." It was enough to satisfy Duke because he felt his mother's love and knew he was safe as long as he remained by her side. She had ensured his every happiness.

As he grew up, she relied on him more and more, leaving more responsibilities to him as her health declined. She continued to teach him how to be a man, guiding him through his wild emotions as a teenager. He did not need to prowl around town looking for trouble because his mother sent him into the woods to hunt and build shelters out of branches. As soon as he had one structure built, he would lead her out to show his accomplishment and she would instruct him to tear it all down so that there was no trace of their presence by the end. The effort to do both exhausted him, but he found himself grateful to her whenever he read about the strange circumstances other teenage boys found themselves in, such as Holden Caulfield in <u>Catcher in the Rye</u>. Duke knew that he was no Holden Caulfield. And thanks to his mother's guidance, he never would be. She provided his only source of education and only allowed him to read books and newspapers of which she approved.

"Dark magic," she had explained to him, "is present in everything. You have to be careful!"

It wasn't until his teenage years that he started to sneak books out of the boxes he found in the attic that she disapproved of. And even then, he always read while constantly glancing over his shoulder, anticipating her arrival and the resulting punishment at any second.

It was because of her that he spent so many hours sculpting his body into the muscular shape he had now. She had given him a book about calisthenics and another about building muscle, so he used what he could find in their home to create the physique that pleased her. As a teenager he started humbly with cinder blocks and old logs to lift weights, but as he experimented further with the boundaries of his strength, he began to use household furniture. He even designed a harness around his chest to drag his mother's van a few times, walking the length of the driveway pulling it behind him. Duke knew he was above average in height, so his muscular stature looked fitting, and his mother praised his efforts up until her illness confined her to bed. She delighted in the strong man he molded himself into being.

Duke reached the small clearing where he stowed the trees he fell. He liked it here because he could see a small stretch of the county highway that led to his home, but he knew from the road, drivers could not see him. It felt like camouflage, like a safe space meant to obscure him from the real world. He worked on one log, then a second, carelessly throwing the pieces into a rusty wheelbarrow, but his mind continued to run on overdrive. What would Mother say when he told her his plan was not working? What if Mother said he was not a strong man?

Mother had only whipped him when absolutely necessary, but no matter how frail she became, when she reached for a belt, Duke knew he had it coming. He had received several whippings that left his back bloody for days, but it never occurred to him to lie to her. No one should lie to their mother. Duke understood it as a necessary act for a parent when their child misbehaved; Mother reminded him of that every time she raised her hand to him. She took no pleasure in doing so.

"'He who spares the rod hates his son, but he who loves him is diligent to discipline him,'" Mother always quoted. All her beatings were really an act of love. Only parents who loved their children bothered to discipline them.

Now was a time when Duke deserved to be whipped; he was failing as a man. He needed to tell her, but that would also mean telling her that Alessa was in their home, something Duke suspected would upset Mother more than his failure to court her properly. His mother loathed outsiders and had not left their home in years. She had never allowed him to attend school and instead taught him to read herself. According to her, as long as anyone can read, books will teach them everything they need to know.

Except no book ever truly prepared him for the way he felt about Alessa or how to make her return his love.

"It has to be that damned spell!" he whispered savagely. Mother taught him about the magical influence certain people wielded to compel others to act a certain way or say things they didn't mean. Every time Duke read her an article about a political dispute or a catastrophe, Mother always commented that it was the dark magic at work. That was why she hated anyone outside their own home. You never knew what kind of magic they possessed.

Clearly this Harrison person had a strong spell to still influence Alessa after death. Perhaps Mother could help him break through to her after she punished him. Yes, that is what he would do. Confess, receive the whipping he deserved, and then beg for her help. Mother could solve everything.

Feeling relief for the first time all day, Duke pushed the wheelbarrow back towards the house. He quickly stacked the wood in the small shelf near the stove and ran upstairs to the second floor.

His mother had not left her bedroom in several months, which was the only reason Duke was able to spend so much time following Alessa. A large growth had developed along his mother's abdomen, rigid and painful, preventing her from moving well on her own. Twice a day he carried her to the adjacent bathroom to use the facilities and sponge bathe her, but otherwise she remained in her bed. Most of the time she slept, but he brought her newspapers and books when he could find them. She barely ate anything anymore and had wasted away before his eyes, making it easy for him to carry her around like a child. Her hearing was all but gone, her skin sallow, and her eyesight had started to wane. More and more she requested that Duke read to her, which he did without complaint. He had dreamt of the day when he could take Alessa up to introduce her to Mother and see her proud smile knowing her son was a man now at last.

Now, his mother's breathing came in short, shallow huffs as he gently held her hand upon entering her bedroom. He pulled her into an upright position and fluffed the pillows behind her head, adding a few more for comfort. Her eyes fluttered open and she looked at Duke for several moments before she seemed to recognize him. "My baby boy?" she asked. "Is that my Dukey boy?"

He nodded, smiling lovingly at her pet names. Why couldn't Alessa cherish him like his mother did? "Yes, Mother. Can I get you anything?"

She shook her head. "No, my dear. I am comfortable resting for the time being. Tell me, have you been a good boy?"

Duke gritted his teeth. It was time for the truth. "I have not, Mother. I have failed at becoming a man."

This seemed to get her attention. She straightened more on the pillows and peered into his eyes, surely seeing straight into his soul. "My baby boy, you are not a man. You will never be a man. You are not big and strong like real men are. What have you done?"

Tears streamed down his cheeks as if she had slapped him. If she could see the tears, she probably would have slapped him for being so emotional, he thought. "I want to be a man, Mother. I want to make a woman love me."

"No, only I can ever love you, Dukey boy. Girls are foolish, wicked things. They have dark magic. They will trick you. You cannot be a man if you want a girl to have feelings for you."

She might as well have punched him. Duke was stunned into silence. Alessa had dark magic? Was he in danger? He wanted to be a man so badly, but if Alessa's love prevented that, was it worth the cost?

"Has a girl started talking to you? Filling your head with lies, no doubt," his mother continued. "You can't listen to her, my Duke. Promise me you won't listen to her!"

Duke hung his head. "I want to be a man, Mother," he said quietly.

"You want to be a man? Is that what you said?" she replied loudly, then tilted back her head and laughed. His mother was actually laughing at him! "You tell this girl to jump off a bridge and leave you alone. You don't need anyone to love you but me. Who will take care of me if you are distracted by love? Who will love me if not you? Your job is to honor and protect me, Dukey boy, not be a man. You're my boy, and you'll stay my boy forever. Whoever this girl is can take her magic elsewhere!" She nodded emphatically as if that settled the matter.

"But Moth—" he began.

She interrupted him immediately. "' Honor your mother, so that your life may be long in the land that the Lord your God is giving you.'" Another Bible passage she often used whenever he dared to question her as a child.

He couldn't believe his ears. Mother wouldn't let him be with Alessa because she thought he would no longer love her? Was she going to keep them apart? Alessa could not be filled with that kind of vile magic; how would he feel such passion from her if that were true?

For the first time in his life, Duke thought his mother might be wrong. And that made him very, very angry. Slamming his fist down on his thigh and breathing hard through his nose, Duke sputtered, "You're wrong, Mother. She loves me. I know she does. And I'm a man, not a boy."

She laughed again. "That's something only little boys would say. I am your mother, and I say you're a boy and you will leave this girl alone. She's already using her magic to turn you against me—your own mother!" Her eyes narrowed and the laugh left her face. "Do you understand me, young man? The girl goes. That is final!"

Duke recognized the tone in her words. There would be no more talk on the subject. Rage simmered just below the surface. He had never experienced this kind of hatred towards his mother. A boy, indeed! He was a man and he would prove it to her. Once he broke Harrison's spell and made Alessa love him, his mother would eat her words.

In the meantime, his mother expectantly held out her right hand. Duke knew this meant he was about to be punished. It happened every time he dared to disagree with her. Without another word, he crossed to her bureau and withdrew an old leather belt from the top drawer, a belt she kept solely for this purpose. The black topcoat had long since worn off and the tarnished silver buckle still held remnants of his blood from past whippings.

He hung his head even lower as he placed the belt in her outstretched hand, then kneeled at her bedside. She cleared her throat, her only instruction that he was to remove his shirt. "Sinners always pay the price," Mother told him. It was the same admonition she gave every time he kneeled before her for as far back as he could remember.

As the first blow struck his back, Duke felt the sharp sting of the buckle break skin, but it also solidified his resolve. His mother was wrong, he was certain of that. He needed to prove to her and to Alessa that he was a true man, someone who deserved to be loved and treated as such. The only way to show them both was to break Harrison's spell. Alessa was not full of any kind of magic; she was an angel, his angel, and she would be his salvation.

He reminded himself of that over and over again as the blood began to trickle down his back.

1990

Edwin shoved his chair back from the desk and rubbed his face gruffly. He was bone tired from poring over society columns, press releases, and notes from previous interviews with those closest to Harrison Pierce. A quick glance at the clock on the wall told him that it was nearing three in the morning. He debated whether to pour himself another cup of coffee or call it a night.

His partner sat at the new desk facing him, absorbed with the information on his screen. Maintenance had rearranged the office to accommodate Gaines and his computer set up. After their eventful conversation with Franklin McElroy, Gaines sought a warrant from the judge to seize all of Pierce's banking information. He had been poring over bank statements and Pierce's investments on the computer ever since.

"Pulling an all-nighter or heading home?" Gaines asked as Edwin stood and gave in to the need for caffeine.

Edwin grunted. "Nothing to go home to. I'd rather find a lead in this case."

"Yep. Me, too," Gaines agreed. He stretched his hands back over his head, then stood up and grabbed a mug for his own coffee. His hand slipped and coffee spilled over the table. "Shit," he muttered. Gaines reached to the first drawer in sight and pulled it open, looking for paper towels or napkins of some kind. As he pulled out a stack of cheap takeout wipes, a framed photograph caught the light.

"Who is this?" he asked, holding the frame up for Edwin to see.

Edwin's face drained of color and he snatched it from his partner's hand. It was an old, faded picture from the day Edwin was promoted to detective, with Shelley assigned as his mentor.

Ever since Shelley's passing, Edwin couldn't bear the reminder of how greatly he had failed his former partner. They had both been filled with such hope that day, such pride at his promotion and delight in being paired together after becoming fast friends in the Police Academy together. And it had all been dashed to pieces so soon after.

Gaines looked at Edwin steadily for several moments without blinking. He turned back to the coffee spill and began to mop up the mess. "That was your old partner, wasn't it? That's why you didn't want to work with me." He said it with an edge to his voice, as if the words embarrassed him to admit out loud.

Shaking his head, Edwin sat back down at his desk, the photograph in his lap. It was the first time in years he had looked at it and it suddenly struck him how different Gaines was to Shelley. Shelley would want Edwin to mentor Gaines, to show him that there was more to solving crimes than the recognition Millhouse had undoubtedly promised him. Shelley would have been the more tolerant one, the detective open to collaborating with others and extending olive branches to those outside the unit in order to facilitate a smoother working environment. He would have pegged Edwin right away as the stubborn ass he had become…and that thought both flustered him and amused him at the same time. Edwin could just imagine Shelley's eyes rolling as he told Edwin that jackasses belong in barns, not the police force.

"Yeah, that was my partner," Edwin surprised himself by saying. "James Shellenbarger, class of Amherst Police Department 516, though everyone knew him as Shelley." He hung his head again. "I always called him Shelley."

Gaines quietly sat down at his own desk. He did not comment on the moisture pooling in Edwin's eyes, but allowed Edwin a few moments to collect himself. After Edwin huskily cleared his throat, Gaines whispered, "What happened to him?"

Edwin didn't answer right away. He couldn't. He spent so much of his time actively avoiding the memories of that day, ignoring how freshly the pain still stung. And since Edwin worked and lived alone, no one ever pestered him *to* talk about it.

But Gaines' earnest face watched him wistfully. Rationally, Edwin knew it wasn't his new partner's fault that Shelley died. Gaines hadn't done anything to make Edwin doubt his commitment to the case. So far, he seemed only eager to please and willing to learn. Gaines earned the right to know why Edwin continued to keep him an arm's length away.

The veteran detective sighed, grief sharply overtaking his senses. It simultaneously felt as if losing Shelley was a lifetime ago and a day ago. "We were working a case on a serial child abduction. Shelley suspected it was a human trafficking operation, but I thought that was a bit too much for our area. All of the kids were taken from the same five mile radius and had the same physical characteristics; none of the abductions looked like crimes of opportunity. Or so I argued." Edwin gave a sad half smile, his gaze lost in the memory. "Some clues led us to a home at the edge of the city limits. We didn't have enough to get a warrant, but he didn't think it would hurt to go to the house and poke around. At least ask some questions of the guy who owned the place. I told him we shouldn't go, that it was too soon and we would waste our time, but he was adamant.

"As soon as we pulled up, something didn't sit well with me. There was no car in the driveway and there weren't any lights on inside. The place needed a lot of work, and it didn't look like anyone had lived there in some time. We could see several cages on the back of the property, but there were no animals in sight, nothing to indicate there were any animals around. There was a large shed that was missing a door and several shingles on the roof. It looked like one good storm would knock it down, it was that rundown. We heard what sounded like whispered voices coming from it, so Shelley headed towards it while I knocked on the front door. No one answered my knock and I followed him to the shed. There were six kids inside, chained by the ankles to one another, and then chained to the walls of the place. They were scared shitless." Edwin's voice broke here and he could not stop the tears running down his cheeks, remembering their dirty, gaunt faces looking up at him from the mud on the shed floor.

"We dispatched the call for backup and had just gotten done with bolt cutters on the last kid. I had the other five waiting in my vehicle; the one boy told us there were more kids in the basement of the house, but we had to wait for backup and a search warrant. We got out of the shed, with the boy in my arms and suddenly heard gunshots coming from behind.

"I didn't check on Shelley, I didn't communicate with him like I should have. I took off for cover, shielding that little boy with my body. It wasn't until I got at the back of the house that I realized Shelley wasn't behind me. When I looked around the corner, trying to locate the shooter in the tree line, Shelley was already on the ground, face down. I could see the blood spurting from his neck from ten yards back. He hadn't even drawn his weapon. He stepped in front of us when the gunfire started, protecting me, protecting that kid." Edwin was crying in earnest now, sobs shaking his shoulders. He hastily wiped his blotched cheeks with the back of his hand, then grabbed a hankey from his pocket and blew his nose.

"After I shot the guy and he went down, I fired the rest of my rounds into his chest as I stood over him. It is the only time anger has ever compromised my ability to serve and protect. I violated my oath that day, my need to slaughter that son of a bitch more important than our laws of justice. I could never trust myself to work with a partner again."

The air rippled with the heaviness of Edwin's shame.

"That day has haunted me for nearly thirty years. And not a day goes by that I don't regret not checking on Shelley. I should have had his back the way he had mine." Edwin noisily wiped his nose with the back of his hand and hung his head. He couldn't believe he was even telling someone about that day, a day which had always been his greatest failure.

Gaines leaned back in his chair, surveying Edwin with sympathy. "I'm sorry for your loss." The admiration in his voice was evident and Edwin could not question the sincerity in his tone. "I can't imagine what that feels like, and I hope I never have to find out. But I promise I will have your back. Your oath to serve and protect still stands with me. And I will do whatever I can to be a great partner to you. We are in this together, Edwin."

It was the use of his first name, something reserved for only those closest to him, that calmed Edwin's racing heart. He offered the young detective a watery smile. "Yeah," Edwin concurred, "I suppose we are. And you can call me Ed."

2011

Stella seethed as she made her way out of the administrative corridor of the hospital. She didn't even deserve to be called down to Human Resources. The Barbie nurses were targeting her because she was different. "Story of my fucking life," Stella mumbled miserably.

She stormed into the locker room used for employees to change their clothing and keep their personal belongings before going through security into the main hospital. Thankfully, Stella was alone, although this wasn't completely uncommon since so few employees ever used the locker room. Several wallets and cell phones had been stolen before, which defeated the purpose of a "safe place" for employees to store their belongings.

She yanked her scrub top off, desperate to get any feeling of Malcolm Glasswell off her skin.

It was no surprise that he manipulated sex out of her. Men had been doing that her whole life. Stella had never had any kind of significant other or real relationship before, yet she had more than triple the average number of sexual partners, starting with Mr. Barton when she was thirteen years old. Men always noticed her, no matter how she dressed or how little she returned their advances. She had accepted long ago that it was simply how the world worked. And she would be lying if she said she had not always used it to her own advantage. How many classes had she passed in high school by sucking off nerds in exchange for papers? And how could she forget Mr. Thompson, her chemistry teacher sophomore year, getting caught with her on his lap after school? He was still on the sex offender registry because of it. None of it was something she was proud of, but if the system was going to screw her over, she may as well try and get something out of it first. She couldn't bring herself to feel any remorse for her actions.

Stella turned to the full-length mirror hanging on the wall, staring critically at her reflection. Her dark hair fell in waves down her back, almost to her waist. She had pale skin, wide hazel eyes, and round, full lips. It was her hourglass figure that made it impossible to hide from the prying eyes of predators. Although she was short, only a few inches above five feet, Stella's breasts had filled out quite early in puberty, and she had a round ass that Mr. Barton always told her deserved to be spanked. If she truly was just meant to be ogled, why not use it to her benefit? Love only existed in fairy tales anyway.

Turning slightly to check her back in the mirror, Stella concluded there were no signs of what Glasswell had done to her. And he was right, wasn't he? No one would believe her if she told the truth because it would not be her first time having sex while at work. She had been caught with the janitor just a couple months ago after Mary started looking for her; one of her patients had choked on his lunch and Stella had not been there to save him.

Like anyone in this hospital should be saved, she thought wryly.

Stella had been stuck on third shift for weeks after that incident.

She pulled a new scrub top out of her backpack and then yanked on a clean pair of leggings. Leggings violated the dress code, too, but at this point, what did it matter? She slammed her locker shut, not caring if anyone stole anything inside, and shuffled out to the elevator for her floor.

Mary eyed her carefully after Stella made her way through the security checkpoint and approached the nurse's station. She didn't say anything but waited for Stella to speak. She could wait all day for all Stella cared.

Finally, huffing impatiently, Mary declared, "I want you to stay away from Veronica and the others. I am assigning you to Room 216 again since there isn't much you can do to screw up in there. You need to keep your head down and your mouth shut, do you understand?" Her lips hardened in a firm line. "You may not be the nicest gal out there, but there's no sense in losing a job over this, Stella."

Mary slid Avery Winslow's chart over to her. "Just stay out of trouble!"

Stella rolled her eyes as she accepted the chart. "Don't kill the mute. Got it."

Room 216 was in the same condition as Stella always found it. Eerily silent, with Avery's dark eyes bored into her face the moment she entered. She laughed at this, fighting off the irritation that still grated her every time he refused to show signs of weakness. "We're gonna have some fun today," she told him.

Pulling another scalpel out of her scrub pocket, Stella pulled back his blanket. Large scabs lined the fingernails on his right hand. The ring finger looked like it was starting to swell, a sure indicator of an infection. It was something she should record on his chart and report to a nurse to further investigate, but since Mary had warned her to stay out of sight and keep her head down, it seemed better not to notify anyone. Further investigation of the man's body showed that blood had gathered in his catheter, and the bag was leaking slightly with the overflow of urine. Stella grinned wickedly at him. "Pretty gross, huh?" Using both her hands, she pulled upward on his hip bone to check his backside and saw several bedsores festering along the underside of his buttocks. Mild green pus oozed out of one of them.

Stella withdrew her hands quickly, letting him fall hard back on the bed. He blinked rapidly several times before turning his stare back on her.

"You're a nasty son of a bitch," Stella whispered vehemently at him.

She lit a cigarette and blew a puff of smoke in his face. He didn't even flinch. Grabbing the scalpel, she yanked the blanket down far enough to expose his thighs. With the blade moving awkwardly in her hand, it took several attempts to get the first letter right as she cut an F into the skin. Euphoria took hold at the blood dripping down his thigh from her work. She felt powerful. She could do anything to this man, unlike all the other men who made her do whatever they wanted.

After several minutes, Stella took a step back to admire her work. "FUCK UP" was carved angrily into the patient's left thigh. There was a lot of blood, but Stella knew from experience that it looked like a lot simply because of the way it spread. She had not hit any major arteries or veins, she was sure of it.

However, the real triumph came when she turned to his face. Avery Winslow's mouth hung open and tears streamed down his face. He looked like he was on the verge of speaking, but continued to silently stare at her without blinking. The pain in his eyes was apparent.

"You didn't like that, huh? Does it hurt to be a fuck up? To be a fucking freak?" Stella felt her blood pressure rising as she glared at him. She pulled the top of his hospital gown down over his chest and stubbed her cigarette on his chest. A tiny tendril of smoke twisted in the air as her nose scrunched at the faint hint of burnt flesh. Avery's head pushed backward as his body reacted to the burn.

"Don't ever forget that you're a fucking nobody! There's not a single person who cares about you!"

Stella hastily grabbed a rag, the last one in the drawer, and wiped the blood off his leg. Just as she predicted, the blood was manageable after wiping away the initial wave. She settled back in the chair by the bed, allowing the air to hit the wound to stall the scabbing process. Periodically she wiped another layer of blood off the cuts, examining the depth of the words. Her satisfaction skyrocketed when she realized it had been deep enough to scar. Now the asshole would always remember he was a fuck up.

Adrenaline rocked Stella to her core. She had never felt so high, not even when she first experimented with LSD after leaving the group home. This was the ultimate rush, knowing she could inflict any kind of pain and punishment she wanted on this man, and there was no one to stop her. Nobody else ever checked on him and no one was going to check on her, Mary would see to that. Stella was free to do as she liked. What was he going to do, tell on her?

1990

Duke thundered down the steps into the basement. It was time to prove to everyone that was a man, no longer a little boy. He was no longer going to use that meddler's mask to break his spell over Alessa, his love would do it for him. There was no place for Harrison Pierce in their future, so he would not continue to allow his magic to ruin Duke and Alessa's present.

He threw open the double doors that spilled out into the back of the hill upon which the house was situated. The basement originally served as a storm bunker that was detached from the home, built into a natural hill that occurred on the property near the tree line for the woods surrounding the house. According to Mother, his father had reconfigured the house, adding on a bigger kitchen and then creating a direct stairwell down into the bunker, labeling the space as a basement instead. It allowed Duke easy access to drag Alessa and Harrison's bodies when he first brought them here.

Now, however, Duke needed to focus on getting Harrison's body out. No doubt Harrison's magic continued to permeate the space and thus keep the hold over Alessa. Grunting slightly, Duke dragged the body's dead weight outside. Alessa whimpered as she shielded her eyes from the bright sunlight.

Squatting down and heaving at the waist, Duke deposited the body into the wheelbarrow. He hastily shut both the doors to the basement and placed the chain lock on for good measure. The chain was only there whenever Duke was not inside as an extra precaution in case Alessa managed an escape attempt again, although her wrists were still tied above her head, and he did not believe she could pull free. He gleefully anticipated a day when he would no longer need such security because Alessa would admit her love for him.

It would take an enormous amount of strength, but there was a large meadow more than a mile behind their home. It was part of a national park, but there was no fence or gate and Duke knew there was next to no chance of being found because the area did not have any hiking trails or camping amenities that close to the border. Park visitors never ventured that far out when there was nothing special or unique to see. It was as good a place as any to bury the body.

Burying Harrison Pierce took several hours, between the harrowing hike with a heavy wheelbarrow and digging a grave deep enough to satisfy Duke. Although he knew it was unlikely that anyone would find the body, it wasn't worth taking a chance. Duke dug a deep hole more than six feet down. He created small crevices in the side as a step ladder of sorts to get himself out. Soon a fresh mound of earth covered the body, which Duke attempted to conceal with branches, pine needles, and other debris from nearby. Quizzically, he circled the area and examined his efforts from several angles. Unless someone knew what to look for, Duke was certain no one could notice the grave.

Hiking back felt like walking toward redemption. He could not explain it, but he felt certain Alessa could forget about Harrison Pierce now and they could focus on their love for each other. Mother would realize she was wrong and Duke could have the life he always dreamt of. It was so tantalizingly close he could practically reach out and touch it. This was the last obstacle he needed to overcome and now there was nothing preventing his union with Alessa. Even she would see that now.

Although he yearned to immediately retreat to the basement and consummate this victory with her, a quick shower was in order first. He didn't bother dressing afterwards, opting to descend the stairs with a towel wrapped around his waist.

Alessa's body shook with silent sobs, but she stopped at the sight of him. He heard her sharp intake of breath and realized she was truly looking at him for the first time. He could not help but flex slightly, showing off the hard muscles he worked for hours to achieve. This is what real men look like, Duke wanted to say.

"What did you do with Harrison?" Alessa rasped. Her voice sounded gravelly after weeks of silence and little to drink. However, Duke was elated at the progress. She had not spoken to him until this moment, so clearly the magic was beginning to wear off.

Calmly Duke approached her before kneeling at her level. The towel fell open and he noticed Alessa flinch as his knee touched hers. "No one will bother us anymore, my love," he vowed. "It is just you and me now."

Thick tears ran down her cheeks. "Please," she begged. "What did you do with him? Why are you doing this to me?"

Duke hushed her, dragging his finger softly over her lips. "We are meant to be together, Alessa. You will see that now." His fingers trailed down her jaw to her neck, ignoring the bruises there from when he last held her down. He hated the way her breasts were starting to droop and her ribs had begun to show. She refused to eat and her body reflected that. She needed to regain strength, but Duke did not know how to make that happen.

She shook her head wearily. "I could never be with a monster like you." She said it quietly, like a tragic admonishment to herself as she accepted a fate worse than death. Her head hung down and Duke saw another fat tear fall onto her chest.

It was the sight of the tear that enraged him coupled with her insult. *He was a monster?* With everything he had done to prove to her just how much she meant to him?

This was the dark magic Mother meant. Women were cruel creatures who sought to harm others. And Duke had allowed her to infiltrate his heart and worm her way inside!

He allowed his rage to manifest and slapped Alessa's cheek with as much force as he dared. Alessa's head swung back and blood seeped out from a fresh cut on her lip. The vacant gaze returned to her eyes as Duke tugged the chain off the hook overhead to release Alessa's body to the floor. He kicked her onto her stomach and enjoyed the crack that echoed as one of her ribs broke. A fitting punishment for such a witch.

Her naked ass extended in the air triggered a primal instinct deep in his gut, however, and he found his erection growing despite himself. Without much thought, Duke allowed instinct to take over as he kneeled behind her and drove his cock inside. Alessa started to fight but Duke struck the base of his palm into the center of her spine. The new angle allowed him to adjust her legs wide enough for Duke to enter fully. Duke thrusted aggressively again and again into her folds, using his hands to pin her upper body to the ground. His whole body shuddered as he released into her.

Now that he saw Alessa's true colors, he hated how much his body reacted to her, how he still felt a sense of marvel at the way their bodies fit together. She was so achingly beautiful. But how could he even think that after she called him a monster?

He thought back to the story of Odysseus and the sirens he read about as a boy. Perhaps Alessa's magic was like a modern day Peisinoe, sent to tempt him into ruin. His entire life had been turned upside down by this vixen. He had allowed her to consume his every thought, drove himself to near insanity at the thought of her touch. He brought her into his home, something neither he nor his mother had ever done with another person. No, she would have to pay for her dark magic. A deed like this could not go unpunished.

Gripping her hair, Duke yanked her head up sharply so her face was only inches from his. Her lip quivered. Blood was smeared down her chin and there was an indent from how hard he had pushed her head into the pavement before. "Now I'll make you suffer like you have made me suffer," Duke declared ruefully. "You will regret putting me under your spell."

Rather than returning Alessa to her previous spot on the dirty mattress with the chain holding her hands above her head, Duke dragged her to the center of the room where he had first tied her up. Even with her arms fully extended out of her dislocated shoulders, Alessa's toes barely skimmed the ground.

He rushed up to his bedroom and pulled one of his old leather belts out of his closet. Once he returned to the basement, he stood behind Alessa's hanging body, clutching the end of the belt tightly in one hand. "Sinners always pay the price," Duke declared darkly. He flinched as the belt buckle made its first strike against her pretty skin, but swallowed back the emotions gathering in his throat. This siren had to learn. She had to be punished.

1990

The sound of a desk chair scraping along the floor woke Edwin from his stupor. After poring over hundreds of documents throughout the night, he had allowed himself a brief cat nap in his desk chair, which offered surprisingly good lumbar support. Gaines stood over at the coffee pot, pouring more grounds into the filter. The kid looked rough, clearly not used to staying up all night inspecting evidence. Edwin felt a glimmer of guilt, but shoved it down after recalling Gaines' promise that they would solve this case together. He might be young, but Gaines was eager to prove himself and earn Edwin's trust. Babying him would only insult the kid.

"Hey," Gaines said by way of greeting. "Sorry, I didn't wanna wake you."

Edwin shook his head, his eyes still laced with sleep. "It's alright, I need to get up." It was going to be another long day. Standing, he stretched his arms over his head and loosened his shoulders. A quick glance at the clock told him it was barely 7 a.m. "Let's head out to the Pierce estate. I wanna talk to that housekeeper of his again."

Despite hours of searching, neither of them had found a shred of evidence that there was a woman of any significance in Harrison Pierce's life. None of the society pages had linked him with anyone, there were no photographs of him with a woman on his arm, and none of the previous interviews with staff mentioned a woman. Edwin had realized early this morning as he reread all of his notes, however, that he never came outright and asked if Pierce was dating anyone. He had asked everyone if there was anyone close to Pierce who might know anything about his disappearance, but with a man who valued his privacy so much, staff on his payroll would never share much information. Since there was still no body discovered, perhaps there was a chance that Pierce had simply charted off to an exotic island with a lover in tow and had not yet returned. Eccentric millionaires could do that sort of thing, Edwin supposed.

Gaines nodded. "Is it okay if we stop by my house on the way? I didn't bring a change of clothes with me." He looked a little sheepish at his rookie mistake. Edwin grinned and grabbed his jacket off the back of the chair.

Gaines' house was a one-story brick building on the poorer side of town. A rickety metal fence surrounded the front yard and the gate creaked as they entered. They could hear music coming from the inside, which Gaines explained came from his mother's radio that was never allowed to be turned off. The smell of bacon frying wafted out of an open window. Despite Gaines' assurances that there were no small children at home, several old bicycles, hula hoops, and sporting equipment littered the lawn. There were weeds sprouting from all the flower beds, but great flowering bushes threatened to bloom at a moment's notice. Edwin immediately felt a sense of comfort about the place as though the house itself was happy with the manner in which the occupants lived.

As soon as they entered the cramped hallway, a little girl's voice cried out, "Kevin's home!" A young girl, approximately ten years old, hurtled herself into Gaines' outstretched arms. He swung her up easily, enveloping her in a bear hug, her light brown hair cascading around both their shoulders. She eyed Edwin suddenly over Gaines back and asked curiously, "Who are you?"

Before Edwin could answer, a woman close to his own age came around the corner into the hallway. She was clearly Gaines' mother; her son looked just like her. She squealed in delight at the sight of her oldest child, rubbing his back and pulling him towards the kitchen. "My special detective! You must come eat something!" She did not skip a beat as she gestured to Edwin. "You come, too! This must be your partner, Kevin. Welcome!"

Mrs. Gaines gently shoved her son and Edwin into chairs around a table already ladened with food. A man who could only be Mr. Gaines sat at one end of the table reading the newspaper, but he rose and slapped his son on the back with a wide smile as the officers sat down. "Working all night like a champ, huh, slugger?!"

The little girl who met them at the door slid into the seat next to Edwin with a grin while Gaines returned to his seat. Another girl, probably closer to sixteen or seventeen, smiled shyly in Edwin's direction and nodded in greeting. There was hardly any room to move around in the tiny kitchen, but the smells made Edwin's mouth water. Plates of waffles, bacon, and scrambled eggs littered the table and a large jug of orange juice stood on the counter. Before he could protest, Mrs. Gaines carried a plate heaping with food and set it down in front of him. "If you're going to protect my Kevin, you have to leave with a full stomach!" Her eyes held so much love and pride at addressing her son's partner that it rattled Edwin. When was the last time someone looked at him like that?

Her husband held out his hand across the table. "I'm Ronald Gaines," he said by way of introduction. He also eyed Edwin with admiration. Edwin shook his hand and thanked them all for the hospitality. Gaines chuckled at Edwin's incredulity over their sudden transition to the breakfast table.

Gaines' youngest sister kept her head cocked to one side as she assessed Edwin. He noticed her eyes dart down to the holster at his side. She laid her hand over his wrist and demanded, "You a cop?"

Everyone else around the table burst into laughter. "Rosie," Gaines chuckled. "This is Detective Greene, my partner. We're both cops."

Her grin revealed a mouth full of pink braces. "You're just Kevin. He's a real cop." Everybody laughed again.

Edwin could not remember when he had last had a homecooked meal like this. He had been single and childless for so long, he took it for granted that others had families. Even Shelley had been single up until his death. Both of them considered themselves married to the job. It was too difficult to maintain a relationship when you were constantly working. Edwin had an older sister who had gone away to Indiana for college and never moved back home. They occasionally spoke over the phone, but family dinners had long been a thing of the past.

He could not conceal the smile from the love and warmth surrounding him. The Gaines family spoke to and teased one another with an easy grace he envied. No matter how the conversation ebbed, laughter constantly rang out. Little Rosie enchanted Edwin the most; now that he had passed whatever test existed in her mind, she became glued to him and peppered him with questions.

Gaines' middle sister, Claire, stood up and heaved a giant backpack over her shoulder. "Come on, Rosie," she prompted her sister, "We've gotta make it outside to the bus stop. Stay safe, Kevin." She kissed her dad on the cheek and gave Gaines a one-armed hug. "You, too, Detective Greene."

"Aw, do I have to? I wanna stay here!" Rosie protested.

"We have to get going anyway," Edwin replied. "And Claire, you can call me Ed."

Rosie and Claire both beamed at him. Rosie leaned in to give Edwin a hug before hugging everyone else goodbye. There was a brief moment of chaos as they collected lunch boxes and forehead kisses from their mother before the screen door slammed loudly behind them as they both ran out the back door.

Mrs. Gaines sat down in Claire's vacant chair. She had already tried to make Edwin accept a third helping of everything on his plate. He would need a crane to lift him out if he ate much more. "You will take care of our Kevin, right?" Edwin could hear the worry lacing her voice. "It is a big step up for him to become a detective."

His partner blushed a deep crimson. "Ma, don't embarrass me," he chided her. He left the table, muttering about changing his shirt.

"I don't mean to baby him, sir," Mrs. Gaines told Edwin. "We are just so proud of him. He is the first one in our family to go to college and now he is a detective! He's worked so hard."

"I will take good care of him," Edwin reassured her. "He is a great kid." Both parents looked relieved.

At that moment, Gaines himself came down the hallway and stopped in the doorway, adjusting the collar on his button up shirt. Edwin stood up, offering to help wash the dishes before excusing himself. Mrs. Gaines would not hear of either man doing anything and instead kept trying to shove a brown bag full of sandwiches into Edwin's hands. Gaines' father clapped his son on the back and wished them both a good day as he followed them outside to his truck to head to work at the factory.

Edwin excused himself, shaking Mr. Gaines' hand again, and left the father and son to talk. He watched the two from his car window as Mr. Gaines pulled his son into a warm embrace. Edwin wondered if Gaines had any idea how lucky he was at having such a loving family around him. It reinforced Edwin's determination to protect the kid. He would never let something happen to Gaines like it had to Shelley.

Gaines clambered into the passenger seat and grinned sheepishly at him. "Sorry about my family, man," he said. "They like to blow things out of proportion."

"It's good that they all understand the risks of your job. Don't ever take it for granted that they care about you," Edwin replied.

This statement made Gaines blush again and they rode in companionable silence for the remainder of the drive.

The Pierce residence was located in the foothills south of the city. Where McElroy's estate looked like an old French chateau, Pierce's looked more like a monument to modern technology. It was almost entirely made up of glass and black metal, offering breathtaking views of the forest beyond the home. Gaines whistled in awe as they approached.

As Edwin turned to Gaines, his partner held up a small notebook. "I came prepared," he said with a small smile.

Edwin couldn't stop the grunt of approval. He clapped Gaines on the shoulder good-naturedly. "Now you're getting it, kid."

Edwin rang the doorbell and turned to an intercom next to the front door. It squawked a moment later, asking for identification. Helen Rory, Harrison Pierce's housekeeper, answered the door immediately afterwards. She took a few steps into the foyer of the home, completely open to the living room and kitchen beyond before stopping short to face the two men. The hard look on her face made it clear that this was an unwelcome intrusion.

"I see you haven't located Mr. Pierce," she said coldly. She clasped her hands in front of her hips and her back went rigid. "We have not had any new information regarding his whereabouts."

Out of the corner of his eye, Edwin could see Gaines' eyebrows raise. He had a similar reaction when he first met Mrs. Rory.

"What can you tell us of Mr. Pierce's dating history?" Edwin asked.

She snorted derisively. "Mr. Pierce does not date. Ever." Her tone had a finality to it as if the subject were closed.

"We have reason to believe otherwise," Gaines said gently.

Mrs. Rory's eyes narrowed. "I have cared for the Pierce family for over forty years. I was there when Mr. Pierce took his first breath in this world. I can assure you, Detective, if he had dated anyone, I would know about it."

Edwin tried a different tactic. "Do you know Franklin McElroy?"

This did not shake the woman at all. "I know many of Mr. Pierce's associates, Detective Greene," she said.

"Then do you know why he would allege that Mr. Pierce had a woman in his life?" Edwin pressed her.

She shook her head. "I do not. I don't have anything further to add to the previous statement I made to you. It is time for you both to leave." She gestured towards the front door, abruptly ending the interview.

The front door had barely slammed behind them when Gaines commented, "Such a charming lady."

The assessment made Edwin smile. "That she is. Good pay will keep most people loyal, though."

He entered his car wearily. If the housekeeper's statement was true, Mrs. Rory was closer to Harrison Pierce than anyone, yet she didn't know of a girlfriend in the past or present. Who could McElroy have been referring to then? And if a girlfriend did exist, why had Pierce gone to such lengths to shield her identity from everyone, including his own staff?

They were running out of time and options; it had been almost four weeks since Harrison Pierce's estimated disappearance. Without a body or any real proof of foul play, the department would transfer it to a cold case file soon unless something concrete kept the case open. Edwin could not shake the feeling that they were missing something. There was no reason for McElroy to send them on a wild goose chase over a mystery woman unless he was somehow involved, an occurrence that was entirely unlikely since McElroy had solid alibis for the timeline they estimated in Pierce's disappearance. They simply had to keep digging.

"Let's get a few hours of sleep and meet back at the office this afternoon. This time you read through all my notes from earlier interviews and I'll take a look at that damn computer thing of yours," Edwin said drily. He could practically feel Gaines smiling beside him as he energetically launched into an explanation of how computer technology would change the way they solved crimes. Edwin still tuned in and out of the conversation, but he knew showing any interest at all was all the ammunition Gaines needed to share his ideas.

A fondness for his partner began to fester deep inside his chest, and in many ways that scared Edwin. Now that he had met the entire Gaines family, he knew he had to honor his promise to them and keep Gaines safe. He couldn't let another false sense of security lull him into dropping his guard and compromising their partnership. He couldn't face another loss like Shelley's. Come Hell or high water, Edwin would protect that rookie.

CHAPTER
TWENTY

1990

Duke leaned back into the bathwater and contemplated what to do. He couldn't let Alessa leave, not after taking her from her work and killing Harrison Pierce. She would go straight to the police, Duke was sure of it. And yet the thought of her following Pierce to the grave made Duke's heart sink. Try as he might, there was still something inside him that assured him Alessa was an angel meant to change his life. She was his in every way and continued to consume his every thought. More of her witchcraft, no doubt.

Mother's call came from down the hall and broke his reverie. It was unlike her to need him at this hour. He snatched a towel from the rod on the wall and tied it around his waist. She didn't like to be kept waiting.

Her chest heaved in harsh breaths as he entered the room. He could hear the rattling sound of the phlegm that clogged her airways and wondered again how much longer he had with her. Creeping silently, he sat on the edge of the bed and took her cold hand in his. Her eyelids fluttered at his touch.

"Mother?" he whispered. His fear prevented him from jarring her awake lest he face another punishment for disturbing her.

She turned her head away from him and moaned. "My Dukey boy. Save me from this pain!"

Duke obediently went to the drawer in her vanity that contained her medicine and looked for the pain pills the pharmacist had recommended to him. Mother still did not know he was lacing her food with it each day in the vain hope of easing her agony. She would have punished him severely if she knew the extent to which he had ventured into town, a pharmacy with drugs being high on the list of forbidden places. All Duke wanted to do was please her, but as he got older and discovered more about the world outside their home, the more he realized that Mother shielded him from a lot of information. He wanted to believe it was out of her maternal instinct to protect him, but ever since he met Alessa and realized his life's true purpose, he wasn't entirely sure. Alessa was the other half of his soul, yet if Mother had her way, Duke never would have met Alessa since nothing was allowed to penetrate the confines of their life. It made his head spin, and he continued to grapple with indecision in regard to his feelings.

He crushed several pills at once and stirred them into a glass of water sitting by her bed. Trying to ignore the sharp crease of her shoulder blades, Duke used one hand to ease her forward and the other hand to hold the glass to her lips. She drank greedily and sank back into the pillows with a sigh.

Lovingly, she brushed her fingers along his jaw. "You take such good care of your mother, sweet boy," she whispered. "I am so lucky to have someone like you to love."

Duke's heart melted at the compliment. This is what he dreamt of hearing from Alessa's lips. She was his soulmate if she would only accept it.

"Mother," he began, "do you think anybody else will ever love me? Even if it's not like you do?" He held his breath, fearful for both her answer and risking her displeasure.

Her eyes snapped open and she studied his face critically. "Since I know I am dying, I am going to tell you something, Duke," she said fiercely.

He began to refute her statement, but she would not have it. "I am and it's foolish of anyone to say otherwise. This ain't living, being stuck here in this bed all day, too weak to even fetch my own water. But you listen here, son, and listen good. All women who aren't mothers are evil. They will tempt you with their tricks and catch you up in their spells, and there's nothing you can do about it. Satan himself made women. None of 'em change until they become mothers themselves. Don't worry about trying to get any of them to love you. You go on trying to become strong and someday you'll be a man, and you'll be alright." She settled back into the pillows and closed her eyes again.

It was not enough of an explanation to satisfy Duke. He needed to understand. "So if a woman becomes a mother, she loses her magic?" he inquired quizzically. That did not seem logical to him, although most of the world seemed illogical to Duke.

"More or less," replied his mother. Her chin began to droop onto her chest, a sure sign that she was on the brink of sleep. "'He gives the barren woman a home, making her the joyous mother of children. Praise the Lord!'"

"But how does the woman become a mother?" he pressed her. Perhaps that was the key to breaking Alessa's curse and any lingering magic Harrison still had over her.

He tried to wrack his brain for a Bible verse on creating children and could only summon the memory of the many times his mother quoted Proverbs 22:6. "Train up a child in the way he should go; when he is old he will not depart from it."

Mother rolled her to her side as she muttered, "The man possesses her, of course."

TWENTY-ONE

1990

Even a run could not help Edwin relax. He slowed his pace to a walk, approaching the end of the greenway where he preferred to exercise. Upon arriving home to his empty apartment earlier that day, sleep evaded him like a lead in the case, so he did the only thing he knew how. He ran.

He had been a runner since junior high, competing in track all through high school. It led to a scholarship at Kent State before an injury his sophomore year benched him for the rest of the season. He left school to return home and joined the police force instead. Although he could no longer run competitively, several years of physical therapy had allowed Edwin to hit the pavement again. Running felt like the easiest way to clear his mind. All he had to do was focus on putting one foot in front of the other to keep his momentum going. Nothing else mattered during his runs because it was like nothing else existed.

Edwin stretched his long legs before climbing in his car to head home. His apartment was small, although he never had any visitors to justify needing more space. The one time his sister came she had insisted on hanging some old family photographs in frames on the wall above his couch, but Edwin hadn't bothered to change out any of the photos in more than 15 years. Even the furniture was placed in the original floor plan from when he moved in. He was the only detective in the department who didn't own a house, a large purchase he could never quite commit to with the knowledge that if anything happened to him, it would end up being a legal hassle for someone to handle. Edwin lived to work, his desire to solve crimes more potent than any other dream.

The only part of his apartment he actively decorated was a shelf in the hallway adorned with the flag from Shelley's funeral along with a framed article from the local paper about the child trafficking ring that ended as a result of their final investigation together. The article declared Edwin and Shelley were both heroes and went on to inform readers of his partner's ultimate sacrifice, laying down his life to protect the boys the officers found in the shed. Shelley's parents had given him the flag after the funeral, saying it was only right that Edwin keep it to honor Shelley's memory. Most of the time Edwin walked down the hall with his eyes downcast to ignore the ghosts the relics stirred. However, today he found himself stopping at the shelf and gently sliding his fingers along the fold in the flag.

"I wish you were here to give me some advice," Edwin whispered to the newspaper photograph of Shelley when he graduated from the Academy.

Except that was a foolish wish, because had Shelley been there, Gaines wouldn't be his partner. Hell, Edwin might have actually moved up in rank without a ghost's memory keeping him stagnant.

He sighed heavily and wondered for the umpteenth time what Shelley would do in the Pierce case, and what he would think of Gaines. Edwin missed his partner fiercely in moments like this where he wondered if he could solve a crime and bring justice to the victims. It felt like trying to catch smoke, as though the clues hovered right in front of him and Edwin couldn't grasp them. Gaines was eager to learn and eager to please, and Edwin had no doubt that Shelley would've found the puppy dog comparison amusing. Enthusiasm wasn't enough to locate a missing billionaire, though, and Edwin didn't know how to work effectively with Gaines yet.

It wasn't fair to the rookie, but Edwin couldn't help comparing him to Shelley. Their partnership had been the sole core of his life for so many years that it felt like a harder burden to let go of his memory than to accept the possibility of forming a new partnership with someone else. He was a traitor to Shelley, who had been promoted to detective first and mentored him when he was still too green to understand how the world worked. Now he was just going to pass down Shelley's legacy to someone else?

After a long, hot shower the loud beep greeted him to announce the voicemail waiting in his message box. It was Gaines; he asked Edwin to pick him up because he had an idea. Edwin noted the hesitancy in his partner's voice and grinned despite himself at what sounded suspiciously like Mrs. Gaines in the background encouraging her son to call.

Grabbing his duty belt and retrieving his weapon from the lockbox, he drove to the Gaines home in record time. Mrs. Gaines greeted him fondly, enveloping him in a hug that smelled like cinnamon sugar. She pushed him into a kitchen chair again and placed a plate with three heaping sandwiches in front of him. "You're too thin!" she scolded him. "Eat something!"

Gaines joined him with a plate of his own. "In Pierce's financial statements there were several transactions at a coffee shop near the university called 'Groundbreaking.' It's a popular place for college kids, locally owned—not really the kind of place you'd expect a millionaire to frequent."

Gaines took an enormous bite of his sandwich that made Edwin raise his eyebrows in surprise. "I started looking more at the dates of the transactions when we got back. It turns out he was going there daily whenever he was in the area. All of the dates coincide with the rough travel estimates Mrs. Rory gave us. Figure it might be worth a look?"

Edwin smiled at him. "Definitely. Good job, kid."

Mrs. Gaines beamed at them. She pulled a large batch of cookies out of the oven and declared, "Well, my boys can't solve crimes on empty stomachs! I'll bag up some cookies for you!"

After several protests that they could not possibly eat more than three sandwiches a piece, Gaines and Edwin left with a small cooler filled with fresh cookies, potato salad, and leftovers of last night's dinner. Edwin could not remember the last time he had eaten so much food in one day. He found himself smiling inwardly at Mrs. Gaines' kindness for the pair and how quickly she included him in their family. Edwin had never experienced such a thing, not even with Shelley.

Groundbreaking was a small shop on the corner of a busy street just off campus. It seemed quaint, with a black and white awning over the large windows that dominated the front. There was street parking only unless someone wanted to utilize a public parking lot accessible through an alley down the street. There were a few tables out front as well as inside, and Gaines said it was mostly used as a meet up location for students.

As soon as they walked inside a young man behind the counter greeted them and did a doubletake at the sight of their badges. "Oh, good, are you here about Alessa?"

Gaines and Edwin glanced at each other and approached the counter. "Alessa?" Edwin inquired.

The man nodded vigorously. "I told her roommate that I was gonna call and start bugging the cops if you guys didn't start investigating!"

Both detectives continued to glance at one another. Edwin had no idea what the man was talking about, and judging from his facial expression, neither did Gaines.

"I'm sorry, sir, we aren't here about Alessa," his partner started tactfully.

Before he could finish his statement, the worker huffed in exasperation. "Of course not! Nobody ever cares about the little guy, right? Why worry about my friend who has been missing for weeks when you could be out writing parking tickets on campus!" He smacked a wet rag down on the counter in impatience.

Wiping the splattered liquid residue off his face, Edwin eyed him carefully. "You said this Alessa is missing?"

"Yes, for going on five weeks now! She just stopped showing up at work and didn't go to class anymore. Her roommate hasn't seen her either. Alessa isn't the type of girl to pick up and leave like that. She was the responsible one of us, you know?" The man shook his head sadly.

Gaines took out a notepad after exchanging a last heated look with Edwin. "Let's start with your name, alright?" he began.

The employee, whose name turned out to be Colin, had worked at Groundbreaking for the mid-day shift for a year while attending the university. Alessa Meinken was the primary opening employee and according to Colin, one of his very best friends. She was approximately 21 years old with blonde hair, hazel eyes, and a desire to change the world. "She wanted to be a social worker or a teacher or something," Colin said tearfully. He recounted the last time he had seen Alessa, how habitual she was about everything, and how much time she dedicated to her studies. Colin described her as a quiet, but friendly girl who had a lot of optimism about the future.

Sounds like a female version of Gaines, Edwin thought wryly.

When asked about her love life, Colin snorted. "She had some mystery boyfriend who whisked her off for private dinners whenever he came around, but he never met any of us. She made it sound like he was a bit of a celebrity…I always thought she was bluffing. I don't even know his name!" He crossed his arms over his chest, a sure sign of defense. "Could that be the man who took her? Oh my god, is she dead?"

Gaines, who had been taking notes as fast as his hand could write, shook his head. "We couldn't say," he replied.

Edwin took a thoughtful sip on the black coffee Colin had provided him. "Do you know who Harrison Pierce is, by chance?"

Colin's eyes widened. "That wackadoodle gazillionaire who is always in the paper?! Of course! Is that who Alessa was dating?!"

"We are here investigating Pierce's disappearance and it looks as though he came here frequently for coffee," Edwin responded evasively.

That seemed to catch Colin off guard. "I am here almost every day, either working or studying. I have never seen him here. If he came during early mornings, it would have only been Alessa waiting on him."

Edwin shot another pointed glance at Gaines, which led to a furious scribble of notes. "Do you have any security cameras?"

Colin nodded and led them to the back of the kitchen where a small desk was built into an alcove. A grainy black and white image of the front room dominated a television screen on a shelf above the desk. Colin explained that the owner had the employees turn the feed on every morning and then turn it off at night. He kept the videos for a few months before they recorded over them.

"Smart man," Edwin mumbled under his breath.

"We're gonna need all of those tapes," Gaines told Colin.

The employee nodded again and excused himself to call the owner to explain the situation.

Edwin could tell from the look on Gaines' face that they both suspected Harrison Pierce would be on those tapes. Alessa Meinken sounded like the mystery woman in his life, and what's worse, she was missing, too. They now faced a serial kidnapper.

CHAPTER
TWENTY-TWO

2011

Stella gritted her teeth as Malcolm Glasswell's fingers snaked past her panties to find the apex of her thighs. True to his word, he called her back to his office only three days later for another "coaching" session. His malice seemed to grow at Stella's ambivalence, as if she presented a challenge for him to break her spirit. He was barking up the wrong tree because Stella would never allow someone like him to get a rise out of her.

People with suits and titles thought they owned the world, but Stella knew the truth. The lowly miscreants like her were the foundation of the pyramid, and without the foundation, all the power in the world couldn't hold it up. She would let him have his little fun in his office, but in the end, she kept her job, her benefits, and all the freedom those things provided, so what harm was really coming to her with the arrangement? Most of her dignity had been stripped from her long ago.

Turning her head under the guise that she wanted him to have better access to her throat, Stella ignored his panting sighs of desire as his other hand groped her bare nipples. Glasswell's scruffy five o'clock shadow felt reminiscent of her first sexual experiences.

She allowed her mind to wander and thought back to her first night with Mr. Barton. He had been a gruff man of at least forty, always wearing dirty overalls and barely grunting two words. His wife, Mrs. Barton, had been the opposite; the foster children had joked that she must have a word quota to reach every day because she never stopped talking.

When the social worker brought Stella to the Barton's farm, she had been instructed to stay on the porch to wait while the social worker went over the particulars of her case with Mrs. Barton. The sun had been setting and Stella remembered her stomach growling. It had been a two-hour car ride to get there, but the social worker would not stop for food. Mr. Barton clambered onto the porch and stopped short at the sight of Stella standing there, her raggedy duffle bag clutched tightly in her hand. He did not disguise the way his eyes surveyed her body all the way down to her feet before zeroing in on her budding chest. At thirteen, Stella's breasts seemed to have sprouted overnight, but no one had ever told her that she needed a bra or provided any opportunity for her to get one. Her shirts were starting to be uncomfortably tight and a quick glance at her chest revealed tiny peaks where her nipples sprung from the cool breeze.

It was only at the creak of floorboards indicating the social worker was coming out to retrieve her that made Mr. Barton drop his gaze and walk away from Stella. The stench of cheap tobacco followed him. Stella still remembered how distinctly the thought ran through her mind that his behavior should bother her, but it never did. He noticed her body in a way that all the other social workers, foster parents, and group home managers had not. Maybe he would finally help her adjust to the changes puberty brought out.

How naïve she was. Within a week of her placement there, Mr. Barton had pulled Stella aside in the barn and told her she was going to have an extra assignment most nights because she was the strongest. Stella knew it was a lie; there was a foster boy there who was in high school and taller than Mr. Barton himself. However, when he instructed her to enter his toolshed after Mrs. Barton had gone to sleep, Stella did not question him or tell anyone. She obeyed his orders, even when he demanded that she strip naked for him upon arrival.

Most of the nights blended together after that. She would quietly sit by her bedroom door, listening for the sounds of Mrs. Barton's heavy snores and then tiptoe out into the toolshed. Mr. Barton always required her to remove all her clothing and although it hurt at first, he was not cruel in his use of her body. Stella simply accepted that it was a burden she needed to bear.

But when another foster child arrived a few months later, a girl around Stella's age with a body on the brink of transformation into womanhood, she recognized the heated look Mr. Barton kept shooting her way. Stella tried to blackmail Mr. Barton into leaving the other girl alone. It was the first time he had gotten angry with her, and the welt from his hand striking her face took days to fade. Even though Stella did not care about the girl in the slightest, something told her that it wasn't right for anyone else to tolerate Mr. Barton's abuse. That was Stella's responsibility.

Yet when Mrs. Barton saw Stella's red, swollen jaw the next morning, the woman was livid and called the social worker immediately to retrieve her. No one ever gave Stella a chance to explain. Years later she realized that Mrs. Barton already knew what her husband was doing to Stella, and that he had probably done it to many girls who cycled through their farm. It was another harsh lesson for her to learn: women do not protect other women.

Glasswell's body shuddered and brought Stella back to the present moment. He withdrew his erection from her and finished his release along her lower abdomen. Stella's jaw clenched tightly to keep from vomiting. She truly loathed this man.

Sensing her disgust seemed to amuse him because he smirked at her as he tucked in his shirt. Stepping around the desk, he commented, "You're dismissed. We'll have another coaching session soon since you can't seem to get the hang of it."

Stella grabbed a fistful of tissues and tried as best she could to wipe the evidence off. Glaring at him dead in the face, she dropped the sticky mess onto the stack of papers centered on his desk and left the office to the sound of his protests. Today had been her only day off this week, something she was positive he had done intentionally as another power play against her, and she hated that he got off on her helplessness. She felt vulnerable and exposed, like a wounded animal left out in an open field, which made razor sharp tears prick in her eyes. Weakness is the worst thing a solo, petite woman could show and yet here she was giving that to Glasswell in spades. She was disgusted with how easy she made it for him.

Since she was already at the hospital, Stella found herself moving automatically towards the staff locker room and depositing her backpack. They were always so short staffed that she knew she could clock in and no one would argue; in fact, the unlimited overtime to pad her paychecks was the biggest reason Stella wanted to stay. It was the first job she ever had where she could afford to live on her own, albeit a small studio apartment. Right now she did not trust herself to return home. She needed a release for all her pent-up rage and shame, and she knew just how to get it.

Once upstairs at the nurse's station, Stella easily snagged Avery Winslow's chart and headed straight to his room. With a little careful eavesdropping and a few quick checks on the computer with Mary's stolen password in the past couple days, Stella had learned no one else had been assigned to Room 216 in several weeks. He was like a ghost that everyone forgot about. It had made Stella elated to realize the likelihood of her ever getting caught experimenting on the man was slim to none. Even Mary, being in charge of them all, only poked her head in his room once a month or so. Stella was free to do as she liked.

For the first time ever, Avery appeared to be in a deep sleep when she approached. He wasn't fidgeting in his sleep, and instead seemed calm and peaceful. She paused, examining his features closely for the first time. His dark hair was long after years of neglect with his hygiene. No one had bothered to shave his face in quite some time, and his beard grew thick and matted. There were splotches of gray in it. Being confined to a hospital bed had rendered his skin almost translucent, the dismal light highlighting his hallowed cheeks. According to his chart, Avery Winslow was approaching 45-years-old, but he looked nearly 20 years older than that. He had not left this room in over a decade.

In sleep, however, the man looked to be at peace. His eyes no longer stared at her in the way that made her uncomfortable, but Stella found herself preferring that. She longed to see the faint traces of fear she caught from time to time. Under his blanket she knew his right thigh now had the scar from the word "MONSTER" she etched into his skin. His chest was covered with small burn holes, the perfect ashtray for her contraband cigarettes. She had also enjoyed cutting his forearms along the deep blue veins and watching the blood pool in the tray she placed underneath. It still marveled her how much blood the human body could lose. Avery had not said a word, keeping his dark eyes trained on her face every time she sliced him.

Today Stella had her intentions set elsewhere. Festering with rage at Glasswell's assault, she did not stop to think as she threw back Avery's blanket and hospital gown before stabbing the scalpel directly into one of his testicles. His eyes shot open and his mouth dropped. A low hum briefly escaped before he clamped his lips together. There was no mistaking the fat tears rolling down the side of his face.

Euphoria overtook every thought and feeling Stella had. It was the happiest she had ever felt. "I knew you could speak!" she whispered savagely, the blade in her hand still lodged in his testicles.

She had done it. Avery Winslow produced a sound, which meant his silence was a matter of choice. With enough pain and pressure, she could elicit more from him, maybe even discover why he had remained soundless all these years.

She yanked the scalpel out and held it in front of her face, endorphins and adrenaline pumping as the blood trickled down the blade and onto her fingers. His secrets, his future, his very life was in her hands, and that was such a heady rush for Stella to process. Her cheeks stretched painfully in what was her first real smile in years.

The smile must have had an even stronger effect on Avery Winslow because he gave her exactly the reaction she wanted. There was pure terror in his eyes.

1990

The owner of Groundbreaking agreed to bring all of the tapes over to the station the next morning and give as much information as he could about the missing girl. He described her over the phone as one of his best employees and Edwin got the sense that the man was truly worried about her. If his dates were accurate, Alessa went missing right around the same time as Edwin suspected Harrison Pierce had actually gone missing, dates that were approximately ten days off from what his housekeeper reported.

He felt jubilant at finally having a lead. They were actually getting somewhere, and although Edwin hated the prospect of there being another victim in the case, Alessa had a far more rigid schedule and surrounded herself with friends. They could find out a lot more information investigating her side of things. For the first time since he had been assigned the case, Edwin felt a twinge of hope. Perhaps their luck was changing.

Back at the office, Gaines repeatedly pestered him to join his family for dinner. Mrs. Gaines was making her famous homemade meatballs. Since he could not think of a valid excuse to dissuade his rookie partner, Edwin agreed to meet him at the Gaines family home in an hour. He raced home to change and stopped at the corner market to select a small bouquet of flowers for Mrs. Gaines and a chocolate candy for Rosie.

It felt strange to him how quickly he fell into place with the Gaines family. Edwin had never been someone with good social skills; Shelley was the first true friend he had ever had, and Shelley was cut from the same cloth. Neither of them ever really wanted to settle down or have someone waiting at home. It was enough to have each other and dedicate all their time to their careers. Once that was cut short too soon, throwing himself into his work felt like the only option. Shelley would not have wanted it any other way.

Edwin amused himself imagining Shelley sizing up his new partner. Gaines was in many ways the polar opposite of Shelley. Where Gaines used logic and rationale to make his decisions, Shelley always opted to barge in with guns blazing. Shelley had a despicable temper that often got the better of him, especially during college football season, yet Edwin had never seen Gaines lose his calm façade. They would have worked well together, though, Edwin reasoned, because they would have balanced each other out and kept each other in check. Almost like Edwin and Shelley had.

This thought wiped the smile from Edwin's face as grief washed over him again. He realized how much his opinion of Gaines had changed since their breakthrough and how the hope that they were no longer facing a dead end had somehow leaked into the hope that he and Gaines could develop a true partnership. What had happened to his former partner was Edwin's fault, and if he had followed the rules and policies as well as Gaines did, his best friend might still be alive. Gaines would have made the right decision to protect his partner, Edwin was sure of it. He was damn lucky to have a partner like Gaines now.

The front door to the Gaines' home was hauled open to the sounds of laughter and music. Rosie came barreling down the hall and launched herself into Edwin's arms, much to Gaines' amusement. She dragged Edwin down the hall to her bedroom and ordered him to sit at her tea table. As soon as his rear hit the seat, she placed a veiled tiara on his head and handed him a sparkly wand with a star on top. She giggled delightedly.

Gaines' booming laughter from the doorway a few minutes later drew his father and Claire, who joined him in laughing at the ridiculous scene. Edwin's knees were braced against his chest and his thighs burned from the strain of squatting over the little chair rather than risk breaking it under his weight. Rosie sat across from him, sipping primly from a China teacup with a pinky in the air. Dolls flanked chairs on either side of them.

Edwin did not care in the slightest. Rosie was happy and seeing her beam at him over the rim of her teacup was all the encouragement he needed to continue the game. He smiled over his shoulder at the rest of them and turned his attention back to his hostess. Mrs. Gaines came in shortly after, shooing out the rest of her family, and inviting Rosie and Edwin to join everyone for dinner. She pulled Edwin into a tight embrace in the hallway and whispered her thanks in his ear; she was just as gratified to see her youngest child so happy.

The night continued with uproarious laughter. Claire played two songs on her clarinet for an upcoming recital at school and made Edwin promise to attend. He couldn't remember when he last had so much fun. As the evening wore on, Mr. Gaines pulled a few beers out of the fridge and passed them to Gaines and Edwin. Before he knew it, Edwin had polished off three and had quite a buzz going. It made him more verbal than he usually was.

When Mrs. Gaines headed back towards the bedrooms to put Rosie to bed and Claire excused herself to work on her homework, Mr. Gaines inquired about their case. Although he didn't know the details of it, his son must have impressed the importance of finding the missing people. Gaines vaguely updated him on the lead they had found earlier in the day.

"Atta boy, Kevin!" Mr. Gaines chuckled proudly and ruffled his son's hair. "I always knew all that computer stuff you wanted to learn would come in handy someday!"

Gaines grinned sheepishly as he brushed his hair back into place. "If anything, we should be discouraged now. There's another victim! How come we didn't know about her?" He turned his attention to Edwin, who shrugged.

"High profile cases like Pierce tend to get the most scrutiny. Those are the ones who come to me," he explained.

The response made Gaines frown. "But that's not fair. It sounded like this woman's friends were really worried about her and they did all the right things to notify the police. Why wouldn't that be just as important as some crazy millionaire who never goes out in public?"

Edwin shrugged again. He wasn't responsible for how the world worked. "It's just the way it is, kid," he offered.

Gaines vehemently shook his head and stood up, swaying slightly. "No, that's not right! I wanted to become a detective to help real people, not just rich ones!"

His father tugged at his son's wrist. "Take it easy, Kevin. It's not Edwin's fault. He's just telling you how things work."

Gaines went towards the kitchen before turning abruptly on his heel and facing the other two. "I don't have to be complacent with a system that's wrong. Alessa's life is just as valuable as Harrison Pierce's. More so, in my opinion, because at least people like her! Why would we dedicate so much time to someone no one gives a shit about?"

Mr. Gaines sighed wearily. "We've had this conversation before. You know that money talks. If this Pierce guy is really as loaded as you say he is, he's probably got a lot of influence and power. It only makes sense for the police force to focus so much on him. Hell, he's probably paid a lot of money to the city for various things."

Edwin nodded in agreement. "With his name splashed all over the papers all the time, his fame makes his disappearance headline news. If the department can solve a major crime that's on the front page of the paper, it gives people more faith in us."

"But that's wrong!" Gaines snapped. "They're misplacing that faith if it means we don't look out for the little guy! If the only way to get help is to have money or status! It isn't supposed to be that way."

His partner was losing patience quickly. "Take off the rose-colored glasses, kid. This is the real world. Didn't they teach you anything at the Academy?" Edwin snorted in annoyance.

"So you're not bothered at all that no one was looking into Alessa's disappearance after several people reported her missing?" Gaines demanded.

Edwin took a long swig of his beer before answering. "No," he stated grimly. "People disappear every day. We can't help them all."

Gaines stared at him in shock. "No, we're just supposed to," he said and swept down the hallway. A door slammed loudly and Mr. Gaines shook his head.

"Don't be too hard on him, Edwin," he said. "Kevin's led a comfortable life here. We might have kept him sheltered a bit…we didn't want him to grow up before he had to."

This elicited another snort from Edwin. "He definitely has to now."

TWENTY-FOUR

1990

Duke descended the stairs with trepidation building in his heart. Mother's words echoed in his head. How could he possess Alessa any more than he already had? What was missing?

It seemed as if the answer was right in front of him, yet far enough that he could not see it. The frustration nearly drove him mad. This was never the way he imagined a future with Alessa to be. He had anticipated some pushback from Mother because Alessa was far too social to isolate herself on their property as Mother would demand, but Duke had assumed they would settle on a schedule and the storm would blow over. He always pictured both women hugging each other tightly and Mother watching with teary-eyed pride as he and his love entered his bedroom each night. His current situation was all wrong!

Alessa appeared to be asleep in a crouched position, her shackled wrists slightly pulled above her head. Her once blonde hair was now nearly black with filth and a thin sheen of sweat glowed off her skin. There were scabs of blood and deep bruises all over her body, and even Duke winced at the sight. This is not the life he wanted to give her. The Alessa he knew was always impeccably dressed and smelled like berries and vanilla. She never had a hair out of place and joy radiated from every pore of her body. Her strength and beauty didn't waver, not like this. She wasn't meant to be covered in dirt and chained to a wall.

Without thinking about it, Duke opened the padlock chain on the outer door and slipped out to the barn. There was still a large washtub from the few summers his mother had forced him to wash all their clothes by hand outside. Once he had gotten sick and she had to wash the clothes herself, there was suddenly money for an old washer and dryer set. Alessa wouldn't be able to stretch out, but at least he could help her get clean.

He rolled the tub into the basement and then dragged the hose inside. As the basin began to fill Duke returned to the kitchen and boiled a large soup tureen full of water. When he returned downstairs and poured the hot water into the tub along with some of Mother's old bath salts and oils, Alessa was awake and eyeing him apprehensively. The fear in her eyes made his heart ache for their mornings of smiles and wit over a newspaper.

Duke set down a few bottles of shampoo and body wash next to the tub and approached Alessa with his hands up in front of him. "If you fight me, I will chain you again," he warned her.

She didn't respond, but continued to stare as he opened the cuffs on her wrists and held out a hand to help her stand. The attempt was futile as her bruised and battered legs gave out on her as soon as she reached her full height. Duke instead scooped her up, one arm behind her back and another arm under her knees, and carried her to the basin. As gently as he could, he plopped her into the washtub where she kept her knees drawn to her chest.

"Do you need my help?" he asked her.

The only reply was the loud chattering of her teeth. Duke tested the water with his own hand; it was warm enough that she shouldn't shake. He placed his hand against her forehead and couldn't detect a fever.

Joy came when he withdrew his hand and realized Alessa was staring in his eyes. A tiny half-smile had crept onto her face as he assessed her and even that miniscule reminder of whom she used to be prompted an enormous smile on Duke's face. They remained frozen like that, holding each other's gaze, for several moments before Alessa broke the silence.

"Is there a washcloth I can use?" Her voice sounded small and breathy.

Without breaking eye contact, Duke grabbed the rag and the soap he brought down for her. She thanked him and began lathering soap onto her skin. His eyes widened and his cock hardened at the visual; how many times had he fantasized about seeing her in the shower? Despite making love to her for weeks, there was something far more intimate about watching her softly exfoliate her skin. She moved harshly and winced periodically, her shoulders still jutting out at odd angles from where they had not properly popped back into the socket. It wasn't an injury Duke was familiar with, but he had done his best in the hopes of kindling feelings from her.

Emboldened by her compliance, Duke gently pulled her hair away from her face and held her gaze. "Did Harrison Pierce have you under a spell?" he asked.

Her laugh sounded harsh and bitter, seeming offkey from her usual melody. Duke didn't like it.

"I loved him," she whispered sadly. She rested her chin on her knees and stared into the distance.

For once this did not anger Duke as it typically did. He recognized the longing in her face from his own reflection all those nights as he yearned for her. The flare of jealousy was strong in his heart, but he didn't act on it.

He wanted to make her feel that way about him. She didn't know what true love was if she thought what she had with a man like Pierce even compared to what she had now with Duke. After everything Duke had done to prove it to her, how could she still doubt him?

"But I love you," he countered.

She raised an eyebrow. "Who taught you about love?" Alessa challenged.

The question caught Duke off guard. "Mother, of course," he replied. "Don't mothers always teach their children about love?"

Alessa shook her head. "Not always."

A heaviness settled in the air around them as he considered her words. He couldn't comprehend a world in which his mother would not be his teacher in every aspect of his life.

But yet, had she really? Duke had been ill-prepared for his feelings when he first met Alessa, and he must have still been approaching things the wrong way if she continued to pine for her dead fiancé.

Even now, Duke continued to venture into town, despite Mother's hatred for the place, and purchased medicine for her, read newspapers that were previously banned, and interacted with people while out in the community. Mother would never speak to him again if she knew some of the things he had done since she grew too ill to leave her room.

"I want you to love me, too," Duke admitted to her. "The dark magic won't find us here and we can be happy."

"'The dark magic'?" Alessa repeated. "What does that even mean?"

Duke shook his head. He couldn't explain it to her until he broke through her spell. "Harrison wasn't right for you," he offered instead.

She reflected on that for a moment. "He probably didn't seem like it," she admitted. "But I could tell I brought out a different side to him. He was different around me and I'd like to think I helped make him a better person."

"You make me a better person," Duke said quietly. His face burned with embarrassment at saying the words aloud.

Alessa did not comment. After washing the front of her body as best she could, she sheepishly handed him the rag and asked if he would wash her back for her.

Duke gulped loudly. This was the fulfillment of his wildest dream. Gingerly he adjusted himself to his knees and pulled her hair over her shoulder. Although he had touched her bare skin daily for the past several weeks, this seemed like a true test of their love.

It was the first time Alessa had ever requested he touch her, he realized. His hands lingered between her shoulder blades and slowly slid down her spine. Her back was littered with deep purple bruises and dark red welts from where his belt sliced her open.

Shame washed over him in a wave. He had done this to her, marred her perfect skin and introduced her to pain of the acutest kind. He was despicable, every bit the monster she claimed him to be, unworthy to even breathe the same air. Alessa deserved all the stars in the sky and all the flowers in the earth, yet he had beaten her like an animal. No wonder she continued to reject him. He had done nothing to earn her forgiveness, and it wasn't in her nature to accept a punishment when she did not understand the reasoning behind it.

Above all, love each other deeply, because love covers over a multitude of sins. How many times had Duke read over that passage without understanding its true meaning?

Duke had to demonstrate how their love would grow and how hard he would fight for them as long as she submitted to him.

His hands paused near her lower back and without warning, Alessa's head collided with his face. Duke felt his nose snap and staggered backwards onto his back from the blow.

Alessa leapt from the basin and raced towards the door that led outside, her feet limping erratically. A door that was no longer chained in Duke's carelessness!

She only managed to take two steps out into the light when he caught up with her. He grabbed onto her hair and slammed her body to the ground, flat on her back. A gush of air like the wind leaving her body whooshed out of her mouth and she whimpered on impact.

Duke stood over her, equal parts aroused at her wet, naked body beneath him and disgusted that he once again gave her an opportunity to best him. He kneeled down over her and yanked her chin up to look at him. Her hazel eyes flared with anger and hatred, which only made him smirk.

"You're never going anywhere," he promised her. "You. Are. Mine." He punctuated each word by jerking her face closer to his and planted his mouth firmly on hers. Bitter over her lack of return in the kiss, he shoved her head back down and felt a moment of satisfaction when she grimaced.

Inspiration setting in, he clamped one hand over her mouth and withdrew a small knife from his back pocket. His hands muffled her screams as he sliced the word MINE into her stomach just under her round breasts. "So you'll never forget who you belong to," Duke explained deviously. His exhilaration grew as he silenced her screams beneath his palm. It was such a rush to exert his will over her and have her succumb to his dominance.

Blood trickled down her stomach and pooled at her navel. He became hyper-aware of her naked body pinned beneath him and how powerful it made him feel. Without a second thought, the hand that was over her mouth clenched both wrists above her head while his other hand pulled his pants down. He had her right there in the dirt, with the sun cascading warmth down his back and the bees buzzing their approval. Her tender flesh accepted his cock, and Duke knew he was making progress in breaking her because for the first time ever, Alessa's hips rose to meet his. There was no resistance, no fight. The fire of defiance that was in her had finally gone out.

CHAPTER
TWENTY-FIVE

2011

Stella sighed heavily as she scanned the next week's schedule. She had been assigned all night shifts so there was no overlap with any of the Barbie nurses. It wasn't that she minded working overnight, but there would only be one nurse on the floor and one other nurse's assistant to divvy up the work, which would mean less time to spend in Room 216 and far more vomit, piss, and blood to wipe up. The patients knew the ones working overnight were running on caffeine binges and the last fumes of patience, so they tended to act out.

It's a punishment, Stella realized. Mary's way of making Stella suffer for saying those things to Veronica.

"This is not a punishment," Mary said from behind her. Stella whirled around wildly, startled at how Mary predicted her thoughts.

"You gave me the worst shift!" Stella argued. "How is it not a punishment?"

Mary darted a glance in either direction before leaning in close to whisper. "I am helping you keep your head down so there's no chance of getting another complaint. If you work nights with Riley and Deb, you'll come out of this just fine."

Stella rolled her eyes. "Yeah, because neither one of them ever do anything and I'll have all the work every night."

Her boss huffed in exasperation and threw her hands up in defeat. "Then I won't try to help you anymore!" She grabbed her beloved clipboard and headed off to do her rounds.

Part of Stella recognized the truth in what Mary said. She needed to avoid getting in more trouble, and if she worked the opposite shift from the Barbie nurses, she was far less likely to have a run in with one of them. But the resentment bled deep. Veronica and her crew would come out of everything unscathed, like always, while Stella would have to eat crow to salvage another chance. Although she didn't take any particular pride in her job, it would be nice to just once have someone take her side. Life never worked like that, however.

Stella rolled her head to loosen some of the tension in her neck and took a few steadying breaths. She had no choice but to accept it and move on.

Snatching the schedule from the nurse's station, she headed down to the elevator so she could grab her backpack from the employee locker room and go home for a few hours' sleep.

When she returned later that evening to start her shift, Deb was already in a foul mood. Deb could be considered Mary's second in command in that she had been at the hospital just as long as Mary and was often the head nurse on overnight shifts, but unlike Mary, Deb's attitude toward the place had long since soured. Any respect she once held for the doctors, nurses, and other staff had disappeared years ago, making Deb as helpful as a cactus when it came to getting anything done. She didn't ever hurry to address an issue with a patient, even if the patient was coding, and snapped at anyone who challenged her. Yet her eidetic memory made her a valuable asset in care and communication…as well as enabled her to blackmail about half the members of management for their minor policy violations. Therefore she stayed and ruled the night shift with an iron fist of sarcasm and cynicism.

Deb immediately began barking orders at her upon her arrival. Stella's hand twitched longing at the cigarettes in her back pocket, but she knew better than to refuse Deb's assignments. It was going to be a long night.

The next several hours were spent cleaning up a patient who contracted some form of the flu and had uncontrollable diarrhea. He had managed to spray his fecal matter all over the floor, the wall, and into the crevices of the hospital bed. When Stella managed to get him up to walk him towards the toilet, he promptly vomited down her torso.

Shuffling into the employee lounge, Stella made to pull her scrub top off when a movement in the corner caught her eye. Riley, the other nurse's assistant assigned to the floor, sat on a broken medical recliner in the corner, eating a bag of chips from the vending machine. Judging by the bloodshot crinkles in his eyes and earthy aroma permeating the room, he smoked a couple blunts before coming to work.

His eyes widened as Stella made eye contact, still pulling the vomit covered top away from her body.

"Um, Riley, do you mind?" Stella snapped.

He chuckled low. "Not at all. You can give me a show."

Riley weighed in the ballpark of three hundred pounds, including a bulbous stomach that always protruded from his shirt and hung over the waistband of his pants. His glasses were perpetually sliding off his nose, and he was a bit infamous for his lingering body odor. He only worked the night shift a few nights a week, devoting most of his time to video games, even competing in tournaments. A "semi-professional gamer" is what he liked to call himself, although apparently even gamers needed health insurance. Stella could not imagine a more disgusting man ogling her, nor could she picture anything less arousing than a woman covered in mustard colored puke.

Stella couldn't stand the stench of vomit any longer and continued stripping it from her body. Gagging slightly, she wadded the top up and threw it toward the laundry chute in the hallway. Riley chuckled again.

"Did you really have to come in while high?" Stella asked. Riley would be worthless for the rest of the night.

He held a finger to his lips. "Shhh!" he stage-whispered, then continued laughing.

She rolled her eyes and went to the small cupboard where there were spare shirts and pants, withdrawing a threadbare top with hearts on it. It looked to be the only one in her size, so Stella would have to live with it. She then went to stand next to Riley, tugging on his upper arm to pull him out of the chair.

"Come on," she grunted. "Get up. You're getting out of here."

Riley threw her arm off. "No, I'm not! I need the hours!"

She crossed her arms in front of her chest. "Then you better get your dumbass up and wash off the smell. I'm getting a buzz just from the proximity."

That made him smile at her again. "I bet you are. I can give you another kind of buzz."

Stella blanched. "I would rather have that guy puke on me again."

Riley's smile turned malicious. "That's not the way I hear it. You've got quite a reputation. You'll sleep with anyone."

His statement landed like a sucker punch to the gut. She stepped back from him, appalled at his accusation. "I wouldn't touch you with a ten cent whore's pussy," Stella swore. "Who the fuck told you any of this?"

It was Riley's turn to roll his eyes. "Dude, everyone knows that's why you have a job here. You're just some dumb slut. All I'm saying is we could at least make this shift a little interesting for both of us." He stood up and leaned over her, his breath smelling heavily of the sour cream and onion chips he held in his hand.

Stella's rage sparked. Just as she opened her mouth to retort, Deb walked in.

"You're not getting paid to make goo goo eyes at each other! Davis in Room 227 needs a bath and Vomit Guy needs new bedding, Stella. Out, both of you!" Deb clapped her hands in urgency.

Stella shot one last look of venom at Riley before leaving the lounge. She changed the bedding as quickly as she could, fighting back tears. After getting the other patient settled, her feet automatically carried her to Room 216. She didn't care what else was going on with the patients and ignored the pages overhead for assistance in other rooms.

The peace from the darkened, soundless room enveloped her like a caress. She sank into the cold chair and drew her knees to her chest. Stella couldn't hold back the floodgates anymore and instead indulged in a crying fit that left her slightly breathless. Her shoulders shook with sobs that she attempted to muffle with a fist in her mouth.

Riley hadn't said anything she hadn't heard her entire life. If she had a nickel for every time someone accused her of being a whore or sleeping her way into some small fortune, Stella could book the trip to Europe she wanted. She knew what her reputation was, and yet she didn't feel it was deserved. Yes, she enjoyed sex free of tangled emotions, but that was just easier for someone like her. Loners didn't do well in relationships and Stella didn't feel like she missed out on anything by avoiding that kind of complication.

In truth, Stella had never met anyone who she wanted to spend more time with, so it didn't bother her. Sex was just sex, a natural urge she ceded to whenever the desire hit her, and even that wasn't very often. Books and movies made love sound so important, but if that were true, she couldn't have survived her entire life without experiencing it. The fact that she was alive and supporting herself proved that love was an unnecessary impediment, one she had no trouble avoiding.

She was being stupid, she knew. Riley's opinion, or anyone else's for that matter, didn't amount to zilch, and sex certainly never opened any doors for her. Look at her current predicament with Malcolm Glasswell. Sex only shifted power dynamics; men had been getting off on that power trip since the beginning of time. Stella had done what she had to, like always, like all women do. She would continue to do anything that made her life easier. Riley's words couldn't hurt her unless she allowed them to.

Brushing her hair back from her face, Stella exhaled slowly through her mouth and lowered her feet to the floor. She realized Avery Winslow's eyes, barely visible in the dim moonlight throughout the room, were zeroed in on her in his usual unsettling gaze. He didn't even blink.

"This changes nothing," Stella said. She wasn't entirely sure if she was directing this at him or herself. "Don't for one minute think this means anything."

He continued to stare at her, eyes shining in the darkness. She hated herself for allowing him to see her in such a moment of weakness. His quiet judgment only served as a mockery of her pain. Quick as a viper, Stella slapped his face as hard as she could. His head snapped to one side before he turned back to her, his eyes boring into her face just as steadily as before.

Stella seethed. "Just fucking speak, you freak!" she demanded angrily. She smacked him again, though this time his head didn't move. This led to another. And another.

No matter how many times she struck his face, he didn't respond. If anything, his eyes held pity. He looked at her with sympathy, as though he wanted to offer some kind of comfort for her despair. It drove her into a frenzy; she didn't want his compassion.

When she didn't have any pain left beyond the stinging in her palm from her strikes against his face, Stella slumped into the chair and leaned against the rail on his hospital bed. Her breathing came out labored and heavy, her body limp from exhaustion. All her rage and sorrow were gone.

In an odd way, she almost felt like Avery wanted her to work out her aggression. He didn't seem to regard her as warily as he usually did. She honestly felt better and his expression made her suspect he was glad of it.

"Thanks," muttered Stella. She patted his chest awkwardly and stood up to leave. Pausing in the doorway, she looked back at him. Even in the filtered moonlight from the window his eyes were vast pools of silent expressions. "We'll go back to our usual tomorrow," she warned him. "You will regret the day you entered this hospital by the time I'm done with you."

CHAPTER
TWENTY-SIX

1990

For the first time he could remember, Edwin dreaded going into the office the next day. Gaines had refused to return to the living room after their argument and even now Edwin was unsure of what to say to his partner. Gaines was young and idealistic, and while those weren't bad traits to have, they would hinder Gaines if he wanted to continue as a criminal investigation detective. His father had apologized to Edwin before he left for the night and promised to talk to his son the next morning.

Gaines already clacked away on his computer when Edwin entered. Neither said anything as Edwin hung up his jacket and poured himself a cup of coffee, coffee that he noted was freshly brewed and hot. Although they didn't make eye contact, Edwin sensed that the rookie followed his every movement like a hawk.

As soon as Edwin sat behind his desk, Gaines turned to him and cleared his throat. Edwin held up a hand to stop him. "We don't need to snuggle and braid each other's hair to make up," he clarified gruffly.

His partner nodded and swallowed hard. "I know that, but I still want to apologize. I shouldn't have walked out last night. We need to trust each other, even if I have some different opinions on the future than you do."

This made Edwin smile. "And what opinions do you think I have of the future?"

Gaines reddened, but stood his ground. "You're okay with letting money determine our investigations. I'm not, and I never will be."

The veteran detective leaned back in his chair and calmly surveyed Gaines. He wanted to phrase things carefully after how badly things went last night. They had too much at stake now to start hating one another.

"I'm not okay with it," began Edwin, "But it does more good for me to focus my effort and energy on the people I can help. If a case is assigned to me, I'm able to help victims and their families and hopefully get a crook off the streets for a little while. That's the prize I have to keep on the horizon."

Gaines shook his head and made to argue, but Edwin cut him off. "Look, kid, bad things happen all day every day. Even if we had a thousand detectives working around the clock on these cases, we couldn't help everyone. Not all cases have the necessary evidence or leads, people lie to protect the perp, witnesses refuse to come forward—the list goes on! As much as I want to help every single person who walks into this building, I cannot prevent the bad things from happening, nor can I alone solve every case that comes through here. I do the best I can with what I have, and I have to accept that that is enough or I will drive myself crazy."

Edwin gave Gaines a very sympathetic look. "You'll drive yourself crazy if you set out to change the world in a single night, kid. Start with the people you can help and go from there."

"But it's not enough!" Gaines slammed his fist on his desk.

Edwin nodded in agreement. "And it will never be enough. There will always be some bastard out there hurting a kid, or snatching a woman, or whatever. The job never goes away. So don't take it home with you. Accept that you are doing as much as you can with the cases that are assigned to you and believe in the difference that it makes. Even if you only find one missing person, that's one life that's entirely changed."

His partner seemed to reflect for a moment on this. "How do you do this? How do you live each day, knowing there are so many horrors in the world and we can't stop it?"

Edwin remembered asking Shelley this one time after they found the body of a woman who had been raped before being strangled and dumped in a park. "You tackle one case at a time with everything you've got," he echoed Shelley's advice. "Gaines, you have so much potential. It's a good thing that you're here for the right reasons. Don't get bogged down with the rest of it—the hypotheticals, the awards, the office politics…it will drown you. And I've seen plenty of cops who had to leave the force because they couldn't handle it anymore. Let's just do our job to find Harrison Pierce and hopefully we'll find Alessa Meinken in the process, okay?"

Gaines nodded before sending his signature sheepish grin down to the floor. "I don't think I'll ever be a cop like you." He pulled at an imaginary thread on the side of his pants and kept his eyes on the floor.

Edwin was speechless. He didn't intend to get so attached to the kid or have this kind of mentorship between them. Even the Gaines family had drawn him in like a moth to a flame. It threw him off balance, and he wasn't someone who liked to be caught off guard. Edwin didn't consider himself an emotional guy, so why was there a lump growing in his throat that made it hard for him to swallow?

"You'll be an even better cop than me," Edwin finally admitted.

The two men smiled fondly at one another for a few moments, the respect between the veteran and rookie only growing. A shrill ring of the telephone shattered the moment.

"Yeah?" Edwin answered. "Yep, we're on our way." The phone clattered back down into the cradle as Edwin snatched his jacket in the same fluid movement. "Get your coat, Gaines. We gotta go pick up those tapes from Groundbreaking."

2011

Stella's eyes fluttered close, despite her determination to keep them open. It had been a long night; a patient attempted suicide by slicing open a wrist with a jagged piece of metal. It took them hours to discover where the piece came from. The patient had somehow managed to take the screw off the bottom of a hospital chair and had been sharpening an edge of the bracket in anticipation. The whole scenario was a nightmare, definitely the type of incident that would get upper management involved. No one liked it when someone from Central Office started poking around and asking questions.

Yet like a fly to shit, Stella was summoned to Glasswell's office shortly after she arrived home. Too scared to refuse, her hatred and animosity continued to grow. Feeling helpless was the worst kind of weakness.

She sat in the glum waiting room until Glasswell's office door sprung open, then bolted upright so her back was ramrod straight. No sense in letting him know her defenses were down. A haughty looking woman in a pinstripe pencil skirt and blazer strode out of Glasswell's office carrying a leather briefcase. Her dark hair was pulled into a tight bun on top of her head, highlighting her angular features. Stella vaguely recognized her face, but couldn't remember where she had seen the woman before.

Malcolm Glasswell emerged behind her, looking harried and stressed. His hair, usually gelled to perfection, sat in disarray and his tie looked crooked. He glanced at Stella and blanched. Angling his body to block Stella from view, Glasswell placed his hand lightly on his companion's back and guided her out of the administrative offices with a fake smile plastered on his face. The woman's stilettos echoed down the hall.

Stella breathed a small sigh of relief. If Glasswell was otherwise occupied, she could go home and sleep. Right as she stood up to leave the waiting area, his head popped in from the hallway. "Go wait in my office. I'll only be a few more minutes," he instructed.

She rolled her eyes, but acquiesced. Disobeying would likely only make things worse. Glasswell didn't need another reason to fire her. Stella threw herself into her usual office chair and groaned. There wouldn't be enough coffee in the world to get her through today.

It dawned on her that she had never been inside Glasswell's office alone before. Maybe if she could find her own form of blackmail, his "coaching" sessions could stop and there would be no need for the hearing.

Stella began pulling open drawers and shuffling through papers. There was a filing cabinet, but it was locked and Stella couldn't find the key. She glanced at the door before attempting to log into his computer. It was also locked, but Stella tended to be lucky at guessing passwords.

She checked the room for clues as to his interests. There were no personal photographs or mementos anywhere. He had a bachelor's degree framed on the wall from a university Stella had never heard of, but that was the only thing that even identified the office's occupant. She halfheartedly tried the password with a few combinations of the school's name without any conviction. There was no way that was his password.

"Looking for something?" a deep voice asked from the doorway.

Stella jumped from the seat as though she were electrocuted. Malcolm Glasswell glared at her from across the room. His jacket was unbuttoned and pulled behind his arms as his hands clenched in fists on his hips. He advanced on her, never blinking, a predator stalking his prey. His wicked smile was enough to stir fear in Stella's brain. She backed up into the second desk along the wall behind her and chanced a quick peek to the right and left, assessing her options.

Meanwhile, Glasswell crossed the room slowly, his dark eyes never leaving her face. He rounded the desk and placed both hands on the hutch behind her, caging her in. Stella's breath caught in her chest and her hands felt clammy. There was nowhere for her to run.

His right hand snaked its way down her body, cupping her breast and using his thumb to tease her nipple through the fabric. As Stella's body betrayed her and she panted, his other hand snagged around her throat. He tightened his hold on her windpipe and leaned in to brush light kisses along her jaw.

"I could do it, you know," he whispered. "I could squeeze the life out of you this very minute and there isn't a damn person who would do something about it. No one would miss you. No one would know you're gone."

Stella's ears rang from hearing her deepest insecurities fall from his lips. He was right. Everyone else at work would just assume she finally quit. Nobody would look for her or give her a second thought. She had no friends, and other than the check she deposited for her landlord on the first of every month, nobody relied on her for anything. She lived a useless existence, bound to nothing. It was a waste to even call it a life.

His eyes gleamed maliciously, thrilled at her fear. He tightened the hold on her throat infinitesimally once more and the edges around her vision began to darken. Desperately she grasped at his wrist to pry his fingers loose. She thought wildly about kneeing him in the balls or shoving him off her, but she had no muscle strength and nothing to defend herself with. Unless she drove a knife through him, he would catch up to her before she could make it to the door.

Glasswell finally relaxed his hand and her body went slack against him as she gasped for air. She felt lightheaded and sick to her stomach. He grabbed her harshly around her biceps and pulled her in close to threaten, "Do not ever touch my things again."

Weakly, she nodded and pulled herself from his grip. "I understand," she whispered.

He smiled cruelly again, the light never reaching his eyes. Before she had time to register what he was doing, the back of his hand struck the left side of her face. Stella's head snapped back and she tasted the bitter blood in her mouth. Her eyes widened in fear as she hugged the throbbing side of her face. It stung, though she could not determine if it was the pain or her pride making her respond as if on autopilot. For once she was rendered speechless.

Patting her on the head, he muttered, "Good girl," before pushing her to her knees in front of him. He lazily pulled open his belt and unzipped his pants where his erection bulged against the boxer briefs he wore. His posture indicated what she was to do.

Loathing herself and what was about to happen, Stella freed his cock from the garment and took him in her mouth. She continued to move as if in a daze. Salty tears coated her cheeks to match the tangy taste from the pre-cum leaking down her throat. Glasswell tugged her hair back, forcing her to look up at him. "Keep your eyes on me and show me you understand," he commanded.

On her knees at his mercy and terrified of what he could do if she disobeyed, Stella swallowed her anger and did as he ordered.

CHAPTER
TWENTY-EIGHT

1990

Duke couldn't believe how careless he had become. For someone who hated surprises, he sure kept allowing Alessa to catch him off guard more often than not. After satiating his lust with her body outside for hours, he had dragged her limp form back into the basement and strung her up from the chain in the center of the room. No matter how many times he lashed out at her back with the belt, he couldn't stop admonishing himself for such an avoidable mistake. Her back, ass, and legs dripped in crimson by the time he was done. He didn't even bother to remove her, but instead allowed her to dangle there in the growing pool of her own blood.

Once he reached the kitchen, his hands started moving automatically to build a fire in the wood burning stove and cook something to eat. However, a low moan from upstairs had him bolting into his mother's room in an instant. Fear gripped his heart as he observed her current state, her eyes rolling in the back of her head as she moaned and clutched at her stomach. Pain was written all over her face, and in his helplessness, Duke couldn't stop it.

For the next few days, Duke stayed by her bedside. Mother's breathing came out in short, shallow huffs. A light sheen of sweat covered her body, though any time Duke attempted to take some of her many quilts off, she begged and pleaded for him to put them back on because of how cold she felt. Her gray and brown hair was in complete disarray and plastered around her face. Duke winced whenever he looked at it because he knew how much Mother hated to be disheveled and unkempt, but when he ran her silver comb through her hair, it scared him to see large tufts of it clump in the brush. A small bald spot had to be hidden on the side of her head and Duke thanked God that her eyesight was too poor to detect it herself.

Duke hadn't been down to see Alessa in several days because he was too scared to leave Mother's side. Any idiot could see that this was the end. Whatever the source of the rigid divide across her abdomen was now so engorged that it stretched along her right side. The rest of her body was skeletal; Duke could count all of the ribs on her left side. She refused to eat anything and he felt a keen sense of failure over her unwillingness to even sip a few spoonsful of broth.

Losing Mother terrified Duke far more than he cared to admit. She had always been such an overpowering figure in his life, and he knew he owed her everything. All he had ever wanted was to become the man she described and to make her proud.

He knew now that she kept him isolated as a child. He had read enough of the forbidden books and newspapers during her illness that he understood most people went to school, had jobs, maintained friend-ships…yet he couldn't even begrudge her choice of isolation because he, too, now saw the world for the dark magic it held. She had been protecting him, like mothers are supposed to do, and Duke loved her for it.

Even so, he was angry with her for raising him in such a manner that left him ill-prepared for the challenges ahead. There were still so many things Duke didn't understand and his ignorance scratched on his skin like an abrasive wool shroud. Had his mother properly taught him about the dark magic with women, Alessa would not be an illusion sent to tempt him. He wouldn't have to resort to pain and suffering to break her spell because he would already know how to tame the beast within her.

His mother failed him, which was a bitter spill to swallow as she laid on her deathbed. Time wouldn't allow for correction now.

Duke squeezed a washcloth into the sink in her bathroom and returned to his chair at her side to lightly wipe the sweat from her brow. It sickened him to see her so weak and frail, his indomitable mother who had delivered so many beatings throughout his life. There were so many questions on the tip of his tongue, but Mother had barely whispered more than five words in the past 24 hours. He was startled when her bony hand closed around his wrist and pulled the cloth from her forehead. He realized her eyes were piercing his with more clarity than he had seen in months.

"I'm dying, Dukey boy," she huffed. Her body began to shake with a coughing fit that rattled the entire bed. He lifted a glass of water to her lips, but she shook her head and pushed his hand away. "This is important, Duke, so pay attention."

Duke's heart fluttered and years of conditioning made him sit straighter in his chair.

"There's a small wood chest in the back of my closet—it's got a little heart on it—that has all the paperwork you'll need. Once I pass, you get that and take it all to the bank. You remember what the bank is, don't you? They can help you from there." Her eyes closed briefly before she looked quizzically back at her son. "You're just a boy. I hate that I'm leaving you so soon." She caressed his cheek with the back of her hand.

Her words stirred anger in his soul. "I'm not a boy," Duke countered. Despite the love behind the gesture, he grabbed her hand from his face and firmly placed it back on her chest. He was in his mid-twenties, yet she still talked to him as though he wore diapers.

Normally such an outburst would have resulted in a whipping at the very least. Were he younger, Duke had no doubt that such a statement would have also included being locked outside without food for a few days, a punishment she resorted to when he was truly wicked. He couldn't believe his own daring to talk to Mother in this manner.

She drew back and seemed to be assessing him for the first time. She didn't correct him or reach out her hand for the belt. Several tense moments passed where Duke waited for her reaction. "No," she finally muttered. "I don't suppose you are." Her brows continued to furrow as she gazed at him.

It was enough for Duke to melt. He allowed the tears to flow down his cheeks and he crumpled his forehead to her side. She absentmindedly brushed her fingers through his hair as his body racked with sobs. For a long time he simply succumbed to the swell of emotion, his love for his mother, his anger at her choices, and the fresh grief of his loss swirling in a vortex Duke could not yet process. The hot tears felt therapeutic and he recognized the baptism of change washing over him. Nothing would ever be the same again.

After he sobbed everything out of his system and his tears dried up, Duke sat up and grasped his mother's hands in own. She smiled fondly at him. "You were the pride of my life, Dukey boy. It's okay to be sad, but don't live there. Move on with your life."

He nodded in agreement. "I will, Mother. I will be the man you always raised me to be."

This made her smile wider. "Yes, you will. Stay away from dark magic and you'll be alright." She gave his hand a quick pat and then settled back into the pillows, closing her eyes.

She didn't open them again as she began to instruct him that the small chest also contained details for her funeral, a thought that had not occurred to Duke. He didn't know of anyone else in his mother's life and wasn't entirely sure that anyone would come to pay their respects. He didn't argue, however, and instead began to sponge the sweat off her face again with the discarded washcloth.

Mother fell into a deep sleep, leaving Duke alone with his thoughts— a dangerous place for him to be.

Duke impulsively decided to go back to the coffee house. Maybe if he returned and learned more about the people who worked there or frequented the establishment, he could learn how to get through to Alessa. Plus, it seemed like the perfect place to go and burn off a little energy, maybe even try one of their pastries for once. Why not people watch and avoid his feelings? With Alessa in the basement recovering, he couldn't distract himself by using her body.

When he arrived there almost an hour later, there was a girl he didn't recognize working behind the counter and he wryly imagined her trying to live up to Alessa's beauty. She was a cheap imitation on Alessa's ugliest day, not that Alessa ever really had any. However, the girl smiled sweetly as she handed Duke his coffee and it was enough to make Duke smile back at her. Craving an indulgence, he took the coffee across the room to the condiments counter so he could try some sugar and cream in it.

The bell over the door clanged loudly and he heard multiple sets of footsteps entering the shop.

"I'm Detective Gaines from Amherst Police Department," a voice said. "I'm here for the tapes."

Duke's heart stopped and a cold sweat broke out over his forehead. What tapes could the police be here for? Did this have something to do with Alessa? He wanted to sneak a peek over his shoulder, but didn't dare draw attention to himself. There was no way they could know he was involved, right?

As subtly as he could, Duke placed a lid on the coffee cup and kept his head down as he approached the door. He didn't want to walk too fast and raise suspicion, but self-preservation dictated he get out of the coffee shop as quickly as he could. Thankfully he had the sense to wear a baseball cap today and he tried to appear as though he was bracing himself to go outside as he pulled the brim down lower over his eyes.

Duke noticed two pairs of leather shoes in front of the counter, though he couldn't see either of their faces as he passed.

It's a partnership, he reasoned to himself.

He whipped around into the alleyway behind the shop and bolted for Mother's van as fast as he could. He needed to know what the police were looking for or his entire plan would go up in smoke.

CHAPTER
TWENTY-NINE

1990

Edwin and Gaines made two trips back and forth between the car and the office to carry in all of the boxes of tapes. It turned out Colin's information wasn't entirely accurate; Groundbreaking's owner held onto tapes for six months at a time before recording over them, however, he had some tapes that went much further back. Nothing was documented since the intention was to record over older videos, meaning there was no way for the detectives to know the dates on any of the videos in the boxes until they watched them. They were in for some long hours over the next few days.

Gaines already had the equipment set up and the pair dedicated all of their time over the next two weeks to the videos. First, they decided, they needed to establish some sort of catalog system to track dates and which videos were which. Then they began to identify the people in each video, making a log of the dates and times where Harrison Pierce was present. Alessa Meinken was easy to identify, and there was little doubt she was the reason Pierce frequented the coffee house. He could be seen kissing her and holding her in many of the films.

It was exactly what Edwin needed to invigorate some hope into his life. The case no longer seemed liked a dead end, and although there was still no sign of either Harrison or Alessa's bodies, they were on track to find something. Dates were aligning and provided a rough timeline that matched what they had already determined from Pierce's banking information.

After several days of watching the tapes, however, cold reality slithered down their backs and enveloped them in a blanket of dismay. The video footage confirmed Harrison Pierce and Alessa Meinken were in a relationship and both stopped going to the coffee house on the same day.

However, there was nothing to indicate they had left in a hurry, a fight, or against their will. Even the video of them from their last day at Groundbreaking showed a couple who an observer would believe to be completely in love. It didn't make any sense.

Wanting to explore the investigation from Alessa's perspective, Edwin and Gaines decided to approach that angle instead.

"Call the roommate and set up an interview. We need to see Alessa's bedroom and learn as much about her as we can," Edwin instructed.

Gaines nodded and picked up the phone to call.

T he next day, the detectives knocked on the door of an apartment in a rundown unit close to campus. Her roommate, a girl named Mallory Jenkins, broke down in such a sobbing fit over the phone that Gaines learned very little other than they were welcome to see Alessa's room at any time. She answered tearfully, her reddish blond hair piled in a bun on top of her head, and waved the officers inside.

The living room looked like a typical college apartment. Most of the furniture appeared dated and well used, most likely second- or even third hand, but the room was clean. A framed photograph of Mallory and Alessa sat on an end table near the door, which Edwin picked up absentmindedly. Both girls beamed at the camera, their arms wrapped around one another.

"I'm so glad you guys are finally looking into her disappearance,"

Mallory gushed tearfully. "Alessa would *never* just pick up and leave like this. She's the most responsible person I know!"

Gaines gave the woman a kind smile. "What can you tell us about her?"

Mallory shrugged. "Pretty much everything. Alessa's my best friend. We've been in school together since the second grade. We both wanted to get away from the Florida heat, so we applied to colleges together, and we've been roommates ever since. I know that girl better than I know myself sometimes."

"Did you know her boyfriend?" Edwin asked, setting the framed photograph back down on the table.

At this, Mallory frowned. "He's been a huge issue between us for the past few months. She refused to even tell me his name, which I told her sounded seriously creepy. He's never come here to my knowledge."

Gaines scribbled frantically in a notebook as he tried to get all the information down.

"Were they serious?" Edwin asked.

"She claimed they were, but how could you marry someone without even introducing them to your best friend?" Mallory pointed out. Another tear rolled down her cheek, but this time she angrily swiped it away. "Alessa has been like a sister to me for most of my life, and yet she didn't trust me enough to tell me his name."

Admittedly, Edwin didn't know much about girls *or* relationships, but it sounded a bit odd to him, too. Harrison's celebrity status might've required some discretion, sure, but to keep even her closest friends and family in the dark? That sounded more than a little fishy to him.

"Can we see Alessa's room?" Gaines asked hopefully.

Mallory nodded and led them down a narrow hallway. While her roommate's doorway featured pictures, stickers, and a Nirvana poster, Alessa's door contained a calendar with a color coded schedule of her work hours, classes, and study groups. A dry erase board hung above the calendar with a bright pink sticker instructing them to "leave a message."

"She looks pretty organized," Gaines commented.

Her roommate nodded in agreement. "Alessa had to maintain at least a 3.5 GPA for her scholarship."

The bedroom was just as neat and organized as the door. Alessa only had a twin bed, indicating she never had overnight company, along with several bookcases. Most contained textbooks, but one closest to the window contained some battered children's books.

"She liked to volunteer at a children's hospital," Mallory explained when she caught Edwin staring at the bookshelf.

A sweet girl...who probably turned Pierce into a caring man, Edwin thought, remembering the conversation with Pierce's business collaborator about their ventures into sustainable housing in Brazil.

"We're gonna take a look around now, if that's alright," Gaines replied pointedly. Mallory took the hint and left the room. "What d'you reckon?" he asked after the door closed behind her.

"Nothing about this girl makes me think she would associate with Harrison Pierce, but I agree with the roommate—Alessa didn't leave on her own free will," Edwin surmised. "Nobody this dedicated to school and work, even volunteering, would take off without a moment's notice."

Gaines didn't reply, but opened the top drawer in the solitary dresser by the door. He hastily shut it, muttering about girls and their underwear. Edwin chuckled softly under his breath.

He moved to the nightstand beside the bed and pointed to the drawer that stood slightly ajar. "Looks like there's something in here."

Pulling a rubber glove out of his pocket, Edwin carefully pulled open the drawer and found a battered leather journal inside. Gaines leaned over his shoulder to get a better look. A capped pen wedged between the pages indicated where Alessa stopped writing. Upon flipping it open, the detectives realized the book was a diary.

"Well that's definitely coming with us," Gaines joked as he held open a plastic evidence bag.

Back at the station later that afternoon, both men took turns reading the passages. Alessa wrote about a man named "H" whom she fell in love with rather quickly. There were several entries that relayed how concerned she was with the differences in their socioeconomic statuses and that she sometimes felt insecure with all of the "gorgeous women" he surrounded himself with. While there was nothing to indicate any problems between them, Alessa also wrote frequently about her intentions to keep their relationship as private as possible, even if it meant keeping Mallory and their families in the dark.

According to the diary, this decision made "H" respect her more because he knew she wasn't after him for status or money.

"She has to be talking about Harrison Pierce!" Gaines exclaimed triumphantly. "This totally links them together!"

Edwin frowned as he read another entry for the third time. "Linking them together isn't the problem. She doesn't have anything in here about fearing for her safety or thinking somebody's after her. The girl practically sounds like a saint!" He threw the book down in annoyance.

An assessment similar to all the others when Gaines and Edwin interviewed people on Alessa's character. Everyone had positive things to say. It was evident that Alessa was well liked and incredibly kind. There was nothing to suggest an addiction or some other dark secret, her grades indicated she was a great student, and she had a typical social life.

Her parents spoke to Gaines over the phone, but Gaines couldn't glean much information from them since they hadn't seen Alessa in over two years. There was never enough money for her to travel home to Florida or for them to visit her, but it seemed as though they were a normal family. Nonetheless, Edwin advised him to run a background check on her parents, just in case.

The only red flag, if it could even be considered one, is that no one seemed to be aware of Alessa's relationship with Harrison Pierce. Although she made references to having a boyfriend—her mother even suggested they were getting serious about planning a future together—Alessa never told anyone his name. Beyond the videos from Groundbreaking, there was nothing to link the two of them together. Even the diary entries weren't enough because a single initial wouldn't count as an identifying piece of information.

Frustrated to his core, Edwin swore under his breath and stood up. He announced his intention to go for a run and take a breather so he could clear his head. Gaines nodded in sympathy and advised Edwin to take his time. He offered to continue watching the tapes while Edwin was gone.

"No, kid, go ahead and take a break yourself. We both need some fresh eyes on this," Edwin countered.

Gaines sighed heavily, but agreed. There was no sense in beating a dead horse.

Edwin ran harder than usual that afternoon, beating his normal pace by almost two minutes. Despite the hot shower afterwards and the indulgence of pizza from the expensive place across town, Edwin couldn't get his mind to quiet down. Those tapes had to have the key and instead they only seemed to confirm what they already knew.

After tossing and turning for several hours, Edwin gave up and accepted that sleep would not come. He hustled into his coat and headed to the office to pour over his notes from the tapes.

He was surprised and grateful to find Gaines had beaten him there. His curls were wet, as though Gaines had rushed there straight from the shower, and he only wore a light sweatshirt and pair of basketball shorts. He had headphones on as he watched the tapes, though they had already ascertained most of the noise was just static. The camera was too high up on the ceiling to capture any real sound from the coffee house below.

Gaines, however, seemed to be fast forwarding through large chunks before randomly pausing and scribbling something on the notepad balanced on his knees. Edwin waved his hand in front of his partner's face to alert him to his presence.

The rookie jumped, unaware of Edwin's entrance. He offered his usual sheepish grin at being caught working on something without his partner. Edwin felt a brief twang of guilt that Gaines seemed to always be embarrassed for working independently, but he brushed the feeling aside until he had time to consider how to address it. For now, they had more important things to worry about.

Edwin shuffled out of his coat and hung it on the hook in the corner. "Find anything interesting?"

"Actually, I think I have," Gaines replied eagerly. "Come check this out." He rose from the chair and pulled Edwin into his vacated seat. Gaines rewound the video to the beginning, dated nearly four months ago.

The grainy footage showed Alessa behind the counter of the coffee bar, pouring a coffee into a mug for a customer. There were two people in line. Based on the light filtering in from the windows, it was still relatively early in the morning. The camera was placed in a corner of the room above the front door. Everything was visible that could be seen from a customer's perspective. Nothing significant jumped out and caught Edwin's attention.

Gaines pointed at a male customer sitting at a table closest to the window facing toward the coffee bar itself. He held a newspaper in his hand and there was a half-filled coffee mug on the table before him.

"See this guy?" Gaines directed. "He's in the coffee shop every morning that Alessa works. She has one day off per week since the place isn't open on Sunday's, and within forty-five minutes of unlocking the door, this guy comes in. From all the videos I've checked so far, he only ever orders black coffee. Certainly nothing that should make him come to the same place every day. He stays for several hours, normally leaving shortly before Alessa's shift ends." Gaines grins pointedly at Edwin as though waiting for him to be as excited about this discovery as he is. "I was just double checking dates—this guy stopped going there on the same day that Harrison and Alessa disappeared."

Edwin couldn't help himself. The smile unfolded across his face and he clapped his partner hard on the shoulder. "Gaines, you're a genius!" he crowed. "Let's find out everything we can about this guy!"

CHAPTER
THIRTY

2011

Stella fumed with herself for what transpired in Glasswell's office. She gave in to that slimy snake's game and allowed him to make her a weak fool practically groveling at his feet. It disgusted her, and she hated that she allowed him to win. And Stella knew from past experience that it would only get worse from there, especially now that he included physical pain in the mix. Her committee hearing wasn't for another few weeks and now that he had seen just how far he could exploit her, the boundary would keep getting pushed further down the path of offensive behaviors. No man deserved to see her on her knees before him. No one was worth that degradation. She had to find a way to put him in his place and make all of it stop.

An idea occurred to her and she grabbed her phone to check the internet. After a lengthy search and perusing the reviews on about twenty websites, she tried not to hyperventilate at the dent in her savings her new purchase had made. A security camera, complete with sound recorder, no bigger than a pen cap was on its way to her apartment.

The harder part would be placing it in his office without him noticing or finding the camera right away.

Slipping the janitor a crisp $50 bill seemed to do the trick, however, because the next night while she was on her lunch break, Luis snuck her the key and vacuumed loudly outside Glasswell's door while she found the right spot for the camera. She settled on placing it over the screw holding the coat rack to the wall next to the door. It blended in perfectly unless you knew what to look for. Stella felt confident it would be the best vantage point in the room.

As soon as she arrived home after her shift the next morning, Stella fired up her ancient computer and logged into the live feed. The video was clear as a bell and picked up everything Glasswell said.

"Money well spent," Stella congratulated herself. She watched him for an hour before giving in to sleep. There was nothing she could use against him yet, but it was harder to plot revenge when your eyelids threatened to close.

By the end of the week, she still didn't have anything worthwhile on Glasswell. He seemed to be rather dull and stayed in the office by himself. Although two other employees came to him for disciplinary action, he simply had them sign the appropriate forms and dismissed them without another word. Stella was apparently the only one he manhandled.

In a way, this caused another form of relief, however, because Stella had been meaning to go downtown to the free clinic and get checked for sexually transmitted diseases. Perhaps she didn't really need to. It also outraged her that she was being singled out again; it seemed to be her lot in life.

The weekend went by in a blur because Stella had agreed to work overtime both days. Even torturing Avery Winslow didn't give her the same kind of pleasure because she was so consumed with ideas on bringing Glasswell to his knees. She needed the upper hand, but nothing gave her that edge.

Monday rolled around and brought her first day off in a ten day stretch. Stella suspected that history would repeat itself and Glasswell's next coaching session would take place that day. She took her time in the shower, softly exfoliating her body with a special body scrub smelling of lilac. Everything that could be shaved or plucked was as clean and smooth as a newborn, and she took the time to carefully curl her dark mass of hair.

Promptly at ten a.m., three hours after the end of her shift, her phone pinged with a notification. Malcolm Glasswell scheduled a meeting with her in his office at 11:30 that day. Stella arched a carefully sculpted eyebrow at herself in the mirror and smirked at her reflection. His predictability made it almost too easy.

Slipping into her tightest pair of jeans before fixing her thick black eyeliner, Stella hoped she could pull this off. The software for the spy camera was already set to record and as long as she played her part well, this would be the last coaching she ever received.

The bus ride out to the hospital made Stella's stomach squirm into knots. She knew what Glasswell's intentions were and how the meeting would play out, but it had to be believable that she was under duress. If it looked for one second as though she was a willing participant, her record would still dictate that she was fired right along with him. And there was no way she could let that happen, not when she was so close to a breakthrough in Room 216.

Arriving with ten minutes to spare, Stella hovered in Glasswell's open doorway for a moment before knocking quietly on the door. He didn't look up from his computer as he directed her to enter and shut the door after her. It wasn't until she sat primly on the edge of her seat across from his desk that Glasswell glanced up, and she inwardly preened with satisfaction at his double-take at the sight of her.

Glasswell leaned back in his chair, absentmindedly tracing his pointer and middle fingers along his jawline as he stared at her. His look made her feel like the only dessert at a buffet in the group home. It gave her a sense of ominous foreboding, like he was already brimming with malice from the dark fantasies unfolding in his head.

Abruptly he stood and circled around behind her, dragging the same two fingers slowly across her shoulder blades. Her hair stirred at his touch and her fragrant scent filled the room. He leaned down over her to inhale deeply, clutching a fistful of hair to his nose.

"Someone's starting to get the hang of this," Glasswell murmured. "Perhaps I should have choked you from the beginning and you would've learned your lesson right away."

He pulled her into a standing position, but Stella turned her body so that she faced him, and therefore the camera, directly. She spoke as clearly as her shaking voice would allow. "I don't want you to touch me," she declared.

Glasswell threw back his head and laughed. "It's a bit late for that, isn't it, sweetheart?"

Without waiting for a reply, he grabbed the collar of her t-shirt with both hands and ripped it down the front. Her breasts were exposed, cupped in a sheer black bra, and Stella could practically feel his mouth salivating.

"You really are a dirty little slut, aren't you!" He leered down at her with an evil smirk.

Stella tried to cover her chest with her arms, but Glasswell pushed them back. On her second attempt he groaned in frustration. "Keep your arms down and let me look at you!" he ordered. When she cradled her arms around her exposed midriff instead, Glasswell reared back a hand and slapped her.

The strike wasn't hard; Stella had certainly been hit worse, but her eyes smarted in surprise. It snapped her brain into focus and she forgot all about filming, only eyeing the monster in front of her.

"You won't touch me!" she roared, pointing a finger in his face in warning.

Glasswell laughed again, but it was hollow and sinister. "I'll do whatever I need to for you to learn your place. This is the only thing your kind is good for." Using both hands, he shoved her backwards onto the desk and ripped her jeans down.

She pushed him off her, indignance bristling along her spine. "'My kind?'" she repeated angrily.

Glasswell rolled his eyes. "Nasty parasites like you, the underbelly of our society. You're a poor, uneducated whore, barely even worthy to spread your legs for someone like me. You'll live your entire pathetic life in the gutter until drugs or some gangbanger wipes you off the face of the earth." He shoved her back down again, harder than before.

Shame was the only thing that made Stella react. Glasswell seemed to know all the insecurities that were always on repeat in her head. He made her feel cheaper than dirt, which she hadn't felt in a long time. His vile words echoed in her head to where she could barely focus on what was happening in the room.

Bracing herself, Stella pulled her body to the right side of the desk, thereby giving a better angle to the video camera on the wall behind him. She allowed the tears to roll down her cheek and repeated the word "no" through gritted teeth. Glasswell either didn't hear or didn't care, forcing his erection into her, balls deep.

Perhaps the bra was too much for him because this time Glasswell came inside her before falling onto her breasts as though they were the only thing available for him to eat. There would be red teeth marks on her flesh for weeks, she was sure of it.

Stella pushed him off her and tried to tighten the remains of her shirt over her chest. How dare he ruin her clothing! Not that she had much sentimental attachment to clothing, but still. Wasn't it bad enough to replace her dignity? Did she really need to scrounge money together and replace all her clothing, too? Somewhere along the line tears had begun streaming down her face, and she hastily swiped at her cheeks while trying to cinch the remnants of her shirt closed. It was the first time he truly made her feel violated.

Glasswell gave her a side eye that indicated how strange he found Stella to be. "You seem to be awfully uncompliant this time. What made today different than last week?"

She huffed, panic fluttering her heartbeat. "You mean what makes raping me today worse than all the other times you raped me?" She shrugged her purse over her shoulder and managed to clamp the sides of the t-shirt shut.

He didn't reply to her outburst, merely continued to eye her suspiciously.

After several moments where Stella waited with bated breath, Glasswell withdrew his wallet from his back pocket. He threw a couple $20 bills on the desk. "Go buy yourself a pill or something. Make sure you don't wind up pregnant."

Vomit crept up the back of her throat. "I would need a prescription for something like that, asshole."

He smirked at his computer, not bothering to glance in her direction. "I'm sure seedy women like you know where to go to buy that kind of thing." The finality of his statement was punctuated by the clack of his keyboard. "We'll have another coaching session soon since you seem to have regressed back into your old habits. Close the door on your way out."

He didn't need to tell her twice. Leaving the money on his desk, Stella tucked her head onto her chest and swept from the room as fast as her legs could carry her. She felt equal parts triumphant and equal parts appalled. Glasswell spoke to her as if she were dog shit coating the bottom of his shoe. It had been years since someone talked down to her that way, and it mortified her that she had allowed this man access to her body.

Yet that was all about to come to a screeching halt.

Rain poured outside the hospital, so although Stella needed to catch the bus, she hovered in the front lobby until it was almost time for pick up. The glass antechamber had several framed photographs on the wall identifying the top five tier of Central Office administrators, which she now read out of boredom as she waited. She recognized the second from the bottom as the woman from Glasswell's office the week prior; it was none other than the assistant deputy director, Jessica Hemmings.

Stella beamed. *This was about to get a whole lot more interesting.*

The camera worked beautifully. As difficult as it was to watch and then again to burn it onto a disk to drop in the mail, Stella knew she needed to do it if she was ever going to get the Glasswell monkey off her back. She slipped the envelope into the priority mailbox, care of a Ms. Jessica Hemmings, and waited for the magic to happen.

It took almost two weeks for any kind of follow up. Stella was subjected to his vile sessions and putrid breath another four times in the interim. Then on a dreary Thursday morning where the temperature flouted between chilly enough for snow, yet warm enough for rain, she exited the bus in front of the hospital to find Hemmings herself standing under an umbrella by the front door.

Stella smoothed her hair back and wiped her sweaty palms on the backs of her thighs. This would be the moment of truth.

Ms. Hemmings must have recognized Stella because as soon as the bus door shut behind her, the assistant deputy director careened down the sidewalk in her tall stilettos. "Miss Andover?" she asked.

Stella could only nod.

"Follow me, please," Ms. Hemmings instructed. Stella followed her through the front doors and into one of the empty conference rooms just off the lobby that were typically only used when a bigwig like Hemmings came for a visit. A man in a black suit and a woman in a blue dress sat on the opposite side of the table with a stack of papers in between them. An empty seat separated the two.

"This is Carl Burnwright from Legal and this is my assistant, Didi Porter. She will serve as your witness. Please have a seat there behind the papers," Hemmings stated.

Stella didn't move from the doorway. Having the legal department involved made the whole thing sound a lot more serious.

"Miss Andover," Hemmings prompted. "We don't have much time." She gestured to the empty seat between her companions.

Realizing she didn't have much say, Stella sank into the seat and pulled her backpack into her lap like a shield.

With the help of the attorney, Ms. Hemmings glossed over several documents in front of Stella, explaining that Malcolm Glasswell would no longer be employed at the facility or with any State department. Stella would be fully reinstated, all complaints stricken from her record, and a full apology was issued on behalf of the hospital administration. The committee hearing had already been canceled. The State was willing to foot the bill if she decided she needed any counseling services and any absences for such services would not count against her paid time off.

There were many pages that required her signature, which Didi would notarize afterwards.

Stella couldn't believe her ears.

A sheriff suddenly walked into the room, shaking water off his face from the gale outside. His brown skin glistened in the fluorescent lighting.

"Ah, Sgt. Hendricks, right on time," Ms. Hemmings said.

The badge shining on his belt sent a shiver up Stella's spine and without meaning to, she scooted her seat back from the deputy. *Why was he here?!*

She gulped loudly. "Um, ma'am…" was all she rasped out.

Ms. Hemmings waved her hands at Stella. "Oh, no, dear, he's here to arrest Malcolm Glasswell. We all appreciate your cooperation in signing the statement and providing clear video evidence of his crime. We take these types of things very seriously," she added solemnly.

Glasswell was being arrested? When did Stella sign a statement about the events of the video? And yet, as the idea softened in her mind, she realized that he deserved to go to prison. What he did was wrong, so why shouldn't he be punished for it? No one else in her life had ever faced consequences for what they did to her. It was only fair that Glasswell be held accountable.

Stella finally nodded and shifted her gaze down to her hands in her lap. She heard Ms. Hemmings lead Sgt. Hendricks from the room. After a tense second, Ms. Hemmings reached her hand back through the doorway and snapped her fingers, making Carl Burnwright leap to his feet.

"You know, you could sue the hospital and make a fortune," he whispered to her. He pointed his finger to his temple as if advising her to think about it and followed Ms. Hemmings from the room.

Stella's eyes widened. She didn't want to sue the hospital, just make Glasswell know he couldn't threaten her and get away with it. However, the threat of a lawsuit that could potentially bring the hospital to financial ruin must have been Central Office's main concern. It loosened the vice grip of anxiety around her heart by a fraction.

Didi seemed to sense the direction of Stella's thoughts. "It would be a publicity nightmare," she explained as she filed documents into a leather briefcase similar to the one Hemmings had carried the first day Stella saw her. "No one blames you, though, dear. Take them up on their offer and get some help. He's being taken straight to jail right now."

That made Stella throw her backpack to the ground and scramble to the window. She made it just in time to see Sgt. Hendricks place a hand on Glasswell's head and guide him into the sheriff's vehicle with Glasswell's hands in cuffs behind his back. As the door snapped shut and the sergeant moved to shake Ms. Hemmings' hand, Stella caught Glasswell staring at her with venom in his eyes. Unable to help herself, she smiled cheerfully and waved back at him. She hoped he met his match in prison.

THIRTY-ONE

1990

It took Edwin and Gaines almost three days to go through all the videos and focus on their mystery male. Each detective wrote down various clues as to his identity, but they hadn't come up with much so far. He appeared to always pay with cash and merely sat with a newspaper during every one of Alessa's shifts. His body stayed angled in a manner that allowed him to view the entire coffee shop, and there was never anyone who joined him. There were frequent interactions with Alessa, none of which could really be heard on camera, but there was nothing in their movements or body language to indicate intimidation.

The only time the video showed any sort of abnormal behavior, if it could even be construed as such, was the first day Harrison Pierce was present at the same time as the mystery man. Gaines ruefully pointed out that the man seemed to act out of character by spilling his drink, but everyone has an accident now and again, don't they? Neither of the detectives could really find any significance in the event. Edwin speculated that the man recognized Pierce from the newspaper and reacted out of surprise. It didn't mean anything.

Edwin wearily leaned back in his chair and rubbed his eyes again. Every time they had a break in the case, another obstacle stood in their way. The fact that this man so abruptly stopped visiting the coffee house on the same day that their missing persons disappeared couldn't be considered more than circumstantial, at best. No judge would back a warrant on something that could just as easily be a coincidence. The more Edwin watched the tapes, the more he began to doubt that there was anything noteworthy about the guy. He might be any other regular customer. And since some of the footage had already been taped over, there was a considerable possibility that the mystery man frequented Groundbreaking for years as a regular and they just didn't know it.

Gaines was determined to see the man as a lead, however. He painstakingly tracked the man's movements, outfit choices, and even tried to determine what paper the man was reading. His notes filled an entire notebook, but the more that Edwin told him it wasted time, the more adamant Gaines became that it all meant something.

They were approaching the deadline where everything would be transferred to a cold case file. Already the media had moved onto other headlines, ignoring the fact that an eccentric socialite's body had never been recovered. Harry Millhouse had even stopped by at one point to advise Edwin that it was time to wrap things up and start taking on more important cases.

As much as it killed him, Edwin recognized that it was time to throw in the towel. Their expertise would be better served elsewhere and without a body, there wasn't even evidence that a crime had been committed. Harrison and Alessa had simply ridden off into the sunset together.

He began packing his notes into a box and marked the case number on the side with a Sharpie.

Gaines huffed indignantly. "We can't give up, Ed!" he argued. "We are so close to breaking this case, I can feel it!"

Edwin rolled his eyes. "Your gut feelings don't determine investigations, kid." He continued to file paperwork inside the white box.

His partner shook his head. "No, look at this." Gaines turned the computer screen towards Edwin and pointed at a grainy black and white image of a white van. "I was able to access some of the security cameras from the surrounding buildings and I think I have a partial ID on the guy's license plate."

Edwin rounded the desk and came to stand behind his partner, examining the image. "When did you go ask the other building owners for their security footage?"

Gaines face flushed and he looked down at the keyboard as he typed. "I know how to pull up some stuff with certain types of camera systems," he mumbled. He was barely loud enough for Edwin to hear, but Edwin heard enough to fill in the blanks.

"Isn't that called 'hacking'?" Edwin sputtered. "That's illegal, Gaines, and unethical! We could jeopardize the entire investigation doing things like that!" He idly wondered if he had entered an alternate universe because it didn't make sense for logical, systematic Kevin Gaines to do something so reckless.

His admonition lit a fire in the rookie, however. Gaines jumped to his feet and threw his hands up in the air. "Do you wanna find Alessa and Pierce or not, Ed? What would Shelley do, huh?"

Judging by the stricken look of horror on his face, Gaines knew immediately that he had crossed a line. Edwin's face went white and his body tensed. He took two steps towards Gaines, drawing up to glare at him nose to nose.

"Shelley would NEVER do something to compromise an investigation." Edwin's voice sounded like icy steel and it took every inch of his self-control not to throttle his young partner. "Don't you EVER bring Shelley into our cases again. You are nothing like him!"

He turned abruptly on his heel, ready to storm out of the office and give himself wide berth to cool off.

Edwin paused at the doorway, however, when he heard Gaines' voice crack behind him. "Yeah, well neither are you."

The veteran briefly glanced over his shoulder, hardly believing Gaines would dare to say such a thing, before sweeping from the room. Nothing good would come from letting the rookie seeing just how much his words rattled Edwin to his core.

1990

Duke showered for longer than he normally dared, for once not caring if his mother needed him. He was so ashamed of his failure in breaking Alessa's spell that Duke felt sure someone was already on the way to take her from him. He also had the overwhelming fear that at any moment a police officer would show up and start asking questions.

Maybe Harrison Pierce would emerge from the afterlife, a rotting ghoul, with demons from Hell at his heels, to seek retribution.

It would certainly be a fitting end, Duke thought bitterly. Shame made him want to hide himself in his room rather than attempt to beat Alessa's magic again. Fear of being caught made him want to spend every moment of every day breaking through to her so Alessa could tell the authorities that no crime had been committed.

Assuring himself that Mother was settled, Duke contemplated what to do. Clearly the spell would ever be broken; Alessa couldn't be possessed or help him become a man. Whom he believed to be an angel was really a devil in disguise and Duke fell right into her trap.

But had he?

Duke reflected back on their romps that afternoon. She hadn't resisted once as his hands traced her body, nor on the many times he entered her. He had even experimented once by placing his cock in her ass, though he found the sensation too tight and dry for his liking. Alessa hadn't protested, and it had been days since she tried something foolish like urinating on him.

He sat upright in bed as the epiphany came to him. He felt most alive when he sensed her fear. Whenever he felt the power of her life flow through his hands, when he punished her and heard the resulting sounds of bones breaking, or better yet, when he observed the blood flow from a wound and accepted the heady knowledge that he caused it, that was when the world became clear and bright. Their salvation lied in him correcting the bad behavior out of her and showing her a woman's true place in the world. Punishing her was really a necessary evil in achieving bliss with Alessa at his side, much like that of a parent to a child. That was how he would break the spell.

Excitedly, Duke threw the covers off and raced down the first flight of stairs, then into the basement. The small lantern had nearly burned out, but it was just enough to make out Alessa's curves as she dangled from the ceiling. Her head lolled against her chest and although her skin was a milky white, deep pink patches colored her cheeks.

He quickly struck a match and lit some of the candles he had placed around the perimeter of the room. She didn't stir, even as he approached her. Gently, he stroked the back of his fingers between her breasts, over the now scabbed flesh, and past her navel. She startled awake right as he pushed two fingers inside her sex, rubbing slowly. He had discovered over the past several weeks that having some kind of lubrication made it easier to make love, a lesson magazines and novels had never fully explained. It still awed him that he could make Alessa's body work in such ways.

Alessa began to cry, dry sobs caused by dehydration. "Why are you doing this to me?" she whined. "Please just let me go."

Duke snorted derisively. "Didn't I make myself clear? You're never going anywhere. You belong to me." He pulled his t-shirt over his head and discarded it on the ground near the stairs, then pulled her legs around his waist. He didn't step back far enough for Alessa's arms to strain, but one movement was all it would take. "You're going to learn what the true meaning of punishment is, my love. That's the only way we can truly be together."

This statement amused her and a maniacal laugh escaped Alessa's mouth. "The only punishment is being here with you, you sick asshole."

Anger blazed in Duke's chest. Grabbing her thighs, he jumped backwards, delighted at the sounds of her screams echoing in the chamber. Her shoulders were so far removed from their sockets, Duke didn't know if they could ever properly go back. "You were saying?" he asked.

The next several hours went in much the same way. Duke construed new ways to torture her, leaving bruises and blood all over her body. Whenever Alessa started to black out from the pain he would use his fingers or his tongue on her sex so the pending orgasm returned her to the present moment. When he could no longer function with an erection hard enough to break glass, Duke dragged her mangled body to the mattress on the floor and used her blood as a lubricant to have his way with her. The pain in her eyes made him triumphant, the cum seeping down his leg made him jubilant. *Surely this was what it meant to be a man.*

And so it went on for days. Over a week had gone by and Duke found that if he held Alessa's head in a tub of water until she choked, she became much more agreeable to eating. She finally regained some color and her breasts no longer drooped. Although she always did as he asked, Duke found minor discretions as justifications to punish her. The reward of releasing himself in her never grew tiresome. His obsession still felt as strong as the day they met.

As the days passed, Duke became far more confident that the police weren't going to locate them. He had never told anyone his name, even Alessa, and he never noticed anyone following him. They didn't even receive mail at the house. Everything went to a box at the post office.

As a precaution, Duke stopped going into town and relied solely on the provisions they had at home. Thankfully the garden still had ripe, fresh vegetables despite his neglect all season, so he was able to scrounge up enough to eat for them to get by. He knew he needed to hunt for deer or at least set up a few traps to catch rabbits or squirrels, but he didn't want to take any time away from his work in the basement. Alessa became his main priority again.

His mother's condition, however, began to worsen, no doubt due to the increasingly poor care she received. Duke didn't want to be bothered with her now that he was manifesting his future. This was what it meant to be a man, after all. His size and strength were finally at the necessary level to fulfill that lifelong dream, and Alessa became more compliant with each passing day. However, it didn't take long for guilt to seize him as he noted his mother's deteriorating symptoms.

One night he broke away from Alessa long enough to spend the evening with his mother. Duke was certain all of the bones in Alessa's left leg were shattered and even he knew it was better if he gave her a day or two of reprieve to heal.

In order to prove to both women that he was truly capable of caring for their needs, he set Alessa's leg in a coarsely made splint and loaded her up with painkillers before entering his mother's room with a newspaper tucked under his arm.

Mother's breathing slowed to the point where Duke placed his hand along her throat to find a pulse. She stirred at the contact and pulled her son's hands over her heart. "This is where you'll always remain, my boy," she murmured.

Duke's heart swelled. He leaned down and placed a tender kiss on her forehead. "I love you, Mother."

She gave him a fleeting smile and fell back to sleep. He waited a few moments to see if she roused again before quietly creeping from the room as her breathing evened out.

With Alessa still recovering in the basement, Duke found himself jittery with restless energy. Pacing did nothing to calm his nerves and it was too late in the evening to go for a hike. He needed something to do or someplace to go. It had been too long since he left the house, a privilege he had already grown accustomed to in his mother's hermitage.

All things considered, he felt proud of himself. He had demonstrated to both of them how well he could take care of their needs, being the head of the household like the men in the Jane Austen novel he read to his mother once. This was what it meant to be a man: to teach the love of his life where her place was and to care for his mother on her sickbed. He had accomplished something and achievement made him feel bold.

Boldness could easily turn to recklessness, however. That was a lesson Duke would learn the hard way.

2011

Stella had learned very early on that money solved most problems. One older kid at her last group home summarized it as, "Money can't buy happiness, but poverty can't buy nothing!"

She hoarded every paycheck like a crackhead hoarded needles. It gave her a tremendous thrill to check her savings account on payday and see the numbers rise. College had never interested her, and she accepted very early in life that she had no real marketable skill set, but that never bothered her. Working a blue-collar job wasn't the worst thing out of life. As long as she lived frugally, she could still build up her wealth.

When a social worker had stopped by the group home with a series of pamphlets on trade schools they could attend on Children's Services' dime, Stella enrolled for the shortest one, figuring it would give her a foot in the door somewhere.

Once she found a job working for the state, however, she had really lucked out. Her current position came with a salary set at 37.5 hours a week, with anything over earning her time and a half. And there was no shortage of overtime. It felt like the lottery to see some of her paychecks go well into four figures. Not to mention, she finally had healthcare that didn't suck. Foster kids tended to get shuffled around so much that they did not always get consistent doctor's appointments, and they could forget about seeing a dentist. One of the first things Stella had splurged on was a set of invisible braces to fix her crooked teeth.

Her favorite perk had to be all the free stuff the state agencies were constantly handing out. Memberships to zoos, golf courses, and amusement parks, tickets to special concerts, and a lot of free food. Most of the time Stella only attended the events for the food, why buy groceries if someone else would provide it for her?

The free item she took the most advantage of, though, was the membership to the art museum. Amherst had a smaller museum that didn't get a lot of foot traffic, but Stella found herself there on just about every day off, wandering the halls and gazing at the paintings on the walls. Art was the one thing of beauty she allowed herself to enjoy, and she had faint aspirations to travel to all the major museums in Europe someday. If she kept building her savings, it might be a possibility.

Stella's triumph over Glasswell emboldened her to march into the breakroom the following Monday in search of Mary and her infernal clipboard. She had accepted the paid time off and taken a mini getaway over the weekend, staying at a shady hotel in the inner city of Detroit and visiting close to a dozen art galleries. The trip hadn't been as expensive as she anticipated, mostly due to her frugal nature, and she felt heady with excitement over successfully taking her first trip. All of her overtime was worth it if it enabled her to travel like that. She was on top of the world.

This was the nature of her impromptu meeting with Mary. Stella decided it was time to return to her normal schedule and leave Deb and the rest of the overnight crew in the dust.

As soon as Mary caught sight of her, however, Mary squawked and practically tripped in her haste to engulf Stella in a hug.

"Mary, you're hugging me," Stella stated awkwardly, her arms pinned to her sides as Mary enveloped her.

She cringed even more with awkwardness when Mary pulled away and Stella realized there were tears welling in Mary's eyes.

"I just can't believe what you were going through!" Mary wailed. "You must have been so frightened!"

Stella didn't know what to say to this because no one had ever cared before when something happened to her. All the jubilation left her and she shuffled her feet unnecessarily as she decided how to respond.

Thankfully Mary saved her. "Do you need more time off? We had another nurse quit, housekeeping is on strike because their pay raise didn't take effect when it was supposed to, and two assistants are out sick today. I could really use another set of hands."

Stella breathed a sigh of relief. "Does that mean I'm back on day shift?"

Mary snorted. "Honey, you can work around the clock for all I care! We need double the staff we currently have and they don't even have any interviews lined up!" She started floating around the employee lounge, throwing trash in the garbage can and pushing in chairs.

Stella smiled inwardly, then tried to sound as nonchalant as possible. "So how is our quiet friend doing?" She fumbled with the buckle hanging off her backpack and kept her eyes on the floor. She didn't trust herself to hide the bubble of panic in her eyes from Mary's shrewd observations.

Instead Mary paused and blew Stella's mind. "You really are taking things with him so seriously, Stella. I am so proud of you."

If Stella had a million guesses, she never would have chosen those words to be directed at her. Nobody had ever been proud of her, especially not here at work. It spooked her because it felt like a set up. Mary hated her, Stella was sure of it, so why was she acting like a clucking mother hen now?

She started to respond, but Mary cut her off with a wave of her hand. "I don't wanna hear a word from you. Winslow is your special case, so you go ahead and look after him. I just poked my head in from time to time while you were gone. It's nice to see you accepting responsibility for a change. Skedaddle! Get to work!"

Barely believing her own luck, Stella did precisely that. *Yet another score for complacency!*

Heading down the hall to Room 216, she almost found herself humming. Life had never worked so much in her favor. If this is what it felt like on the other side, Stella completely understood why people worked so hard for advantage and opportunity. She could definitely get used to this.

The room was quiet and bathed in filtered light from the small window, like always. A bright sun finally shone outside now that spring started to yield to summer, and the brightness mirrored the joy in her heart. Stella almost felt a fondness for Avery Winslow and genuinely smiled when she saw him. His eyes, however, widened in alarm, which made Stella chuckle.

"Surprise!" she cackled, waving her fingers by her face like jazz hands. She quickly pulled down his blanket to assess how the scabs and scars were fairing. It seemed pointless to have a hospital gown on, so she went ahead and pulled that off, too.

He watched her warily, eyes never blinking but following her every movement. His gaze didn't unnerve her the way it usually did.

She snorted. "Time away must have been good for me because it doesn't even bother me that you stare like a fucking freak." Stella grabbed a pair of rubber gloves from the box on the wall. "Why don't we go ahead and make up for lost time?"

Practically giddy with excitement, she withdrew a thermos with hot water in it. She hoped it was still close to boiling temperature and grinned when the water hissed as it made contact with Avery's chest. He gritted his teeth and turned his gaze to the ceiling. Stella then twisted the cap off his full urine bag and giggled as she lazily poured the contents onto his raw, puckered chest. His mouth opened, jaw clenched, but no sound came out. The rancid smell was enough to turn anyone's stomach and Stella had to stop herself from gagging as the scent hit her nostrils.

Too happy to be disappointed, Stella merely whistled. "You're gonna challenge me today, huh? Do I need to get creative?" She returned the urine bag to its proper place and used both hands to forcefully twist Avery's head towards her. His eyes held reproach, but he didn't utter a word.

A page went out through the overcom directing all available personnel to respond to a Code Blue in Room 228 and Stella knew she needed to go or Mary would come looking for her. She hastily threw the blanket over her patient and smacked him hard on the chest, promising more to come as soon as she was able. She scurried from the room to reach the code as quickly as possible.

And so the day continued. Stella returned to Avery's room as often as she could, frequently using the brief reprieve as a smoke break. Although she didn't have enough time to do more than use him as a human ashtray, she made sure to threaten him with wicked images of slicing and dicing his body in all manner of inhumane ways. It gave her a quiet thrill to see the blood leave his face after every promise.

By three in the afternoon the rumbling from Stella's stomach could not be silenced or ignored. She had been running around like a madwoman all day to clean up spills, replace bedding, and transport patients to different areas of the hospital. They had a security breach for a short period where a patient who was being transported to the psych hospital up the road got loose and ran down the corridor naked. Stella didn't think she could ever get the image of his saggy butt cheeks out of her mind.

Although she had been utilizing Room 216 as her new cafeteria, the smell of burnt skin, stale urine, and cigarettes was not particularly appetizing. Stella raced into the employee lounge with the intention of scarfing down a Pop-Tart before torturing Avery some more.

For she recognized now that what she was doing to Avery Winslow constituted as torture. Rather than bringing a sense of shame or guilt, it only empowered her to the point of recklessness. Mary misguidedly placed her faith in Stella to care for that patient, and for the first time in her life Stella had the freedom to act on her darkest fantasies. She pictured Malcolm Glasswell, Mr. Burton, and all the other creeps from her past in Winslow's place. The fear and disgust she saw in Avery's eyes only heightened the glory and pleasure she felt from watching his blood trail down his skin or seeing a wound begin to scab. She reaped endless amounts of power from her place at the top of the ant hill and intended to find the strongest magnifying glass she could to blaze her way to infamy. She held his fate, his very life, in her hands, and it was a hell of a potent high. For the first time ever Stella had a way to balance all the pain, injustice, and hatred that had brewed in her heart her entire life.

Stella had only just fed her dollar into the vending machine when Veronica walked into the lounge, flanked by two other Barbie nurses. She recognized one as the Bible thumper who clutched her cross at their previous encounter. Stella rolled her eyes as the girl immediately backed away from the corner of the room where Stella stood.

"Well, well, well," Veronica crooned. "Look what the cat dragged in. Didn't they arrest you along with Glasswell?" She smirked as she languidly sat down at one of the tables facing Stella.

The third nurse, who Stella believed to be named Brittany, tittered at Veronica's comment and sat down next to her at the table. All three of them waited to see Stella's reaction.

A large *thunk* informed Stella that her snack had dispensed and she grabbed it before walking slowly and deliberately to the table. She leaned over the table menacingly, her face only inches from Veronica's. The other Barbies drew back in surprise and although she did not retreat, Stella could tell from the slight quiver of Veronica's bottom lip that she was not prepared for Stella's proximity. Stella sneered at her, finding the nurse's trepidation almost comical.

She's just as pathetic as the mute in 216, Stella thought.

"Go ahead and say something to me," Stella said, her voice low. "I dare you." She put as much threat and venom into her face as she could, holding her breath for the Barbie nurses' response.

Veronica's face blanched and her mouth dropped open in shock. She looked truly fearful, and rather than arguing with Stella or making another snide remark, she gathered her things and slid out from the seat.

"Come on, guys," she said to the others. "We don't need to be with her." She eyed Stella apprehensively before sauntering out of the room with the other Barbie nurses in tow.

Her shoulders heaved as Stella released the breath she had been holding. Veronica clearly got the message. She knew it was too much to believe that the Barbies would never bother her again, but for now, it was enough that she stood up for herself and put the bitch in her place. Stella could not imagine having a better day.

"What's next, am I gonna win the lottery?" she asked aloud to the empty room.

Her elation triggered warning bells, however. No good thing ever lasted. Stella knew that firsthand. If luck was finally on her side, that meant there would be a price to pay later.

1990

Edwin was still reeling from his fight with Gaines. He had crossed a line that was unforgivable. Shelley's memory was sacred to him and Edwin would rather have a white-hot poker shoved into his ear than to ever hear a bad word against his old partner.

But, as the smoke cleared and his racing thoughts caught up to reason, Edwin had to admit Gaines did have a small point in that Shelley didn't always follow the rules when it came to their cases. He never blatantly stepped over the line into illegal, but nobody could ever say Shelley swore by the rule book.

Regardless, it wasn't Gaines' place to bring his old partner into their current investigation. If they really were going to continue working together, they had to reach a certain level of respect and trust. That was pretty difficult to achieve if dead people were going to be brought up as emotional missiles to win an argument. Edwin knew they needed to talk it out, but he wanted to be prepared with the right thing to say. Since he was such a burly old man himself, communicating on this level scared the hell out of him. He had the fleeting suspicion that this conversation could make or break their partnership.

There was also the matter of what to do with Gaines' information.

Although hacking into a security camera was not the right course of action, if it led to a lead or at least gave them a suspect, it would be enough to keep the case open and continue the investigation. While Edwin didn't necessarily think the customer from the coffee shop would amount to anything, he didn't want to discount Gaines' instincts either. Hadn't he had a gut feeling before they approached the house where Shelley died?

So while he didn't agree with Gaines' methods, Edwin *did* want to locate Pierce and Alessa. If they ultimately found them, they might be able to gloss over the incident with security cameras by saying they found a partial plate image on one of the tapes from Groundbreaking. It was a long shot, but Edwin reasoned that for someone like his partner to take such a risk, there must be something really nagging at him to do so. Edwin tried to ignore the sneaking guilt that the nagging entity was Gaines' desire for his own approval.

After taking a long lunch at the diner near the precinct, Edwin finally decided it was time to head back to the office. He couldn't accomplish anything by avoiding the conflict. He threw his bills down on the counter and walked briskly back to his partner.

As soon as Edwin opened the door Gaines popped out of his seat and began swearing apologies profusely. His whole body vibrated with remorse, and he followed Edwin from the coat rack to his desk chair repeating his sincere promise to never speak like that again. Any other time it would have made Edwin chuckle.

Now, however, he merely gestured for Gaines to return to his own chair across from him.

"Kid, listen to me," Edwin began. "Whatever happens between us is for us to work out. You don't need to bring Shelley into anything ever again-"

Gaines cut him off. "I know, it was so stupid of me! I can't believe I said that! I had no right-"

This time it was Edwin who interrupted. "Stop talking and let me get this out. We have to work together if we are gonna be a team. It doesn't matter what Shelley would have done or said because he's not here." A pang of grief made Edwin gulp before continuing. "The bigger issue, as I see it, is what to do about what you've done. Breaking laws can't become the norm, but we both know how important it is to locate these people. So while I am willing to do a little digging on what you've got, I gotta tell ya, you and you alone will be taking the fall if it all goes to shit, you got that?"

If Gaines were a puppy with a tail, Edwin was sure it would have been wagging a mile a minute.

Gaines burst into an enormous grin and slapped the desk with glee. "I'm so glad you said that because I called a buddy down at the DMV and got two names from that partial. Wanna check them out?"

Edwin smiled back. "Let's go."

The first address took them to a large two-story residence in one of the smaller suburbs outside Amherst. A gate blocked the driveway and a large iron fence surrounded the property. Compared to the rest of the homes in the neighborhood, the placed looked rundown. It hadn't been updated like the neighbors' homes on either side. Balls, bats, and other children's sporting equipment littered the lawn.

After honking the horn a couple times in quick succession a harried-looking woman frantically ran out the front door to open the gate. She didn't approach the vehicle after they pulled in, but merely pulled the gate closed. She wiped her hands on an apron around her waist and came to the passenger side window with a smile on her face.

"What can I do for you fellas? I didn't have anyone scheduled for a walk-through today," she said jovially.

"I'm Detective Gaines and this is my partner Detective Greene. We're with the Amherst PD," the rookie said.

The smile melted off the woman's face instantly. "This is about the paperwork, isn't it? Oh my god!" she cried and raced back inside.

Gaines and Edwin exchanged a puzzled expression before following after her. Before they could knock, an equally anxious-looking man flung open the door and stepped out onto the porch. He had square glasses that looked far too big for his face, and he was well below the average height for a male. Edwin knew immediately he was not the man from the Groundbreaking tapes.

"Yes, uh, officers? What can I do for you?" the man said. He crossed his arms over his chest, but circled his arms farther back, as though giving himself a hug.

Edwin glanced at his partner, unsure of whether to laugh or draw his weapon. Gaines looked like he was tickled pink.

"What is your name, sir?" Edwin asked.

The man looked down at his feet and shuffled in place. "My name is, uh, David Hollingsworth."

Gaines covered a laugh with a cough.

"Mr. Hollingsworth, I'm Detective Greene and this is my partner. We just wanted to ask a few questions about a van that's registered to a Patsy Hollingsworth?"

The man visibly relaxed and exhaled a shaky breath. "Okay, hold on and let me get the missus," he said. He leaned back and opened the door, poking his head in to call for Patsy. The same woman as before came outside, her eyebrows nearly reaching her hairline, and nodded towards the detectives. She had smoothed back her brown hair a little bit and removed the apron.

Her husband only said they wanted to talk to her and went back inside, promptly shutting the door. Gaines and Edwin exchanged another look of confusion.

Mrs. Hollingsworth smiled at them and apologized for her husband's erratic behavior. "Poor David doesn't do well talking to people. How can I help you?"

Gaines jumped in. "Mrs. Hollingsworth, do you own a 1982 Ford Econoline?"

She nodded. "I do, it's parked behind the house. What is this about?"

"We are simply investigating a disappearance and trying to follow up on something. Are there any other male drivers besides your husband?" Edwin asked.

Mrs. Hollingsworth shook her head. "No, it's just us. We hardly ever go anywhere." She seemed perplexed as to why the detectives were asking such things, cocking her head as she eyed them suspiciously.

"Does your husband ever get coffee at a place called Groundbreaking?" Edwin inquired. Mr. Hollingsworth didn't match the physical characteristics of the man from the video, but they had to cover their bases.

She shook her head again. "David doesn't drink coffee and we certainly wouldn't waste money to get it from a coffee shop. That money is far better spent elsewhere!" Mrs. Hollingsworth laughed and swatted the air, pleased with her own joke.

A loud bang came from inside the residence and Mrs. Hollingsworth stood ramrod straight. A guilty look crossed her face, but it was gone as quickly as it had come. Edwin could hear what sounded like Mr. Hollingsworth inside shouting something.

Edwin paused a moment, waiting for her to voluntarily explain the commotion. She merely smiled apprehensively toward him as she backed up to the door. "Is that all, detective?" she asked.

Her hand had barely touched the doorknob when the door flew open and a young black teenager with Down Syndrome waved at the officers. Mrs. Hollingsworth looked frightened and told the boy to go back inside. Instead he pushed past her and went to embrace Edwin. Startled, Edwin looked to her again for an explanation.

Mrs. Hollingsworth's shoulders sank. "This is Daniel," she said quietly. "He loves police officers."

Gaines, who was trying not to laugh again from the look of shock on Edwin's face, replied, "Then it's nice to meet you, Daniel." He looked at Mrs. Hollingsworth. "Is he a friend of yours?"

She glanced back inside and her husband appeared at the doorway as if summoned.

"We are trying to get a home started for kids like Daniel," Mr. Hollingsworth explained. "Our own son has Down Syndrome, too, and when we tried to find support groups, a lot of other families just wanted someplace to send them rather than keeping their relatives themselves. So we decided to take them all and take care of them here."

"We don't necessarily have all the paperwork in order just yet," Mrs. Hollingsworth added while biting her lower lip.

Edwin's features smoothed and he smiled down at Daniel, who let him go and pointed excitedly at the badge clipped to Edwin's belt. Gaines followed his lead and asked Mr. Hollingsworth if any of the other kids wanted to meet a police officer. Three other teenagers came outside and crowded around the detectives, focusing mainly on their badges. All of them wanted several hugs a piece from Gaines and Edwin, and didn't stop until Mr. and Mrs. Hollingsworth peeled each child off and directed them inside.

Mrs. Hollingsworth could barely contain her tears. "This means the world to us, sir!" she gushed. Shaking Edwin's hand wasn't enough for her. Instead she threw her arms around his neck and whispered her thanks in his ear. Edwin had never been hugged so many times in his life.

As the detectives finally headed back to the car, Edwin caught Gaines giving him a funny look out of the corner of his eye. "What?" he gruffly asked.

Gaines shrugged nonchalantly. "I just never figured you'd do something like that," he replied.

"Something like what?" Edwin countered.

"A random act of kindness. Believe it or not, you're kind of a hard ass."

Edwin glanced at him for only a moment before both of them burst into deep belly laughs. Neither of them could stop, and it left Gaines gasping for air. This only made Edwin laugh harder.

All the tension from their argument earlier dissipated and they were left with only the camaraderie they had been developing from the beginning. Before he knew it, all Edwin's anger and disappointment with Gaines was gone, and he was only left with the same fondness that had been growing with each passing day.

Gaines was his partner, his mentee, and most importantly, he was becoming Edwin's best friend.

1990

When Edwin could finally rein in his laughter, he wiped the tears from his eyes as he asked Gaines, "So now where to?"

Gaines continued to grin as an errant chuckle escaped. He glanced at the paper he printed off from the DMV and stated, "The other address is out on the other side of the county, almost at the county line. Perhaps we should stop at Groundbreaking and ask about this guy?"

His question sobered Edwin fast. "You haven't done that yet? We've been chasing this lead of yours for weeks now, but you haven't bothered to talk to anyone at the coffee house about him? That could be the owner himself for all we know, Gaines! Why the hell are we chasing around false leads?!"

Gaines' face flushed deep red, but his eyes darkened in anger. "You never instructed me otherwise."

Edwin sighed in exasperation and yanked on his seatbelt harder than was necessary. "That's not an answer!" The tires peeled as he backed out of the driveway and sped towards the highway.

They rode in heated silence for several minutes, the tension nearly crackled with lightning inside the vehicle.

As if Gaines couldn't contain himself, he burst out angrily, "I was only doing what you asked!" He grasped the dashboard as Edwin lunged the car onto the shoulder and slammed on the brakes.

Edwin's composure snapped. "Damn it, kid, you don't need my approval! Stop acting like you need a gold star at the end of every day. You are a cop. Not only that, but you were also promoted to detective! That means you're a damn good one! You've got better instincts than I did when I first joined the force, and the only reason we've made it this far in the Pierce case is because of what you've found! You are worthy of being here—with or without me!"

Gaines gaped at him like Edwin sprouted a third arm out of his forehead. The poor kid opened his mouth several times to respond but no sound came out. A faint blush grew deeper as the seconds ticked by. Edwin's chest still heaved as his frustration abated.

Finally Gaines seemed to realize Edwin was no longer yelling at him. He shook his head to clear his thoughts and looked down at his hands in embarrassment. "But you always make it sound like Shelley is the only one you could work with. I never thought you even liked me," he admitted sheepishly.

This frustrated Edwin as much as it shamed him. He had been trying to prevent himself from an attachment to Gaines, but he didn't want it to come at the expense of Gaines doubting himself. It wasn't personal, at least to Edwin, but as a professional, Edwin found Gaines to be insightful and dedicated. Yet every conversation, every time he noted a change in Gaines' technique or behavior, all he felt was a surge of appreciation and fondness for the kid. Their partnership had already crossed the line into personal, and Edwin didn't know what to do about it.

Except…was their friendship really so bad? Edwin couldn't deny that he enjoyed being around Gaines and his whole family. Despite his best efforts, he was getting attached. He cared about Gaines and wanted him to succeed.

"It's not you, Gaines," Edwin finally said. "Shelley has been all I had for a long time. I just don't know where you fit into the picture."

"Do you even want me in the picture at all?" Gaines asked quietly.

Edwin paused at this but chose not to answer. He threw the car back into drive and merged onto the highway. Gaines nodded to himself before looking out the window. Neither said a word for the remainder of the drive.

The street was almost deserted by the time the detectives pulled up to Groundbreaking. Later afternoon sunlight sent long shadows to follow in their wake, and they found the coffee house to be empty of patrons. According to the sign on the door, it would be closing soon for the day.

The two walked inside and found Colin behind the counter again. He did a double take upon seeing the officers there again, but quickly set down the tongs he used on the bakery display case and approached them while wiping his hands on his apron. Colin's demeanor was much more subdued this visit. He braced himself against the front counter as though he expected bad news.

"Good evening," Edwin greeted him. "Do you have a moment for a couple more questions?"

Colin nodded. "Have you found Alessa? I miss her so much."

Edwin glanced at his partner as he shook his head sadly. "We haven't yet, but we are still investigating. That's actually why we're here—do you know who this is?"

Gaines pulled grainy print out of the mystery man from the surveillance tapes and handed it to Colin. Surprisingly, Colin snorted.

"Alessa's biggest fan?" he joked. "He was only ever here on days when she was working. We all noticed how he had the hots for her, but she denied it. The guy is totally harmless." He handed the paper back to Gaines.

"How do you know he was harmless?" Gaines asked.

The barista shrugged. "Just a vibe, I guess. He always seemed really awkward. Like he didn't know how to talk to people. He was amazed one day when the phone rang and Alessa answered it. We all laughed about it for a while."

Edwin's eyebrows went up. Mystery Man didn't know how to operate a phone?

"Why did you feel it was Alessa he was attracted to?" Gaines asked.

Colin shrugged again. "His eyes just always followed her. Like he couldn't believe she was real or something, I don't know. She was defi-nitely his favorite."

Gaines nodded as he scribbled more notes on his pad.

Edwin asked, "Did you ever get a name on him?"

Colin shook his head. "I didn't, but Lauren is here. We can ask her. Hey, Lauren!" he called towards the back.

A young girl with curly blonde hair and a face full of freckles came out of the back kitchen. She had on the uniform apron like Colin but looked to be a couple years younger. She merely raised her hand in greeting as she joined the group.

Gaines handed her the photo print out at the same time as Colin laughed, "Check it out, Lauren. The cops noticed Alessa's imaginary boyfriend."

Lauren giggled. "He was kind of obsessed with her," she told the detectives.

"Why do you say that? Did you ever feel he might've been stalking her?" Edwin asked. Although he tried to hide the exasperation from his voice, he found it rather difficult. Their friend went missing and they never bothered to mention that she had an obsessed customer watching her every move?

Lauren shrugged. "No. I sort of thought he had a crush on Alessa, but didn't know how to ask her out. He barely spoke a word and when he did, it was only to politely answer a question Alessa asked him."

"From what we saw on the tapes, it looked like he always paid in cash?" Gaines confirmed.

Both of the baristas nodded. "Just black coffee. No sugar or nothin'!" Colin cried in alarm.

Without meaning to, a sigh escaped Edwin's lips. Although Mystery Man sounded creepy, they were no further ahead. He thanked them both and turned towards the door.

"Hold on," Gaines stated, holding up a hand. "When is the last time you saw this guy?"

Colin held up his hands in an I-don't-know sort of gesture while Lauren scrunched her face in concentration. "He was here a few weeks ago, actually. He came later in the day than he usually does and he had a baseball hat on, but I'm pretty sure it was him. He drives a white van, right?"

Her statement made Edwin turn sharply from the door and Gaines raise his head in alarm.

"You've seen his van?" Edwin inquired.

Lauren and Colin both looked at the cops as though they were crazy.

"Yeah," Lauren said slowly. "He pulled up right out front. Actually—you know what? I think it was the day you guys came for the tapes!"

Gaines and Edwin exchanged a startled look. Without saying another word, Edwin proceeded to the car, leaving Gaines to sputter out a brief "thanks" before hightailing after him. Before they could get inside, Edwin rounded on him.

"We need to head there straight away!" Gaines insisted before his partner could say a word.

Edwin shook his head. "No," he said emphatically. This reminded him too much of the evening he lost Shelley; they needed to play by the rules this time and wait for a warrant and back up. "We are going back to the station and doing this the right way."

Gaines swore and kicked a tire. "There isn't enough for a warrant right now, and you know that! It's all circumstantial, at best! Don't go soft on me now."

His statement enraged Edwin, who didn't trust himself to speak. He got into the car, slamming the door so hard he was momentarily afraid he knocked the windowpane out.

Gaines scrambled around to the passenger side and dove in after him. He, too, slammed the door as if emphasizing his point. "Alessa Meinken could be in danger right now. You heard how they described this guy! If he was obsessed with her and saw Harrison Pierce as a rival, he could have done any number of things to them both. Jealousy is a helluva motivator!"

There was a war going on in Edwin's brain. While on the one hand, he agreed with the urgency of the situation and wanted to act as swiftly as possible like Gaines did, on the other hand a bright neon sign flashed a warning to him. There were so many things that could go wrong and they did not have a concrete plan since they didn't even know what they were walking into. It could be the key to solving the entire case or it could be another dead end. Edwin wanted to find Alessa and Harrison, but cutting corners and taking risks was no longer the route he could take. Jeopardizing the entire case certainly would not help.

Yet the need to protect weighed heavily on him. This Alessa girl had friends and a family who cared about her. They were desperate for answers, and if Edwin's gut told him this mystery man had the answers to her sudden disappearance, he owed it to her loved ones to find out as soon as possible. The clock was already ticking against them; it had been too long since either Harrison or Alessa were seen alive. Edwin knew the statistics around abductions and the odds were not in their favor.

Considering what Shelley would do in this case didn't really help because the last time Shelley was in a similar situation, Edwin lost him forever. They rushed in like hotheads and Shelley paid the ultimate price for it. The risk of repeating history nagged at the back of Edwin's mind like the pull of a magnet.

His silent contemplation seemed to be too much for his partner. Gaines threw up his hands in frustration and angrily asked, "Do you want to save a life? Isn't that our job?"

Edwin dragged a hand down his face before turning the key in the ignition. "Fine," he agreed, "we will go out there, but just to look around. If there is anything that puts us on notice, we return to the car and wait for back up, got it? I mean it, kid. This is not the time to play hero." He backed out of the parking space and circled towards the county highway.

Gaines rolled his eyes. "I'm not playing anything, Ed. I need to know that someone cared about this girl enough to do something. It's not about Harrison Pierce for me. And I don't care if you tell them I said that."

"'Them?'" Edwin repeated while slamming on the brakes.

The rookie's skin bloomed as red as a cherry. It was too late for him to backtrack from his slip now. "Millhouse has been asking me about the case…and you," Gaines admitted. His eyes stayed glued to the floor as shame rolled off him in waves.

Edwin's worst fears were confirmed. Gaines had been placed with him to spy for Millhouse, to report to him on Edwin's capabilities and performance so the higher ups could justify pushing through his retirement paperwork. His entire career was about to end, his entire way of life, all because of a few interpretations from a young kid who hadn't even worked a full case yet.

The roaring in his ears drowned out all other thoughts. He couldn't believe his worst fears were true.

"We do this my way, Gaines, or we don't do it at all," Edwin replied slowly. His voice sounded tight and foreign even to his own ears.

For once, Gaines did not comment, but simply nodded. He angled his body so it faced towards the passenger window, away from Edwin's reproachful stare.

As they pulled out into the street, the fluttering of Edwin's heart didn't stop. An annoying thought looped on repeat like the score of a basketball game on the bottom of the television screen.

Nothing would be the same after this.

1990

W*hat were the police doing at the coffee shop again?*

Duke could barely breathe as he drove past Alessa's workplace and saw two cops standing by a gray sedan. They appeared to be in an argument, with the younger one gesticulating wildly, their badges glinting in the late afternoon sun.

Duke had to get out of here immediately! He was only driving by on his way back from the post office, but he instantly forgot his other few errands at the sight of the officers.

Duke's mind raced the entire ride home. Why would the police be at the coffee shop again? Were they still looking for video surveillance? Was there footage of him taking Alessa? Did the police know who he was?

Although Duke knew in his heart he hadn't done anything wrong, Mother taught him well enough to know other people could never understand his true intentions. And, as much as he hated to admit it, even Duke knew that what happened to Harrison Pierce would be labeled as "murder" in a newspaper. Nobody would understand the necessary lengths Duke had to take to secure his place in Alessa's heart. The outside world didn't understand their own inclination to wickedness and sin, just like Mother always said.

Oh no…Mother, Duke thought.

Murderers went to a bad place; Mother always said there wasn't a fit punishment for it. She never specified whether allowances could be made if the person deserved to be murdered. Would Harrison Pierce's dark magic and sin make a difference?

The realization that he might have disappointed the most important person in his life made Duke start hyperventilating. He hastily pulled along the shoulder of the road. Mother deemed murder unforgivable. How could he redeem himself if that were true?

Alessa. She was equal parts his ruin and his salvation. Surely there had to be an exception for an act committed out of sheer love. It was his desire for her that overruled all common sense. She was the reason his desperation peaked to the point of Harrison Pierce's downfall. Mother would certainly understand that, Duke reasoned. She might blame Alessa, but that would have happened anyway, based on their conversations thus far. Duke couldn't even refer to Alessa by name in his mother's presence.

The first thing Duke needed to do was return home and ensure Alessa remained chained in the basement. Seeing the police had spooked him, and he could no longer remember if he had clamped down until the padlock clicked. It would be better if Alessa's restraints had an additional lock. And perhaps something to clip around her ankles.

Duke smiled at the image.

He swerved back into traffic and sped home. Thankfully there were no signs of the police or anyone else around the property when he pulled up. Just to be safe, Duke parked the van further behind the house than usual and immediately checked the lock around the outer doors to the basement. Duke made a mental note to drag one of the larger fallen timbers in front of the doors as an additional barrier. He would no longer use it as a point of entry after this. All the better for it to be concealed.

While the house had been a stately farmhouse at one point in time, the exterior long since gave away to the elements. Shutters hung haphazardly from several windows, which had more than one pane with cracks or holes in the glass. All of the siding needed a fresh coat of paint from the buildup of dirt and scratches from the low hanging tree branches.

Hopefully they'll think the house is abandoned, Duke thought wildly.

Once inside, Duke ascended halfway up the stairs to the second floor to listen for his mother's faint breathing before descending down into the basement. The lantern had gone out and it took several minutes for his eyes to adjust to the darkness.

Alessa remained chained in the back corner of the room, her wrists bound above her head. One leg jutted forward due to the makeshift splint he had applied the day before, though it didn't look as though the knee joint had set properly.

He lit a few candles near the staircase and carried one over to her sleeping form. Her lock remained securely fastened as the chains cut into the flesh of her wrists.

She shifted in her sleep, aware of his presence even in her unconscious state. The movement drew her blonde hair off her shoulder and exposed her breast, leaving Duke once again in awe over her naked form. No matter what, she was perfect. He would never stop wanting her even if he had one hundred lifetimes to fulfill his every fantasy.

Leaning down, he carefully kissed her forehead without jostling her broken leg. The caress made her eyelids flutter open and she stiffened beneath him. Their eyes locked, Alessa's filled with apprehension, and Duke's stomach turned. He didn't want to cause her pain, only teach her true submission. It wasn't his fault that he happened to enjoy her punishments.

"I need you to be very quiet, my pet," he cooed. "If you're good, you'll be rewarded."

Alessa snorted. "Is that what this has been?"

Duke smiled indulgently. "Would you prefer to have the gag back in your mouth?"

She blanched and shook her head. He was delighted with her acquiescence and planted a firm kiss on her mouth, ignoring the way she tried to pull away from his touch.

"I will see you soon, love. Get some rest," he said. She didn't close her eyes again, but leaned her head against the stone wall behind her.

Duke returned to the kitchen and boiled the water for tea. Although he knew his mother would not eat it, he poured some applesauce into a bowl as well. Once inside her room, however, it was apparent that no matter what he brought her it would remain untouched.

Mother's eyes rolled back in her head and the splotches in her cheek were a bright red in her lifeless face. Her breathing was forced and rattling, each inhale cinching in her chest in great heaving sighs.

When he tried to grab her hand, she couldn't bend her fingers to grasp his. Duke asked if he could get her anything, but received no response. He kneeled by her bed, holding her hand to the top of his head, and screamed his pain into her bedding. Something told him this was the end. She would finally be at peace and his entire world would shatter.

"I love you, Mother," Duke repeated over and over again in a passionate whisper.

What could have been several minutes or several seconds passed. Duke couldn't bring himself to check the time if it meant he missed a single moment. Each breath stalled longer than the one before as he tried to count the seconds in between. She shuddered and grew still, another heaving gasp echoing throughout the room.

Suddenly, a noise outside made Duke's heart jump to his throat. Gravel sifted along the driveway. There was a car pulling up. He didn't need to go to the window to know there were police officers inside.

2011

Stella moved through the next two weeks as if in a dream. The Barbie nurses didn't bother her, she no longer had to contend with coaching sessions from Human Resources, and the sudden downsizing of hospital staff meant she could work as many hours as she wanted again. She exploited this down to the minute; her paycheck rivaled those with a college degree. As long as she kept her head down and didn't do anything to raise suspicion, Mary left her to her own devices.

The problem was there was very little time to be on her own. Less staff meant more work, and shots of espresso became a standard routine in her day. Stella hardly had time to check on Room 216, let alone experiment on him in any way, and she found herself longing for the quiet solitude of his room as her scalpel grazed a vein.

She did manage to glean some new skills during her overtime streak. One doctor, exasperated with the staff shortage, held a small instructional seminar on the proper way to suture wounds for all the nurses willing to learn and agreed to sign off on approval if any of the nurses gave stitches to a patient. Stella wore her best set of scrubs that day to blend in and sat in the back of the room, tucking her head down if anyone glanced her way, but she was able to understand the technique from watching the nurses practice in front of her. On her way out, she quickly snatched two of the banana practice dummies as well as a basic suturing kit before anyone noticed.

Life was going well and she didn't know what to make of it. Contentment unsettled her as it felt eerily similar to waiting for the other shoe to drop. Yet Stella couldn't deny the satisfaction she felt at the end of every day when she clocked out and read the total accumulated hours for the week.

She even dared herself to check the price for flights to Paris. If she kept this momentum going, it might actually be possible for her to visit the Louvre. The thought made her so happy she could hug herself.

It therefore came as a shock to her one day when she reported to work and saw her schedule started the day in a private meeting with Mary. Stella couldn't think of anything that might have raised alarm, no matter how hard she racked her brain. She had been careful, checking on Avery Winslow every chance she could, while simultaneously preventing anyone else from entering his room. There was no way she could have gotten caught, and the Barbie nurses avoided her like she carried typhoid.

The meeting had something to do with Room 216. That was the only conclusion she could draw. Somehow another staff member saw or heard something and now the truth would come out.

Stella entered the employee lounge filled with doubt. If anyone stood next to her, they would definitely hear the whirring from the gears in her brain turning as each explanation she concocted in her head became more far-fetched than the last. She braced herself for impact, glancing around for a sheriff deputy who would surely be there to arrest her.

However, it was only Mary, crouched over her beloved clipboard, sitting at the table on the opposite side of the room. Stella cleared her throat to announce herself and tried to ignore the way the lump settled in place instead.

"Go ahead and shut the door, hon," Mary instructed. She gestured to the seat across from her.

Dread rising deeper with every step, Stella sank into the chair with bated breath.

Her boss didn't even look up at her as she began to explain. "We should've done your evaluation a little while back, but with us being so busy and all, it's just taking me forever! Now that your probationary period is over, Central Office is really laying the hammer down." She slid a document in front of Stella and began to go line by line through her employee evaluation. Stella deflated like a balloon.

"So that's that. Just sign here," Mary said as she slid a pen over. She smiled fondly at Stella for a few moments. "Can I just say how proud of you I am? You really are trying, and I can see that. I hope you noticed how much that's reflected in your evaluation."

A new lump formed in Stella's throat, one that had nothing to do with guilt. For once she was at a loss for words. It had never occurred to her that Mary would see a positive difference in her behavior, especially after the last incident with the Barbie nurses. While Mary had said she was trying to help Stella stay under the radar, Stella didn't consider the ways in which it had. She had been able to skate by with none the wiser as to her extracurricular activities in Room 216.

But now Mary misinterpreted that as some sort of profound change in Stella's character. No one had ever told her they were proud of her, what did she even do with this information?

Stella had never sought anyone's approval before, and although she didn't believe Mary's opinion meant anything worthwhile, there was a small part of her that felt happy to be noticed at all. Stella wryly wondered if it was how the Grinch felt when his heart finally grew.

Mary looked at her expectantly as though waiting for Stella to agree with her. She hoped it was enough to smile and nod because the whole scenario began to make Stella uncomfortable.

Her awkward grimace did the trick, however, because Mary smiled at her before gathering the remaining papers from the table.

"Now, this next thing I'm going to say strictly off the record." Mary leaned in conspiratorially like they were old chums. "I know you've had a hard life, Stella. There's no sense in beatin' around the bush about it.

But you've gotta know, having a bad past doesn't mean you have to have a bad future. You can do just about anything!"

Stella suddenly found her hands firmly clasped in Mary's. The nurse gave her a final squeeze before pulling her glasses back on her face and leaving the room.

The ringing in her ears was only matched by the weight on her soul. Kindness wasn't something Stella was used to, but she was surprised at how unsettled Mary's words made her. Although the fondness would never be reciprocated, Stella didn't relish the idea of disappointing Mary now. And that was exactly what would happen if Mary discovered the truth of the mute in Room 216.

It meant that the only way out of her predicament was to succeed in making Avery Winslow speak. Stella had to make that bastard sing like a canary or else Mary's faith in her would be foolishly misguided. She shook her head violently to dismiss the thoughts from her mind.

Thoughts that sounded a lot like guilt.

1990

Duke blinked several times, willing himself to wake up from this nightmare. How could the police have found him? Why were they knocking on his front door so late in the evening? He slid down the stairs as quietly as a doe in the woods, keeping his back pressed against the wall as he tried to listen over the erratic rhythm of his heart in overdrive.

As foolish as it was, Duke cowered down behind the living room chair and pulled the cord to extinguish the lamp. The room was now bathed in shadow, the only light coming from the porch sconce and the bright moon peeking out through the trees. Duke could hear one of the officers comment on the sudden darkness, a sure sign that someone was inside. He didn't care, however, because he needed them to leave. He knew from reading the newspaper that police needed something called "warrants" to search homes, although he didn't know how they obtained such a thing or what it even meant to have one. From context clues, Duke gathered that warrants were issued when it was suspected there was involvement in a crime.

But how could anyone suspect that of him? No one even knew who he was. He had never told his name to anyone, not even Alessa. There was no way to link him to anything.

He crept along the back wall, keeping to the darkest shadows, trying to spy on the men on the porch. Duke saw the older one begin walking towards the sedan parked in the driveway, but the younger one with curly hair gestured around the side of the house. It sounded like he wanted to walk around.

"Shit!" Duke mumbled. Although the basement was a storm bunker at one time, once the double doors had been added into the side of the hill, only cheap aluminum had been used. If Alessa made one sound, anyone standing out there could hear it.

Acting quickly, he turned through the kitchen and scurried across to the back door, bent at the waist to keep out of sight of the windows. He pulled a large kitchen knife from the block on the counter. The knife hadn't been used since the last time Duke sharpened it and the blade glinted ominously in the moonlight.

Skirting around the outside of the property, Duke followed the worn siding around the other side of the house. Old, decaying shrubbery, neglected since his mother's illness, mottled the wall closest to the hill and Duke sought the camouflage in its branches.

An opening just big enough to peer at the cops' faces allowed him to spy. Duke didn't even dare breath in case one of them looked his way.

"Come on, Gaines," the older man said. Duke could hear the weariness in his voice and a hardened edge as though he had survived many battles up to this point. The man waved towards his car. "Let's get out of here. We can't be caught poking around."

The younger one, who must have been named Gaines, shook his head. "I am *telling* you, I can feel something is off." He looked in the direction of the woods behind the house. "Why would that light have gone out inside?"

The older man took a few brisk steps closer to Gaines. "We could jeopardize this investigation if we're seen looking around. There's no good reason to be here. You know that, Gaines."

Even from the distance, Duke could tell that the man's eyes softened as he spoke to the younger partner. This Gaines person was important to the cop.

Interesting, thought Duke.

The older police officer's arguments must have made sense to the young man, though, because he turned and started towards the vehicle. Gravel crunched loudly beneath their feet and Duke suddenly had a startling fear that the sound would wake up his mother. He would be punished severely if she knew police were at their home. An errant thought reminded him, however, that his mother was likely dead; he had scuttled downstairs so fast that he probably missed her last breath.

A howl akin to a wounded animal rattled from behind the home.

"Help me, please!"

Alessa's voice, hoarse and wailing into the night.

Both of the cops turned towards the sound, wordlessly exchanging a heated look, and withdrawing their weapons. Gaines moved faster, rounding the back of the house in a moment. It was now or never, Duke realized.

Pushing through the brush, Duke slid around the corner bathed in darkness and lunged for Gaines. He tackled the cop to the ground, using all of his strength to hammer down the wrist holding the gun. Duke cracked Gaines' wrist against the ground three times before the cop's grip slackened. Duke threw the gun into the woods beyond.

"Hands up, buddy!" The other officer aimed his weapon at Duke, Gaines still pinned beneath him. The kitchen knife pressed against Duke's leg in one of the cargo pockets on the opposite side of the officer. It was too dark to make out much of anything anymore, not that the officer knew to look at Duke's leg for a weapon.

Gaines suddenly punched Duke in the gut, making him gasp for air and fall out of his hold. Duke curled up in a fetal position as Gaines scrambled back a few steps. Although Mother frequently beat him, usually with other objects like a belt or a switch from a tree, no one had ever punched Duke before.

After gaining his bearings, Gaines extracted a pair of handcuffs and advanced towards him. Right as he bent at the waist to pull Duke upright, Duke popped an uppercut into the cop's knee, the resulting crack indicating how hard the kneecap popped in the wrong direction. Duke jumped to his feet and held the knife to the police officer's throat, glaring back at the older man who still aimed his gun. Now his partner's body shielded Duke and he knew that the officer would not fire at him. Not if it would risk his partner's life.

"Drop that knife!" the older cop barked.

Duke noticed that Alessa's cries still rang in the background. The double doors to the bunker were approximately fifteen feet behind him. Once the police found her, Duke's mission would go up in smoke.

"Who are you?" Duke demanded. He used his free hand to twist Gaines' arms behind him, further incapacitating the officer.

"I'm Detective Edwin Greene with the Amherst Police Department," the man replied. His arms didn't waver as he kept his weapon on target. "Drop that knife and we can talk."

Duke felt his fury simmering just under his skin. It wasn't supposed to end like this! Alessa was so close to loving him, he had almost broken the spell!

"You need to leave. Now."

There was an unveiled threat in his words and he felt Gaines straining to pull away from the knife. Duke pushed it further into his skin by the fraction of an inch. A strangled whimper escaped the cop's lips.

"What's your name?" Detective Greene asked. He was stalling, Duke was sure of it. However, Duke needed time to think, so he played along.

"Mother has always called me Duke," he answered calmly. Perhaps if he gave the impression of confidence, they would take him more seriously.

He began taking slow steps towards the woods. No one knew that area like he did. There were hundreds of places Duke could hide. They might take Alessa, but he would find her again, when the time was right. It was the only option he could come up with in the heat of the moment.

"'Mother'?" the older detective repeated. He glanced briefly at the house behind him, on alert for another threat.

The thought made Duke laugh. "It's just us, Detective. No one would ever find you out here."

Detective Greene shook his head and took a tentative step towards the pair, which Duke noted instantly. The officer was aware of his slow retreat towards the tree line.

"We already have back up on the way, Duke. This place is about to be surrounded with cops. Put the knife down and no one needs to get hurt."

This made Duke see red. Mother would definitely notice dozens of flashing lights and sirens outside! He braced himself, momentarily gathering strength for what he knew he had to do, and glared at the detective. The gun had not wavered, but Duke sensed that he didn't want to fire it unless absolutely necessary. These men were prepared to destroy his home and ruin his mother's last few breaths, if they hadn't already. They deserved to be punished.

Stonily staring Detective Greene dead in the eye over Gaines' shoulder, Duke declared, "Sinners always pay the price." With a mighty jerk, the knife plunged deep into Gaines' jugular, blood spurting everywhere.

CHAPTER
THIRTY-NINE

2011

Stella's boots felt heavier than usual as she slid them off to peel her leggings from her skin. Thankfully they were black, so unless someone looked closely, no one could tell the blood that had spilled on them. She had grown careless with her experiments in Room 216, but she couldn't bring herself to care.

All it took was a simple hack into Mary's computer (*who makes their birthday their password anymore?* Stella thought wryly) and Stella had managed to assign herself as the only worker in Winslow's room for the next four weeks. After a few casual conversations with the housekeeper, she knew for certain they would avoid the room—Avery Winslow made all of cleaning staff just as uncomfortable as her with his perpetual staring.

It was the end of her shift and although Stella didn't want to stay at work, she dreaded going home.

Her apartment was okay. A simple studio loft in a rougher part of the city, but since she didn't associate with anyone in or outside of the building, she never really had any problems. Most of her time was spent at work anyway, so it seemed frivolous to have a bigger place or stay in a more expensive part of town.

Stella found herself catching the bus to the museum rather than her apartment as she left work. It would still be open for an hour by the time she arrived and it sure as hell beat staring at the blank walls of her apartment.

Her feet walked automatically to her favorite room, the Impressionism Hall. There was a local artist, Drew Pelego, whose work was featured there and no matter how many times she looked at them, every painting revealed something different to her with each visit.

Her favorite was a piece entitled "The Mind" that presented bold reds, purples, and oranges flying out of a man's head as he lied on the ground. The man was meant to have fallen, based on his pained expression, and the crack on the cement depicted the horrors his mind unleashed as it split open. It drew her in again today, captivating her once more with its vivid collage of color.

She sat on the wood bench a few feet away from the painting and leaned back to revel in its splendor. This kind of peace and euphoria only existed whenever she cut into Avery Winslow's body, a sense of the chaos finally stabilizing. The painting reminded her that she wasn't alone in the madness; there were others out there just as fucked up and beautiful in their darkness as she.

"What do you think of it?" someone behind her asked.

Her head whipped around to see a shorter man in his mid-twenties with rich tan skin and black eyes standing nearby. He had on a cashmere sweater that screamed status to her but his worn jeans greatly contrasted the look. Casually assessing her, the man kept his hands shoved in his pockets.

Stella raised an eyebrow. She had no interest in talking to a stranger, especially when this time it was hers and hers alone. A quiet solitude she rarely found within the walls of the hospital.

He didn't seem to mind her lack of response and instead sat down next to her on the bench, his thigh barely touching her hand that rested on the seat. She quickly sat upright and pulled her hands in her lap. Turning to glare at him, she found him already gazing at her intently.

"It's perfect," she finally whispered, her attention drawn back to the painting.

The man let out a low whistle. "Perfection is a very bold interpretation," he commented jovially. He smiled at her, teeth white against his tan skin.

She rolled her eyes. This was why she didn't want to say anything. Although she loved visiting the museum, she knew absolutely nothing about art and had no desire to learn. Simply appreciating the beauty for what it was had always been enough for her. Now there was some hipster art critic who wanted to lecture her on the techniques behind the style when she never even asked.

"Excuse me," she said. She stood up abruptly and had only gone a few steps when the man's voice came from behind her again.

"I'll be sure to tell my agent you said so."

Stella spun on the spot. "You're Drew Pelego?" she asked.

He held his arms out at his side. "In the flesh," he laughed. "It's always nice to see someone admiring my work."

His smile mesmerized her and she sat down on the bench next to him again. "What does the painting mean?"

Drew shrugged. "I just wanted something to reflect the way I feel." He said it casually, but there was a hint of sadness and pain to his tone that Stella recognized. It made her heartbeat louder in her chest.

Now her new companion became a lot more interesting. She noticed the way his curls sprung out in every direction, giving him an aloof look, like he couldn't be bothered to tame them.

Stella leaned back from him in a way that accentuated her breasts, sending a silent prayer of gratitude that she had chosen to wear a shirt with a deep V-neck today. Her cleavage was on point, a detail Drew immediately noticed. His breath caught and he looked her in the eyes before a wicked smile crossed his face. "Wanna get out of here?" he asked.

"It's like you read my mind," Stella replied mischievously.

It turned out his place was closest, the top floor of an old administrative office in the warehouse district near the art museum. Half-finished canvases in varying sizes covered Drew's art studio, immediately catching Stella's eye when they walked in. There were cans of paint on every surface, including on what looked to be a small kitchenette near the front door. The entire room spanned the width of the building, featuring two enormous skylights and several massive windows on two sides of the room.

The bed shoved into the corner seemed to be an afterthought, but Stella collapsed onto it gleefully as Drew heaved her shirt from her body. He devoured her breasts, releasing them from their lacy cage and licking them with wanton abandonment. Her burning desire made her so clumsy with undoing his jeans that she broke the zipper in her haste to get them off. It was sex in its most frenzied, reckless form and Stella shivered with delight and ecstasy as she rode her high from his cock.

After several hours and positions that stretched muscles she didn't know she had, Stella finally peeled her naked body from his and began to gather her things. Tiptoeing quietly into the small bathroom, Stella splashed chilly water on her face and attempted to shake the tangles from her hair. With a grunt of defeat, she pulled an elastic band off her wrist and piled her unruly curls into a high bun. When she finally emerged from the bathroom, she found Drew awake. He sat up in bed, still naked, leaning back against the headboard. His black eyes raked her body, clearly unsatiated and ready for more.

Despite herself, Stella giggled. "Yeah, that's not gonna happen. I need to get home so I can sleep for a few hours before I head back into work."

He accepted her answer gracefully, though his lips sank into an adorable pout. "Where do you work?"

Stella rolled her eyes. "No place you will ever go," she said.

Drew didn't seem to like that answer. "Well, when can I see you again?"

She shrugged into her leather jacket. "You won't."

He clambered off the bed, pulling the sheet with him and wrapping it around his waist. "So you're just gonna bail like this? I don't even know your name!" He made to block the door, driving her for an answer.

Stella caressed his jaw. "Oh, sweetie," she purred, "that's because I don't want you to." With that, she yanked open the door and sauntered out of the room.

Power over men, Stella realized, came easily when one allowed them to serve her purposes rather than theirs.

1990

An animalistic roar bellowed from somewhere deep in Edwin's chest. Blood sprayed everywhere and quickly soaked Gaines' button up shirt as he dropped to his knees and then fell back onto the dirt. The man, Duke, hastened toward the trees in an all-out sprint. Edwin, however, darted forward and pulled Gaines onto his lap.

The blood made a gurgling sound as Gaines tried to speak, but Edwin shushed him and applied as much pressure to the wound as he could, knowing it was a fool's errand. Gaines' eyes were shifting in and out of focus and Edwin could feel his partner's body shuddering as his lungs gave out. Gaines' warm brown eyes sought Edwin's, and although he wanted to remain strong for his partner, he could feel the hot tears cascade down his cheeks. Edwin pulled the man closer and whispered, "It's okay, Kevin. This wasn't your fault."

Gaines shakily reached a bloody hand towards Edwin's face, but his body gave one last spasm and the hand dropped, limp at his side. Gaines was gone.

Edwin could feel the white-hot lust for revenge taking over his senses. He didn't understand how he let this happen. First Shelley and now Gaines, both gone too soon. Both his fault.

He looked over at the dark wood and could just barely make out the sound of branches snapping in the distance. It was enough, he decided.

Without a second thought, Edwin tore off into the trees after the sound. Edwin's childhood had been spent hunting in the woods with his father, and although the moonlight splintered through the trees, he felt sure of his steps as he wove around the trunks and dodged exposed tree roots. Duke's rustling sounds grew closer as Edwin gained on him before it suddenly went quiet and moonlight flooded the area as clear as sunlight. They had reached a clearing, with Duke only twenty feet or so ahead of him.

Duke glanced back at Edwin over his shoulder as he made a beeline for the other side of the meadow where it looked as if it headed into a steep hill. The man began running faster, which pissed Edwin off even more. The bastard didn't get to run from the chaos he created. He had to pay for what he'd done.

All of Edwin's police training went out the window as Gaines' bloody, lifeless face filled his mind. Without pausing to consider other options, Edwin raised his weapon and aimed center mass at Duke's retreating back. The blast echoed around them in a fierce symphony of power and pain before the man's body smacked the earth. He laid face down in the dirt for several moments before Edwin lowered his weapon and carefully approached him.

The far off sounds of sirens barely registered with Edwin as he knelt down over Duke's body and gave a brief pat down for more weapons. Feeling none, he holstered his gun and used both hands to roll the man onto his back. Duke didn't move, but big anguished sobs had turned his face into a blubbering mess. Edwin ordered him to get up.

Duke's face crumpled even more and a large snot bubble blew out of one nostril. "I can't! It hurts! Sir, it hurts!" He continued to bawl but did not so much as twitch a finger.

Edwin rose, disgusted at the mess the man made. He felt sure this was a ruse to lull him into lowering his guard again. Edwin's radio was back in the car and he needed to return to Gaines' body. Back up should be pulling up to the home at any moment, and then someone else could worry about the crocodile tears.

He rolled Duke's body onto its side and clasped both wrists into handcuffs drawn from the back of his duty belt.

Moving slowly while keeping his face towards Duke, Edwin retreated to the edge of the clearing and paused. The man hadn't moved a centimeter. A bad sign, Edwin knew. His shot had been clean in the dead center of Duke's back, but there hadn't been an exit wound. Duke still lived, which meant the bullet was lodged in his body somewhere.

Edwin turned and raced back through the trees, a longer distance than he had originally noticed, and found several ambulances and police cars with sirens blaring and lights flashing around his vehicle. At least ten flashlights shone on him as he emerged from the woods, his hands up and his badge exposed.

"Greene, is that you?" an officer called out through a megaphone. He was standing next to an EMT moving over Gaines' body.

Edwin approached the officer with his hands still in the air, and the flashlights all pulled away, allowing his eyesight to adjust. The officer's name was John Parker, a cop a few years behind Edwin in the Academy.

"The assailant was apprehended in a clearing about half a mile through the trees there. He's incapacitated right now. Send officers and an EMT team out to collect him," Edwin commanded.

Parker nodded and gestured to a pair of nearby officers.

Kneeling down, Edwin placed a hand on Gaines' chest, the blood still warm and sticky. "End of watch, kid," he said and gently closed Gaines' eyes.

Parker scanned the area around them. "What made you come out here, Greene?"

Edwin shot up and withdrew his firearm from his holster as Parker's question brought him back to reality. This was not the time for grief.

"Watch my six," he said quietly as he approached the set of double aluminum doors to his left. Now that he paid attention, Edwin could hear what sounded like a woman crying and shouting inside.

A thick padlock chain wrapped around the door handles. Three officers, including Parker, stood in a similar formation behind him, and a fourth officer came up from behind with a large bolt cutter. With two heaving cuts, the chain fell free. The officer paused with a hand on the handle, waiting for Edwin's signal. Edwin nodded tightly and the man yanked back on the rusty door.

A small camping lantern hung from a wall in the right-hand corner of the room. An emaciated woman, completely naked, huddled in a squat beneath it, both wrists bound by chains above her head, one leg bound in a crude splint at an odd angle. She was covered in blood and bruises, the sight of which made Edwin's stomach roll. He recognized her immediately.

Alessa Meinken, in the flesh.

Slowly, he lowered his gun and slid it back in this holster as he made a tentative step towards her. The woman began crying again and loudly wailed, "Please help me! Help me!" The chains above her rattled as her body shook with sobs.

Edwin reached her first and placed a gentle hand on the back of her shoulder. "We're here now and no one is going to hurt you anymore. My name's Edwin and I'm a detective," he whispered delicately. He didn't want to scare her any more than she clearly already was.

She cried even harder before lapsing into a phlegmy coughing fit. She spat blood onto the ground and replied, "I'm Alessa." Her hazel eyes locked into his, full of fear and pain.

Without breaking eye contact, Edwin waved to the officers behind him to stand down. Someone brought forth a blanket that he lightly placed around her shoulders, attempting to return a bit of modesty to her. Another officer came forward, and although Alessa jumped and pulled her body away from the man, he was able to use the bolt cutters against the chains on her wrists.

As soon as she was free, Alessa tugged the blanket further around her body and collapsed into Edwin's arms. He gingerly lifted her, disgusted at her featherlight weight, and took her into the back of an ambulance. The EMT's began to assess her, placing an oxygen mask over her nose and mouth, and a cuff around her arm for blood pressure, but her hand darted out and clasped around Edwin's wrist.

"Don't leave me!" she cried. The harsh light of the ambulance threw her bruises into sharper focus, making Edwin wonder what else that monster had done.

He shook his head and sat down on the seat next to her. Carefully taking her hand in his, Edwin promised he wouldn't leave her yet. The EMT nodded at him wordlessly and the unit pulled away to get to the hospital. Even without their confirmation, the worry etched in all three of the EMT's faces told him that she was in a bad way.

Gaines would be happy to know we saved her, Edwin thought. That alone would have made the entire night worth it to Gaines. He had a fleeting image of Shelley meeting Gaines at some sort of pearly white gates and clapping the rookie on the shoulder in welcome. The idea made him choke on his grief.

He hung his head in his hands and couldn't stifle the tears. Gaines and Shelley were both gone, and it was his fault. If he had been a better partner, if he had waited for back up in either scenario, they would both still be alive. Guilt weighed heavily and his shoulders literally sank beneath the load. Some burdens were just too heavy to carry.

FORTY-ONE

1990

Hard hands lifted Duke off the ground and placed him onto a stretcher. Fire burned within his entire body and he idly wondered if this was what the flames of Hell felt like. He didn't think it was possible for his body to sustain this much pain, yet he was keenly aware of his inability to move his limbs. None of Mother's beatings ever left him in this bad of shape.

The voices around him sounded muffled. Lights kept flashing above his head and he felt the sensation of movement as a stretcher took him somewhere, flanked by two police officers and three other people in a matching navy uniform.

The peeling white siding of his home came into view and Duke panicked for a moment that his mother would know what had transpired tonight. Reality set in, however, and he remembered that Mother was most likely dead. Detective Greene and his partner stole her last minutes from him, time that he could never get back.

At least his mother passed without knowing the truth of how he had used her house. She would have punished him for several days if she had known he chained a strange woman in their basement, then punished him again for failing to break Alessa's spell. Perhaps this was one of God's merciful acts.

"Surely goodness and mercy shall follow me all the days of my life, and I shall dwell in the house of the Lord forever." The words of Psalm 23:6 brought Duke a small touch of comfort.

The crew loaded him into an ambulance and he drifted in and out of consciousness. He vaguely recalled hearing someone asking him for his name, but Duke couldn't remember if he answered. Sleep came and he succumbed to the darkness.

His eyelids felt heavy and his head throbbed as he regained awareness sometime later. He couldn't sense any clothing, but a scratchy blanket covered his entire body. There were several different beeping sounds.

Slowly Duke peeled his eyelids apart and raised his left hand to check what felt like a bandage around his head. Or at least, he attempted to raise his left hand. A sharp, cold object jabbed into his wrist. Duke's eyes widened as he realized metal handcuffs locked his wrist to the rails of the bed. He was in what he assumed was a hospital room, having never seen one before, but the surroundings matched those of novels he had read. Tubes came out of multiple points on his body.

A police officer sat in a chair near the door. He stood up quickly when he made eye contact with Duke and stepped out in the hall to call for someone. A man in a white coat and glasses entered the room along with Detective Greene.

"Sir, can you tell me your name?" the man in the lab coat asked. He clutched a clipboard, pen poised in wait.

Duke simply stared at him, wary of the strangers in the room. There was dark magic at work here, he could feel it.

"I'm Doctor Nicholson," the white coat said. "You're at Amherst General Hospital. Do you remember how you got here?"

At this question, Duke's eyes shifted to the detective. *He* was the reason they were here.

Sensing the tension fluctuating, the doctor turned back to Detective Greene. "Perhaps you should talk to him first." He swept from the room, the other police officer following at a nod from the detective.

Detective Greene sighed, his hands in his pockets. His tie was rumpled and his button down shirt needed pressing. Mother would cringe at the man's disheveled appearance.

In the weak light, frown lines creased the man's face and Duke had that same sense of foreboding as when he said his final goodbye to Mother. Nothing would ever be the same after this.

"What's your real name?" Detective Greene began.

Duke tried not to show his surprise. He had only ever heard his full name once. Mother *always* called him Duke. Always. She insisted it was the only name appropriate for him.

A sense of foreboding increased tenfold.

The detective's head cocked to the side, surmising Duke's reaction. "We can't find anything identifying you," he declared. "The house belongs to a Pamela Pauer, and her body was found in a room upstairs. Is that your mother?" Detective Greene paused, giving Duke an opportunity to answer that he didn't take. He didn't want to say anything that would involve Mother.

The detective cleared his throat. "You are under arrest. You are being charged with kidnap, rape, and first degree murder…"

He continued to speak, but the ringing in Duke's ears drowned out his voice. Only criminals were placed under arrest. Was he a criminal? He only wanted Alessa to recognize the love that existed between them. Surely that wasn't a crime.

Wait—Alessa.

"Where is she?" Duke growled. She could put a stop to all of this.

Detective Greene's eyes narrowed. "You will never see Alessa again, Duke. I swear on my life, you will never leave this hospital again unless it is to stand trial. I will make sure you live the rest of your miserable life alone and suffering." The room blazed with the heat of conviction behind his words.

Something lodged in Duke's throat, making it impossible for him to swallow. He tried again to lift a hand and found there was still no sensation in his extremities. Nothing moved.

"What happened to me?" he asked weakly. His eyes were full of reproach as he glared at the detective.

Without answering him, Detective Greene returned to the door and called for the doctor. Dr. Nicholson entered and started down a winding tangent that left Duke bereft. The word "quadriplegic" was interspersed throughout and made Duke's blood run cold. He had read about that before in an article about a car accident victim. It meant Duke was a cripple.

If anything, Detective Greene's reaction made it worse. The shock registered on his face, followed by crushing guilt. It was the shot directly to his spine, the doctor explained. It severed the nerves in his spinal cord instantly. Surgery to repair the damage had been unsuccessful.

The doctor rattled off a litany of other physical ailments currently plaguing Duke, but he didn't want to hear anymore. He kept his attention on the detective, eyes burning into the man's face.

After several more explanations of what would happen going forward, all of which Duke tuned out, the doctor left the room again. The police officer and Detective Greene exchanged a heated argument in the corner before glancing back at him. Detective Greene followed the doctor out. The officer sat back in the chair and leaned his head against the wall, no longer watching Duke for any signs of a threat.

Tears prickled hot down his face as he stared at the ceiling above.

Sinners really do pay the price, he thought.

CHAPTER
FORTY-TWO

1990

Edwin felt sick to his stomach. The words "severed spinal cord" were on repeat in his head. His actions led to a man losing all mobility. Duke would never walk again. He would never be able to sit up on his own or feed himself. He would be entirely dependent on the help of others. All because of Edwin.

Shame overwhelmed him and settled deep in his gut. He knew better than to fire at a man retreating from him. In the heat of the moment, covered with Gaines' blood, it had seemed like the right thing to do, but was it really? Had he allowed his own emotions to override how he handled an assailant? Thirty years on the job had disintegrated with one decision. A decision that had permanent consequences for Duke.

If Shelley had been there, he would've done the same thing. Shelley didn't focus much on the rules when it came to handling criminals. "Right was right and wrong was wrong" was Shelley's favorite justification any time he stepped out of line.

As a younger detective, eager to capture the evils of the world, this logic made perfect sense to Edwin. Now, as a seasoned veteran, witnessing all of the horrors people could inflict on one another, he knew the line between right and wrong was often blurred. Still, it comforted him somewhat to know that Shelley wouldn't have blamed Edwin. Shelley would've congratulated him on executing real justice, not the public's watered-down version.

Edwin, lost in thought, found himself pulling into the police precinct and parking in his usual spot. He let his feet carry him to his office and blindly poured himself a cup of stale coffee.

Gaines' empty chair made his throat go dry; had it really only been a day since they sat here pouring over video footage? It didn't seem real. He knew he should return to Duke's house and help with searching and cataloging evidence, and there were probably about fifty new crime scene photos in an envelope waiting for his perusal, but he couldn't bring himself to care. Gaines was gone. Nothing else really mattered in comparison.

A knock on the door jerked Edwin back to the present. Harry Millhouse stood in the doorway, his face somber. He didn't ask for permission but entered the room and gruffly clapped Edwin on the shoulder. It was his own way of offering solace, Edwin knew, but he resented the man's presence at the moment. Millhouse would only want to rewrite the narrative in his favor.

Yet his question surprised Edwin. "Would you like to go tell the Gaines family about Kevin?"

The floor might have fallen out from under him. There was no greater punishment than bringing their worst fears to light, but Edwin knew he had to be the one to do it. He owed them the truth. He owed them an apology for misplacing their faith in him; he swore to keep their son safe, and instead Gaines would never grace their home again. This day's burdens would leave their mark for the rest of his life.

Edwin nodded to Millhouse. "I'll go now. Let me straighten up first." He went to a small wardrobe in the back of the office where he kept spare clothes for the days he worked around the clock and pulled another dress shirt out. He changed quickly, withdrawing a matching tie, and started towards the door.

He paused next to his superior and stated quietly, "Please consider this notice of my retirement. I'll have the paperwork on your desk by tomorrow."

Millhouse gave him a look filled with pity. "We'll discuss this in a few days," he offered. "Take some time first, Ed." He clapped Edwin on the shoulder again before sweeping from the room.

Pulling up to the Gaines' home felt like Edwin was walking to the electric chair. Dread was an ugly monster and right now it swallowed him whole. He couldn't bear the thought of looking Mrs. Gaines in the eye and telling her he broke his promise. Their whole family was so warm and inviting, everything he had always wanted but never pursued. They didn't deserve such a tragedy.

He realized in the gray morning light that it was still too early for anyone to be up. The sun had barely peeped over the horizon. Before he could even knock, Mr. Gaines opened the door. He didn't say anything, but looked Edwin down from head to toe and pulled Edwin into a rough embrace.

"My boy's gone," he whispered flatly. A statement, not a question.

Rosie came flying around the corner from the kitchen, followed by Mrs. Gaines. Seeing her husband's fierce grip around Edwin was enough. She burst into tears and leaned into the wall for support. Claire came from the hallway leading towards their bedrooms and grabbed her mother's hand.

Edwin pulled away from Mr. Gaines and approached his partner's mother. "I'm so sorry, Laura," he breathed.

Sobs started to choke him. Mrs. Gaines only shook her head and sank into his open arms. Mr. Gaines came around them and began to rub his wife's back at the same time he pulled his girls close to him. The five of them held this position in the tiny hallway for several moments, grief poisoning the air.

Claire broke the spell first, moving into the kitchen and starting the coffee machine. She gently guided her weeping mother into a chair and placed a bagel in front of her. Mr. Gaines followed, sinking into the chair with a weariness Edwin knew came from the soul. Edwin sat down between them.

Claire turned back to him. "What happened?" she asked tearfully.

Edwin recounted the lead they had gotten, Gaines' desire to set out right away to talk to the man in question, and the resulting aftermath. He paused at the end, wanting to spare them the nasty details. Mrs. Gaines continued sobbing next to him, but he realized her hand still held his in a vice grip. She didn't need to hear the worst of it. Edwin assured them that he stayed with Gaines until his very last breath. He didn't die alone or afraid.

Mr. Gaines exhaled shakily. "Did you at least catch the son of a bitch?"

He nodded. "I shot him. He's currently being treated at the hospital until he can be transported over to the jail to await trial."

"Thank God you're alright, Ed," Mrs. Gaines whispered, patting his arm gently.

Her kindness unleashed the floodgates of emotion that Edwin had been trying to keep at bay. Even after breaking his promise to keep Gaines safe, this woman cared about Edwin's wellbeing, too.

His whole body racked with sobs as the sadness poured out of him. No one in the family said anything, but they all moved to comfort him, even Rosie. She crawled her way into his lap and locked her arms around his neck. He let all the tears fall, succumbing to the guilt and hate and despair lodged inside his chest. Something inside of him had broken, but the Gaines family's sincerity in their concern for him might be enough to parse pieces back together. They made him feel like he belonged, and surprisingly, he liked it.

Using the back of his hand to wipe his face, Edwin sat up a little straighter and realized a doll was wedged into his chest. Rosie pulled back, taking the doll with her, and offered him a watery smile.

"What's this one's name?" he whispered to her.

She leaned into his ear and shared the name like a sacred secret.

He nodded at her. "It's a good name," he told her. He turned her around on his lap so that she faced the rest of the family and apologized yet again. No matter how he phrased the words, it never sounded like enough to convey his remorse.

Mrs. Gaines stood up and walked like someone in a trance towards her bedroom, Claire following after a glance from her father. Mr. Gaines nudged Rosie's knee and instructed her to go to her mother. He turned to Edwin, eyes blazing with anger, and asked, "Can you keep us informed? I want to know the moment this man is on trial."

"Absolutely," Edwin promised. "I'll keep you updated every step of the way. Someone will be reaching out to you soon to…to make funeral arrangements. The department will take care of everything…Kevin will be honored like he deserves." More tears clogged his throat as Edwin struggled to get the words out.

His partner's father nodded. "This wasn't your fault, Ed," he reminded him. "Don't blame yourself." Once more tears began to fall from Edwin's eyes, Mr. Gaines added, "You're family now. Never forget that because we won't."

FORTY-THREE

2011

Stella was no closer to making Avery Winslow speak than she was to being the next prima ballerina in the New York City Ballet. Other than the one time she attacked his penis, he remained as silent as a monk. She didn't dare to mutilate it further because even she could tell that she might have destroyed it beyond repair. Not that it mattered; it wasn't like the quadriplegic was getting a lot of action.

She was the one who felt impotent as the days wore on and there were no signs of Avery's spirit breaking, however. Although he occasionally still showed her a glimmer of fear or trepidation, it no longer gave her the thrill she craved. He did make an excellent test dummy as she practiced her suture skills, though. It took a while because her fingers were not accustomed to the grip the tools required, but it was an immense source of satisfaction to see Avery's teeth grinding under her clumsy care.

One day as she lingered outside the employee lounge to avoid the Barbie nurses, she overheard a conversation that shifted her perspective. They were discussing the recent death of a patient who had an allergy to Benadryl; the poor man had been given a dose after going into anaphylactic shock from digesting an almond and the dose proved to be lethal. It was administered intravenously, resulting in an instantaneous death.

Until then Stella had never considered the possibility of injecting something into Avery's IV. Technically she was supposed to have cleaned the injection site and replace the bandage every few days, but that had never happened. A nurse tended to go in and rotate the IV site every few months to give each vein a bit of a break, but ever since word got out that Room 216 was Stella's special project, no one had bothered with it. It created the perfect opportunity for her to push her experiments one step further.

The trickier part would be accessing the drugs. They were locked in a room behind the nurse's station that only nurses and pharmacists could open with a swipe of their badge. Plus, she realized, she needed to ensure nothing she injected could actually kill him—that would definitely raise some questions she was not prepared to answer.

"Mary!" Stella sang out when her supervisor stepped off the elevator. The high pitch to her voice should have been a dead giveaway that something was off. Mary definitely noticed because her eyebrows met her hairline. She passed through the security checkpoint and nodded to the guard on duty, keeping her eyes on Stella at the nurse's station.

Stella held out one of the two Starbucks cups in her hands.

"I grabbed you a coffee this morning on my way into work," Stella offered. She smiled and had to stop herself from rubbing her cheeks as they strained against the unfamiliar stretch.

Mary huffed, part laugh, part incredulity. "Am I being pranked? Is there poison in this?" She took a grateful sip from the cup despite her comment and snatched her clipboard from behind the desk.

Stella laughed as though Mary said something incredibly witty. "Poison's not really my style," she deadpanned. Inspiration set in and she quickly followed with, "But if I became a nurse like you, maybe I could save you if you were poisoned!"

Her statement hung in the air so long Stella wasn't sure if Mary even heard her. After shuffling through several charts and handing Room 216 to Stella, Mary pushed her glasses on top of her head. "Wait—are you saying you're thinking about nursing school?"

"Um, yeah. I mean—yeah. Yeah, I'm thinking of applying for nursing school," Stella stammered. She couldn't believe Mary was buying into her bullshit, but if this served as a way in, so be it.

Mary's face split into a wide grin. "That's FANTASTIC!" she bellowed. Without warning, she crumpled Stella into a bone-crushing hug. Stella would need the jaws of life to get her out of it.

The situation called for Stella to lay it on thick. She needed her boss to eat out of the palm of her hand. "Well, ever since we had that conversation about my evaluation, you've just really inspired me," Stella clarified. "'Reach for the stars' and all that." She withdrew from Mary's grasp and smoothed her hair back into place.

Her boss's excitement couldn't be contained. She giddily clapped her hands and took Stella by the shoulders. "You can shadow me today and I'll show you how great it can be!"

Thankfully Mary's happiness overshadowed Stella's grimace, which she quickly concealed behind another fake smile. Events could not have played out better if Stella had planned them.

For the next several hours, Stella followed Mary around like a shadow. She tried to simper at the right moments, flatter Mary as much as possible, and asked an obscene number of questions about everything she could think of in order to distract her from the nature of her real inquiry: getting into the locked medicine closet.

Mary, for her part, soaked it up like a wet sponge. The more Stella peppered her with hypotheticals, the bolder Mary became in what she shared with her.

That was how, by late afternoon, Stella could be found measuring out a syringe of liquid Tylenol for a patient on the other side of the floor. The man had a severe allergy to ibuprofen and morphine, and after the Benadryl scare from the day before, all the nurses were taking added precautions when administering medication. As Mary gleefully pointed out, Stella could be her second set of eyes for the patient's chart.

Stella was always one to seize an opportunity. "You've had such a rough day," she commented offhandedly. "I can't believe this is what you do here!"

Mary beamed and waved her off. "It's nothing!"

"No, it's really something! Why don't you go ahead and take a seat so you can get caught up on some of those charts?" Stella gestured to the large stack of paperwork on Mary's clipboard and did her best to appear sympathetic.

She could tell Mary was mulling it over because of the way she chewed on her bottom lip. "I've gotta put this back," she stalled, gesturing towards the tray with the medication on it.

Stella held up both hands. "Allow me! You've earned the break!"

The bottom lip all but disappeared. "I mean, I would be right there at the nurse's station," Mary hedged. "It's not like anything could happen while you put this away." She eyed the patient as if he was judging her choice. "Alright, here is my badge real quick. Just throw this away in the hazard bin inside, okay?"

Stella accepted Mary's badge while internally waving pom poms. The fact that Mary fell for it would make her laugh until she cried when she got home tonight, but for now she would have to act fast. She swiped the badge and noted that the hazard bin was on the opposite wall. There were several rows of medicine along all four walls, two of which looked to be liquid form to inject into an IV. Just beneath those shelves were new syringes in clear plastic. Stella grabbed a few and snatched a few bottles of medicine at random. She slipped it all into her back pockets since her oversized scrub top hit almost mid-thigh.

She darted back out of the room just as quickly and handed Mary's badge back to her. Mary smiled at her absently before returning back to the charts in front of her.

"I'm gonna run to the restroom while I've got a chance," Stella said, hiking a thumb over her shoulder.

Mary nodded sagely. "Take the minute while you can. There's plenty of work ahead of us."

With a quick glance down the hall towards the security guard, Stella forced herself to walk at a normal pace as if she were headed to the bathroom. At the last second, she darted across the hall into Room 216. She released a slow breath once inside the threshold, the familiar barrier of solitude surrounding her. Avery merely glanced at her before returning his gaze to the ceiling. She smiled at him triumphantly anyway.

Stella angled the chair so that her back was to the door and hunched down over her cell phone. She withdrew three different medications from her back pocket and examined their labels closely, the tiny vials cold in her hand. One of them had already been opened, about half gone.

"Is it half empty or half full?" she asked the room. She smirked at her own joke.

The first medication identified it as a blood thinner. A quick Google search informed her that it wouldn't do anything to cause pain, but would simply make Avery Winslow bleed more.

"Like he needs any more of that," she muttered.

The second medication, the one that was already half empty, was actually an antinausea medication. Stella didn't want to waste it in Room 216 after reading about its uses and side effects on her web browser. She would keep it at home for her next hangover.

She typed in the final medication, resigning herself to further disappointment. Pulling medicine at random hadn't been a good idea, she realized, and the entire day may have been a lost cause.

"Methotrexate," Stella tested the word aloud. The website indicated it had been known to induce vomiting, swelling, and severe stomach pains, among other possible side effects. The medicine should only be used in moderation.

"Jackpot!" She grinned wickedly at Avery, pleased to see he was back to watching her. "Let's see if you're my rare occasion."

She stuck a long needle into the bottle, withdrawing twenty milliliters of the drug, and then inserted the needle into the IV port as she had seen Mary do all day. Taking a deep breath, she quickly plunged the syringe down.

The result was instantaneous. Avery Winslow's body began to shake violently, his chest heaving as his head swung from side to side. Tremors shook all the way down to his feet and his eyes rolled back in his head.

Spittle flew from his mouth while Stella watched in wide-eyed surprise. Winslow made a gurgling sound that turned her stomach. His heart rate shot up to the point that the monitor on the wall set off an alarm, but Stella dashed to the button before it could register at the nurse's station.

The seizure ended just as abruptly as it began. Avery's body settled back into the hard mattress of the hospital bed, sweat dripping down his face, with his eyes closed. His breathing became shallow and labored.

Stella paused for a few heartbeats to steady herself. Her adrenaline had spiked in fear and now she was unsure of what to do. She didn't expect a seizure like that, but now that she considered it, she had never experienced a seizure with a patient before. Could they cause brain damage? Would the doctor know what was going on the next time he came in?

Quickly, Stella forced Avery's face in her direction and pulled one eyelid open. His eyeball whirred in the socket before settling on her face. His other eye slowly opened and blinked rapidly as if he needed to focus his vision.

She let out a staggered breath of relief. That had been too close. She didn't want to join Malcolm Glasswell in prison.

She slumped over in the chair by his bed and pulled her long hair off her neck. After a few moments a tiny giggle escaped as she realized the risk had been for nothing. Avery Winslow still hadn't uttered a sound. She glanced up at him only to find his unsettling gaze back on her face, which led to more high pitched giggles. Suddenly she started laughing so hard tears ran down her face.

"Nothing will make you crack, will it?" Stella held the stitch in her side. "I'm either gonna kill you or die trying!"

The last tethers of her patience snapped and she stuffed her fist in her mouth to snuffle the cackles coming from her mouth. She had finally met an iron will to match her own, and it was in the form of a quadriplegic mute!

Coming down from her hormone rush, Stella finally felt her laughter die out. It was replaced with an insane urge to beat Avery at his own game. She couldn't let him win. This was her chance to prove to everyone that she was more than some troublemaking slut, that she was worthy of recognition and praise.

While it had started as an act of boredom and morphed into a questionable form of therapy, now Stella needed it as vindication. She deserved to be appreciated, treated with basic human decency at the very least, and if successfully making Avery Winslow speak was the only way to prove to everyone in the hospital that she deserved respect, so be it. Stella wouldn't stop until he was spitting out his life story.

Avery closed his eyes the moment her maniacal laughing stopped. For once, she didn't feel like waking him.

1990

Around four o'clock the next afternoon, Edwin answered the phone as if on autopilot. He had not been able to sleep and the pain behind his eyes from how hard he cried at the Gaines house had become a permanent fixture in his head. He couldn't shake the images from his mind that replayed Gaines' final moments on a loop, making him relive the horror over and over again.

The call came from a doctor from the hospital. Alessa woke up from surgery and asked for him. Could he come straight away?

Edwin jumped to his feet and ran to the bathroom to brush his teeth and splash some cold water on his face. Although he told Millhouse he intended to retire, Edwin wanted to see this case through to the end. Alessa was the key witness to provide the answers he needed.

Alessa wasn't in her hospital bed when Edwin entered the room, despite the nurse advising him of such. As a security precaution, there was an officer from the precinct at her door around the clock and he indicated no one went in or out in the past hour.

After doublechecking the bathroom, Edwin found Alessa huddling in the fetal position in the farthest corner of the room. He wasn't entirely sure how she managed to wedge herself down there given the bulk of the cast on her leg and both arms.

He reached down to help her up, but as soon as his fingertips brushed her arm she screamed out, "Don't touch me!" Her hazel eyes were wild, not seeing anything in the room.

Edwin's heart sank. As best as he could, he settled himself down on the floor across from her, then held his hands up in surrender. It took several seconds before she was able to shift her focus on him, but when she did, he could see her body slump back in relief. They sat in silence for a long time before Alessa cleared her throat.

"You found me." Her statement didn't seem to be directed at Edwin, but more a reminder to herself.

She cocked her head to one side as she stared at him and he realized every inch of visible skin was covered with bruising of some kind. He counted four bandages and at least two different lacerations that were sewn tightly with stitches in the small spaces of exposed skin between her hospital gown and the casts on her limbs. Her eyes were enormous in her face, once again returning to the wild fear from before.

Someone else entered the room and when Edwin craned his head over the hospital bed, he saw a female doctor in a white coat.

"I'm gonna go talk to her," he whispered to Alessa, but she didn't seem to hear him. She pulled her knees in tighter against her chest and rocked slightly with her eyes out of focus.

"Detective Greene, I am Dr. Lyle, one of Alessa's physicians here," the woman introduced herself. She held out her hand and grasped his firmly. "Could you step out into the hall with me for a moment? I don't think it's wise to discuss things in here."

Once the door clicked shut behind her, Dr. Lyle rounded on Edwin. "Sir, I'm the psychiatrist who came to provide an initial exam for Alessa. She has experienced extreme trauma and isn't ready to answer any questions about the investigation at this time." She frowned at him as though he had personally insulted her.

"I only came because the hospital called and said she was asking for me," Edwin countered. "I haven't asked her anything."

She nodded, somewhat appeased. "And will you promise to wait on questioning her until myself or one of my colleagues clears her? Alessa is in critical condition and is very unstable right now."

Edwin nodded as well. "I would never do anything that might further hurt a victim," he said delicately. "Do you know what all happened to her?"

Dr. Lyle only grimaced and handed him some of Alessa's paperwork. There were 12 pages total that listed broken bones, internal bleeding, and more. Edwin's stomach lurched reading what the poor woman had suffered. One condition in particular caught his eye.

"She's pregnant?" he blurted out, dumbfounded.

The doctor shook her head sadly. "It's too early to tell if this is a result of rape. We don't have any clear answers yet. In the meantime, due to her fragile mental state, we have not yet informed her of her pregnancy. There is still a very good chance that she could succumb to some of her internal injuries, and she must be monitored carefully."

Edwin agreed. "May I stay and sit with her?" he offered.

For once, Dr. Lyle smiled. "Yes, I think that would helpful. We contacted her parents, but they live in Tallahassee and don't know how soon they can be here. Alessa's team and I will keep you updated as we run more tests." She promptly turned on her heel and strode down the corridor, greeting the officer next to Alessa's hospital door as she passed.

When Edwin returned to the room, he found Alessa in the same huddled position on the floor, but her head fell back in sleep. Edwin didn't disturb her other than to gently wrap a blanket over her body. He hoped for her sake that she was free from nightmares like his.

CHAPTER
FORTY-FIVE

Mother had been right. She was always right. The world was indeed an evil place where demons roamed and dark magic poisoned the air. Otherwise, how could he be in such a predicament?

Duke had spent the last several days shifting through his thoughts as he stared at the ceiling. Doctors and nurses came in and out with different medications, asking questions, and prodding him with instruments. He ignored their queries and didn't even look at their faces to see who addressed him. At night, when he was truly alone, he tested his own limitations without any hindrance from someone carrying a pen and a clipboard. He had been pleased to discover he still had some mobility in his neck. He was able to turn his head on his own, though not enough to fully look over either shoulder. Still, it allowed him to examine his room a bit more, and knowing his surroundings slightly eased his anxiety.

Several police officers had been in to see him as well, but that was typically when he closed his eyes and pretended to sleep. Duke had yet to see Detective Greene again and he wasn't entirely sure how that made him feel. On the one hand, he wanted to confront the man who had ruined his life, but as Mother's voice echoed in his head, "evil only triumphs if you let it." This Greene guy would not be given the opportunity to inflict any more spells on Duke.

He hadn't answered a single question from anyone since the first day in the hospital. He couldn't fully explain why he didn't want to speak to anyone except that his senses were heightened on high alert. Instinct told him he was past the point of no return with how deeply he had sunk into their dark magic, so not speaking was another way to prevent them from adding fuel to their fire.

Mother never would've let him speak to this many outsiders anyway. No one bothered to tell him if she was alive or dead, and on the off chance that she was still alive and he got to see her again, Duke didn't want to disappoint her any more than he already had.

Bits of conversation floated around him constantly and Duke had learned how much his continued silence flummoxed the investigators. They couldn't understand it because they only considered medical reasons for his lack of speech, which led to more arguments with the doctors.

Duke had surmised that special accommodations were made for him because one day everyone scrambled about in a state of nervous energy as a judge entered the hospital room. A man in a brown suit with a small stain on his shirt advised him that he was being arraigned on two counts of aggravated kidnapping, one count of first degree murder, one count of second degree murder, and several counts of rape. Duke had no clue what any of that meant, or who the man was, so he opted to remain silent.

Throughout the proceeding, which was relatively quick, Duke learned that the man was named Howard Marginois and he was employed as a "public defender." Duke had the right to an attorney and since there was no indication that he had a bank account or any kind of real money, one had been appointed for him.

The term puzzled Duke even more. Defend him from what? He felt so frustrated at his own ignorance, but it seemed safer to keep his mouth shut and prevent them from realizing how simple-minded he must be.

The judge asked Duke several times if he understood what was happening. Duke simply turned his gaze back to the ceiling.

In his own desperation, Duke found himself wishing for Alessa. The sight of her face could calm any storm and right now, he was pretty sure he was ready to unleash a tornado. She belonged to him. Why could no one see that?! This was yet another obstacle that dark magic had presented to drive them apart.

Whoever believes in the Son has eternal life; whoever does not obey the Son shall not see life, but the wrath of God remains on him, Duke thought.

"We plead 'not guilty,' your Honor," Mr. Marginois stated, drawing Duke back to the present.

The judge then rattled off a date four months out and swept from the room. Most of the others followed, including the public defender, after clapping Duke on the shoulder with the promise that he would see him soon.

As the room cleared, Duke spotted Detective Greene leaning against the far wall, a pensive look on his face. The last person filed out of the room and the detective approached the hospital bed.

"I have the distinct honor to escort you to the prison hospital while you await trial," Greene said quietly. He looked as haggard as Duke felt, with large bags under his eyes and lines permanently etched between his brows. Yet there was also a sense of regret as he looked down at Duke.

The detective hesitated for a moment before withdrawing a small key from his pocket and unlocking the handcuff binding Duke's left arm to the bed rail. "Since there's really no need for this," he explained.

Two young men in scrubs entered the room and began to turn off monitors and disengage Duke from the various wires attached to his body. There was a brief sting as a needle was withdrawn from the crease of his elbow and then one of the men pushed Duke up to a sitting position by placing an arm behind his shoulder blades. The second man brought a wheelchair into the room and parked it next to the hospital bed so the two of them could transfer Duke into it. He had never felt so embarrassed or helpless. Having strange men touch him resembled the same feeling as when bugs crawled over him on the nights Mother locked him outside.

Detective Greene stood watching the entire time, keeping his attention on Duke's face. He absentmindedly swung the handcuffs around in his hands as though he needed to fidget with something in order to keep his mind from wandering.

Once Duke was settled in the chair and the detective signed paperwork the men handed to him, Detective Greene began pushing the chair out of the room. Three police officers flanked them as they exited the room, all of their faces stern with reproach and disgust. No one said a word as they wheeled him down a corridor to a set of glass doors.

There was a van parked outside that read Ohio Prison Association on the side, but it was surrounded by men holding large cameras with flashes that blinded him. They bellowed at him, "Look here! Look over here!"

Panic made his heart race because Duke didn't know what they were doing or why they were using cameras. Flashes went off everywhere at once, nearly blinding him, but he no longer had the use of his arms to block their light. Detective Greene tried to angle his body to keep Duke concealed from the photographers, but they simply moved around the detective for a different angle.

The two men in scrubs from earlier helped load Duke in his wheelchair into the back of the van while two of the police officers entered the front seats. Detective Greene advised the third officer to follow behind them in another vehicle since he was confident he could handle Duke on his own.

All too soon the van pulled away from the hospital, leaving the screaming photographers behind, and Duke's heart sank with the knowledge that he was getting further and further away from Alessa. If he could just see her one more time, just make her understand that everything he had done was for them! She couldn't possibly forsake him like this when he had done everything he could to prove his love. The punishments had finally been working—she was falling into the role of submission he required of her. Had all of that been in vain?

The detective sat beside him, continuing to idly twirl the handcuffs around his fingers. After several tense minutes, he cleared his throat and turned to Duke. "Are you ready to talk yet?" he asked.

Duke couldn't turn his head enough to face him and for the first time, he was glad of his limited mobility. He didn't want the detective to read anything in his expressions. Instead he stared straight ahead, his eyes burning a hole into the metal grate separating the two officers in front from the passengers in the back.

His silence didn't deter Detective Greene. "We found out all about you, you know," he taunted. "I know everything there is to know about you, Duke. All your secrets will be laid bare."

Duke felt his face flush. There was no way that could be true.

Greene sighed dramatically. "The only missing piece of the puzzle is where Harrison Pierce's body is located. You must have had a hand in that somehow seeing as we found his face in your dungeon."

Despite himself, Duke smirked at these words. A dungeon, indeed. Harrison Pierce's face was the least of Duke's troubles, at the moment. That man's fate had expired long ago.

Greene clearly noted the smirk, however, as he leaned forward to face Duke directly. "Where is Harrison Pierce's body? If you tell me where he is, perhaps we can work out a deal where you don't go see Old Sparky."

He had no clue what Greene meant. Old Sparky sounded like champagne from the roaring '20's. Why would Duke have to see anything again if he was in fact going to prison like Detective Greene had explained earlier? Duke had never read anything about jail or prison and didn't have the faintest idea what any of the legal jargon floating around for the past few weeks meant.

Duke allowed the silence to stretch on and thankfully, Detective Greene allowed the same. After what felt like hours, the van slowed to a stop in front of a massive gate surrounded by a stone wall. Barbed wire curled around the top and after a brief conversation between the driver and a guard at the gate, the van was permitted to pull through. Approximately twenty feet beyond the stone wall was another chain-link fence that was also topped with barbed wire. The van drove down a deeply rutted road another mile or so before they drove through a third and final fence. A large, square concrete building loomed ahead. Duke could see a few guards with guns walking outside. One lonely watch tower, a few stories over the roof of the building, hovered in the opposite corner. It made Duke's breath catch in his chest.

For the Lord hears the needy and does not despise his own people who are prisoners.

The next few days passed in a blur. He barely registered being transported from the van to what appeared to be his designated room. Once there, Duke was never allowed to leave it, and a bevy of guards, nurses, and housekeepers cycled in and out without saying a word to him. They laid him in a bed and left him alone. Almost a week had gone by before Howard Marginois, the public defender from the hospital, came to see him.

For once, Duke sat propped up like a doll as Mr. Marginois sat at a table across from him. The man introduced himself again and before Duke thought about it, he asked, "What are you defending the public from?"

Mr. Marginois laughed harshly. "Don't you know how the justice system works?"

Duke shook his head stiffly.

"Oh." Mr. Marginois stared at him for a few moments while he contemplated what to say. "Basically if you're charged with a crime, you get to have someone like me tell your side of the story. I have to make you look as good as I can so that you don't wind up on Death Row."

This confused Duke even further. "What is Death Row?"

Another harsh laugh followed this query. "Keep up the innocent routine, man, and I'll have you sailing out of here in no time." Mr. Marginois shuffled through some papers he pulled from his briefcase and started jotting down notes on a lined piece of paper.

"Now," he continued, "You have been offered a plea deal that would mean life in prison without parole as long as you provide the exact location of Harrison Pierce's body. That information is really your golden ticket, buddy. Keep playing it tight to the chest and they're not gonna touch you."

Duke's frustration mounted. "I don't even know what any of this means!" he burst out.

Mr. Marginois glanced back at the door behind him before leaning in over the table. "It means that as long as you keep your lips shut every time somebody talks to you, you get to stay alive."

His words echoed in Duke's ears, drowning out the roar of fear. Could he really be put to death for what had happened? Was this the dark magic winning? What would Mother say?

If Mr. Marginois truly had an obligation to present Duke in the best light possible, that would mean his advice was best. It would be more beneficial for Duke to remain silent than to say anything to the strangers that would continue to question him.

Mother wouldn't want Duke to associate with any of them. She would hate to see his predicament, but she would blame him for allowing himself to be caught up with strangers outside their home. Ultimately it was Duke's own fault for going into that coffee house all those months ago. Had he never met Alessa, none of this would be happening.

Alessa...he had barely allowed himself to think of her since leaving the hospital. He could never be reunited with her if these demons killed him, but perhaps it was more of her dark magic at work. She was an illusion driving him to madness, a siren worthy of the name. A defiant streak in him didn't want her to win. Her spell would not break him. Yet he wanted nothing more than to find himself sinking inside her to wash away all his pain. She would always be his salvation and his ruin.

It all circled back to the same choice. Reconciling himself to his decision, Duke's chin rose in determination. If he was truly going to beat them at their own game, he knew he had to fully commit and allow himself to succumb to the quiet. He allowed his mind to go blank, the silence encasing him like a tomb. Duke's lips formed a firm line, never to open again.

2011

With a heavy heart, Edwin parked his car in the back of the lot. This day was always rough for him, even twenty-one years later. So much had happened during that time, so much that his partner missed. Just six months ago Edwin sat in the second row of the chapel at little Rosie's wedding. Claire had given birth to her third child after completing her residency at a hospital in Anaheim. She was now a practicing oncologist and sent Edwin photos of her kids every month, which he displayed proudly on his living room wall. Her oldest, a boy named Kevin, had the same lopsided grin as his biological uncle, and loved to talk to "Uncle Edwin" on the phone about what it meant to be a police officer. The Gaineses kept their promise. Edwin was a treasured member of their family.

Edwin could still picture Gaines' face as the knife plunged into his neck and the image haunted his dreams. Although Edwin dreaded every visit, he would never stop commemorating this anniversary and ensuring that bastard remained locked up, unable to hurt another soul.

This visit, however, always brought a twinge of guilt, too. Of course the man couldn't hurt anyone else. Edwin had taken that ability from him permanently. A detail the media hyper-fixated on during the six months of the trial. He couldn't look back at that time of his life without breaking out in a cold sweat. Journalists camped outside his apartment for months, demanding he comment on his recklessness. Edwin was painted as a monster equivalent to that of the one who murdered his partner. Humanitarians argued that serving any kind of prison sentence was inhumane because Duke had already been punished enough, and in many ways, Edwin agreed with them. Ultimately it was watching Alessa suffer that convinced him he had done the right thing. No one should ever experience the trauma she had.

Sighing, Edwin braced himself for the strong emotions that were sure to come from exiting the vehicle. A large sign reading *Danberry Correctional Hospital: Ohio Prison Association* illuminated the space on his right.

The line through the security checkpoint was blessedly short and Edwin scrawled his name on the visitor log hurriedly. The guard presented his visitor pass and directed him to check in with the guard at the checkpoint on the designated floor. Edwin paced in the elevator, unable to calm his racing heart.

Every year was always the same. The anxiety, guilt, and sadness mixed in a cocktail that threatened to suffocate him. He hated the sight of this man, but he hated the thought of ignoring the anniversary of Gaines' death more than anything. All of the emotions would battle for control of his mind until he finally pulled out of the parking lot.

"Good morning, Ed," Mary, the charge nurse, greeted him as soon as he stepped off the elevator. "I expected you an hour ago."

Mary had been running the floor in this unit for the past seven years, working as a regular staff nurse for at least eight years prior to that. Although Edwin had never explained the significance of this date to her, she must have guessed its importance. If the visitor logs were to be believed, it was the only day Duke ever had anyone come to see him. Once news spread that Duke wouldn't speak, reporters stopped trying to get the coveted "inside scoop." The man was just as much of a loner now as he had been two decades ago.

"Yeah, I had a late start this morning," Edwin agreed. She offered him a small smile before handing him a cup of coffee, which he accepted gratefully. "How's our boy doing?"

Mary shrugged. "The same as ever, I suppose. We have a nurse's aide who has been assigned to him for the past several weeks due to a disciplinary issue. She hasn't brought anything to my attention." She nodded down the hall. "He's still in the same room, 216."

Edwin smelled cigarettes as he approached the room. For the first time ever, there was someone else occupying his usual chair in the small prison hospital room. He cleared his throat loudly to announce his presence.

A young woman visibly started and leapt out of the seat as though electrocuted. Her dark, wavy hair whipped around as she turned to face him. The shock registered on her face could only be called a paltry imitation of his own, however, because the face staring back at him could have been the identical twin of Alessa Meinken. Her eyes were even shaped the same, matching Alessa's deep hazel perfectly.

"Who are you?" the look-alike demanded. Her tone had a haughty quality, someone who had been accustomed to making demands and fighting as a result. She clutched something in the pocket of her scrub top and blocked the bed.

It's almost like she's guarding Duke, Edwin thought.

Edwin realized his jaw hung open and snapped it shut. "I'm Edwin Greene, the detective who worked on that man's case. What's your name?"

He knew immediately from her reaction that he had said the wrong thing. As soon as she heard the word "detective" her entire facial expression glossed over and the rigidity in her body disappeared. She hastily grabbed a pile of rags on the floor, all of which looked as if they had blood on them, and swept from the room.

Without so much as a glance in Duke's direction, Edwin followed her. The girl headed in the opposite direction of the nurse's station, towards the employee rooms. "Stop!" he ordered.

Surprisingly, the girl halted. She slowly turned around, keeping her eyes on the floor and subtly positioning the rags behind her hip. Even from a few feet away Edwin could notice her shaking. She didn't say anything, but waited expectantly.

"What is your name?" he barked.

The effort pained her enough that she winced. "Stella Andover," she said quietly through gritted teeth.

Hearing that name struck like a sucker punch to the gut. What kind of divine intervention happened here?

Without meaning to, Edwin stammered, "That's impossible." He thought he was going to be sick.

She finally looked up at him, clearly confused as to what he meant. "Excuse me? It's impossible that I have my own name?"

Edwin could barely breathe. He was transported back to the day almost 20 years ago when he entered the social worker's office at the Children's Services building, a wailing bundle in his arms. The worker had been gruff, recognizing his badge and barely asking questions. She took the tiny baby from him and immediately soothed her in a way that Edwin envied. He had no paternal instincts, apparently.

"Does she have a name?" the social worker had asked.

Gaines' family was fresh on his mind. Stifling back tears at little Rosie's despair over the loss of her brother, Edwin thought of the doll she had kept grasped to her chest all those months during the course of the trial. "Stella," he had replied. "The baby's name is Stella."

The social worker had nodded, asked for his signature for the release of custody, and whisked the baby out of sight. He had never followed up after they called to notify him a few days later of her initial placement with the Andover family. He had assumed she was simply adopted and cared for, never knowing her true parentage.

Now he stared in horror at the young woman in front of him. There was no mistaking her features, which matched her mother's down to her height. She looked to be the right age, too.

This was who had been assigned to Duke's room all this time?

"I knew your mother," Edwin stated slowly. He swallowed hard before adding, "And your father."

Stella stepped back a few paces, utter shock upon her face. Her eyes welled with tears in a way that mimicked her mother so strongly, it was all Edwin could do to stop himself from holding his arms out to her.

"I don't have any parents," she whispered. Her chest heaved as she fought off a panic attack.

Edwin's stomach sank at these words. She had never been adopted, then. But she had also never been told anything about where she truly came from. Perhaps that was a good thing. Did Edwin want to ruin that for her? He could only imagine how shocking it would be to learn you were a product of rape, let alone that your father was imprisoned for it. Was it his place to even tell her?

He held up his hands in defeat and began backing away from her. He wasn't prepared for this. No matter what, this wasn't the right time or place to destroy the poor girl's life.

"Wait!" she called after him.

Edwin didn't wait. He needed to escape this moment before all the horrors of that fateful day came back to haunt him.

FORTY-SEVEN

2011

The only words Stella could process were *what the fuck*. The phrase looped on repeat in her head so loud she wanted to cover her ears to drown out the noise. What the fuck had just happened? She had never in her life had anyone mention her birth parents. Foster families and group homes were all she had ever known until she was emancipated at sixteen.

Digging around in the past to find her parents' identities had never appealed to her. They were gone, so why would it matter to her who they were? She'd seen far too many kids waste away with hopeless longing or endless searching that never led to fruition to find birth parents. It never changed the status quo, so Stella couldn't spend a second thinking about it.

Now, however, the harsh reality that her birth parents existed smacked her in check. She knew the man had answers. The recognition in his face when he first saw her wasn't something he could fake. But how had he known them? He said he was a detective…did that mean her parents were involved in a crime? She needed to know.

She realized she still held a bloody mess of rags in one hand from her most recent experiment. Avery Winslow might be missing a toenail or two at the moment.

"Shit!" she exclaimed, realization dawning on her. That man was a detective trying to visit her patient and she was standing in the hallway holding bloody proof of her crimes in her hands. She darted down the hall to housekeeping, thanking whatever gods she knew when she saw an unoccupied cart outside the laundry room. Pulling the top couple of sheets out, Stella stuff the crimson rags down and threw the other bedding on top.

Heart pounding, she ran back to Room 216. Edwin Greene was standing outside it, head pressed against the wall, one hand gripping his chest. His eyes were closed and didn't open at her approach.

Stella jerked on the leather of his bomber jacket. "Are you okay?"

He started into a standing position and Stella saw silent tears running down his face. He looked so lost and confused as his eyes pored over her face.

Yet there was a kindness to his expression that she hadn't seen in many years. Her gut warned her that he didn't have good information to share. No one ever looked at her like that if they had something decent to say.

"I'm not sure if this is the right place to talk to you," he said in a low voice.

"This is the only place you can ever fucking find me," she growled at him. If he thought he was going to wimp out now that he had dropped a bombshell on her, Stella would lose it.

He looked helpless. "Is there a lounge or something we can go to? I can answer your questions, but it might be better for you if you had some privacy." He added this last bit with a cringe, as though he suspected Stella was the sort of person who didn't react well to bad news. Or maybe the news would simply be that bad.

She rolled her eyes, but gestured for him to follow her. She led him to the break room and slumped into a chair at the table. Stella couldn't believe her luck at the room being empty. No writes up from scaring co-workers out of the break room might've been the only silver lining.

Edwin sat in the chair across from her and began fidgeting with his hands. His discomfort only angered her even more. He was a damn detective! Wasn't he used to crappy situations?

After another minute of awkward silence, Edwin cleared his throat again and focused his attention on her face. "Do you know anything about your birth?"

Stella shook her head. "I was in and out of foster homes my whole life. None of them wanted me because I was a 'difficult child.'" She used air quotations with her fingers at this phrase. It still made her cringe. "I never asked about how I got there or what happened to my parents because it didn't change anything."

He began to reach his hand across the table towards hers, but seemed to think better of it and stopped himself at the last second. "I was the detective who turned you over to Children's Services," Edwin explained. "I named you 'Stella.' Your mother was one of the victims in the last case I ever worked before I retired. Actually, she was part of the reason I chose to retire," he clarified. "She died shortly after you were born."

There was a hint of meaning behind these words, but Stella could barely make it out over the ringing in her ears. Her mother had been the victim of some kind of crime. And now she was dead. She hadn't even named her own daughter, a fucking cop had to do it.

"A victim of what?" Stella pointedly asked. Her voice sounded tight to her own ears.

Edwin grimaced. "Your mother was abducted, beaten, and…raped." The last word came out in a rush. He knew what kind of revelation that had to be, but he told her anyway. Stella respected him for that alone. Most people tried to sugarcoat the truth to avoid setting off her temper. What he was implicitly stating, while dancing around the bush like a cowboy at a square dance was that she, Stella, was a product of rape. She had been conceived during an act of pure evil, a baby born of darkness and horror.

Which meant her father was the devil incarnate, capable of rendering unspeakable acts on the innocent, introducing suffering and misery on those who least deserved it. Her father was a monster in every form of the word. And she had inherited that darkness, her genes yielding to her own monster within. She was a sick case study in the nature versus nurture debate.

"How did she die?" Stella couldn't explain why it made a difference to her now. What would matter if her birth father was a murderer in addition to being a rapist? Yet she needed to know.

He paused before answering, "She took her own life. I don't think she could handle the trauma of what she experienced."

This response was worse, if anything. Her mother had a choice. And she chose to kill herself rather than face what happened to her. Rather than saving Stella from the hardships that her mother knew firsthand the world had to offer.

Bile rose in her throat. Her birth mother had been weak. Yes, she had been raped and beaten. But how many times had that happened to Stella? Stella always dusted herself off and went on with life. Even when tragedy struck, there had to be something beyond it. You couldn't give up. Infuriated, Stella couldn't believe that her mother chose to die rather than save herself.

It wasn't that Stella believed her mother might have chosen to keep her rather than putting her up for adoption. Stella didn't blame her for that choice. Stella had plenty of opportunities to be adopted, after all, and it never happened anyway. Being alone didn't matter to her. It was the failure to triumph over her own demons that made Stella rage at the woman. As an infant, she needed her mother to be strong and instead her mother gave in to her own suffering. It was pathetic.

Was this really all her gene pool amounted to? A rapist and a coward? No wonder Stella was so fucked up. She never even had a chance at living a normal life or being a normal person because DNA predisposed her for chaos. She was doomed to live a life of misery before she took her first breath. What chance did she honestly have of making things better when this is what she came from?

Suddenly Stella felt as though the walls were closing in on her. The air became thick and heavy, and she couldn't make her lungs function properly. She needed to get as far away from Detective Edwin Greene as possible.

Stumbling slightly, she pushed her chair back as far as she could from the table and ran out the door.

FORTY-EIGHT

2011

Edwin rose from his chair as Stella sprinted from the room. He knew it wouldn't be wise for him to follow her. He wasn't the kind of man who offered comfort to a woman when she was emotional. Hell, he barely handled his own emotions.

Still, he hated the anguish he saw in her face after he told her the truth. What a terrible thing to tell her. Watching Stella's face crumble transported him back to the day when Alessa received the results of the paternity test. Alessa wore a similar facial expression of abject horror and disbelief.

And it wasn't even the worst of what Stella had to learn, he realized. There was far more to the story that would absolutely destroy her.

Edwin left the room and followed the hallway back to the alcove for Room 216. It was time to face Duke.

Just as it had every year, the room offered no sound or indication of life. The lights had been shut off, something Edwin hadn't noticed when he arrived earlier, and the only glow came from the modest window at the top of the far wall. He flipped the light switch on and received his second jolt of alarm that morning.

Duke's eyes stood larger than life in his gaunt face. His skin had gone sallow, clinging to cheek bones that protruded more than Edwin had ever seen. The man's hair sat unkempt and wild, jutting out at odd angles from his head. There was far more gray in it than there had been the year before, and his beard now hung in a shaggy and matted mess. He looked fearful as Edwin entered, searching over Edwin's shoulder for a movement or presence beyond.

An unsettling unease washed over Edwin. He had visited Duke every year on this date for over twenty years, the anniversary of that fateful day when Edwin had finally apprehended him and watched in terror as Duke stole Gaines' life before Edwin could stop him. Yet in all that time, every visit had been uneventful. Duke never said a word, always focusing his attention on the dirty patchwork ceiling above while Edwin repeated his promise to keep the man behind bars. This was the first time that Duke looked unhealthy, disheveled, or showed any kind of reaction to Edwin's existence. Something was obviously wrong.

Duke opened his mouth as though he wanted to say something, another act the retired detective had never seen before. Edwin leaned in closer and noticed there was no hospital gown collar poking out above the blanket.

Cautiously, he pulled the blanket down a few inches to check and gasped aloud. Small holes pockmarked Duke's chest, some still festering and raw, some faded and puckered into scabs. A sour odor emanated from him that grew worse as Edwin lifted the blanket. It was worse than body odor, something far more rancid, like mold that had been left baking in the sun.

"What happened?" Edwin asked incredulously. He didn't know much about medicine and had been blessed with rather good health, even now approaching 75-years-old. The marks on Duke's chest didn't look like any illness Edwin recognized. In fact, the more that he looked at them, the more they looked like…

"Are these burn marks?!" The lingering cigarette stench in the air made sense if Duke's chest had been used as a human ashtray.

Edwin rose and started to call for someone when thundering behind him alerted him to Stella's return. She observed the scene with a mixture of horror and guilt.

It was the guilt that stifled Edwin's cry for help. Turning back to the bed, he gently pulled the blanket off Duke's body and wheezed. There were scars along both arms and torso, some still bleeding lightly, evidence of their fresh state. Words had been carved into the flesh on both thighs; one had small amounts of green pus clustered at the swollen skin. He was missing toenails on both feet. The same small, circular burn marks dotted the length of his body.

However, the worst part was inarguably what was left of Duke's penis. Bloody, yellow crust formed at the head where the catheter emerged, but the rest was an amalgamation of flesh, muscle, and blood, swollen and bruised dark purple in places. It barely resembled a reproductive organ anymore.

Edwin fought the urge to vomit, though his gag reflex worked against him. He threw the blanket back over Duke's body and stepped backward, knocking Stella to the floor.

"What have you done?" he stammered. He pulled her off the ground and grabbed her firmly by both shoulders.

The challenge in her eyes appalled him. Not a single shred of remorse shone through her eyes—Alessa's eyes. Stella didn't answer him, nor did she protest at his vice-like grip on her arms.

"He got what he deserved," Stella countered. "The bastard did far worse or he wouldn't still be here!" Her chin rose in defiance, a hint of arrogance tracing her features.

He released her and she backed way until she hit the doorway. Without thinking about it, Edwin stated, "This man is your father."

Stella paused for a moment before a maniacal laugh escaped her throat. "Avery Winslow is *not* my father," she replied. She continued to giggle in a way that told him she viewed the entire thing as a joke. Like the whole scenario could have been an episode on a reality pranking tv show.

He shook his head hard. "When I apprehended this man twenty-one years ago, he went by the name Duke, a nickname used by his mother.

We found his birth certificate when we searched the house, and it was the only thing that provided his legal name. That's why everything for his trial says 'Avery Winslow,'" Edwin explained. "He killed my partner right in front of me before I was able to catch him and save your mother. He had her locked in a storm bunker underneath his house."

At this, Edwin turned to look at Duke. This was a part of the story that Duke never knew. "Your mother was pregnant at the time, after he had raped her repeatedly for months. She committed suicide a few days after you were born, while Duke was on trial for murder, rape, and kidnapping. I took you from her arms myself, Stella."

Duke's eyes had widened to the size of half dollars as his eyes darted frantically from Edwin to Stella. Any color that had been there before was now drained from his face.

Stella, on the other hand, turned a faint shade of green and teetered on the spot, threatening to fall again. She clutched the door frame for support and brushed the hair from her face. "It's not true," she breathed. "It's not true!" Moving as if in a daze, she stumbled out of the room.

Edwin took a step to go after her and stopped short at Duke's voice, raspy from over two decades' worth of silence. He faltered on the words like the use of his tongue was foreign to him now.

After a couple failed attempts, Duke finally managed. "Sinners always pay the price," he ground out.

The words struck Edwin like a blow. Words he could never forget, words that still echoed in his head every night as he woke up in a cold sweat from the nightmares he could not shake. An involuntary shiver ran down his spine.

He found Stella squatting against the wall a few feet from the door. Her hands had pulled her hair back as her elbows rested on her knees. There was a dazed, vacant look in her eyes, staring into space. She rose as he came to stand beside her, bottom lip quivering.

What she had done was horrific. That kind of mutilation was indicative of a budding psychopath.

Like father, like daughter, Edwin thought wryly.

She showed no signs of remorse or regret. In fact, it was apparent how much she prided herself on torturing the helpless man confined to a hospital bed. Edwin suspected she enjoyed every moment of it.

His oath to serve and protect swirled around his head, along with his obligation to report this disaster to the police. He glanced at the guard not even fifteen feet away who read a magazine at the security check-point. Edwin should alert that man right now and get Stella in handcuffs immediately. His own hands twitched towards the back of his belt where his cuffs had hung for over thirty years, muscle memory triggered by the threat of danger. Stella had been unchecked for who knew how long and could escalate at any moment.

Yet she didn't look like a woman on the verge of becoming unhinged. She looked as though the world had slipped out from under her and she desperately sought a place to land. Without meaning to, he placed a hand on her elbow to steady her.

Reproachful hazel eyes glared at him with the touch, but she didn't draw away. She continued to waver on the edge of uncertainty.

Mary came around the corner of the nurse's station and briefly glanced in their direction. They must have created an odd tableau because Mary stopped on her heels and pulled her glasses from her face. She approached them warily, clipboard clasped at her chest. "Stella," she said lightly. "What's the matter, hon?"

Stella didn't respond. There was no indication she even heard Mary's question, so Mary rounded on Edwin.

"What's going on?" she spat angrily.

A loaded question, indeed. Edwin blinked in surprise as he saw the ghostlike forms of Gaines and Shelley hovering momentarily behind Mary. What *was* going on?

Duke was a monster, there was no question about that. He kidnapped two adults in broad daylight and killed Harrison Pierce out of some twisted form of jealousy. The police never found Pierce's body despite almost a year of searching around Duke's property. For months he raped Alessa Meinken while wearing her dead fiancé's skin. Nobody in their right mind could fathom something so grue-some. It had been enough to turn Edwin's stomach over when they found the remains of Pierce's face on the table Alessa had been forced to eat at.

Edwin knew from conversations with her doctors after she was rescued that Alessa had been beaten repeatedly. Duke had caused internal injuries that even surgery couldn't properly heal. Her bones couldn't reset in some places because they had been broken so many times without recovery.

Alessa only held onto life long enough to bring her daughter into the world. And having that physical tie to the devil who tore her life apart had been too much for her. It was too much pain for one person to endure, Edwin had realized much later.

Now the manifestation of that horrendous coupling stood before him in all the sadistic glory of her father. Stella had desecrated Avery Winslow, a quadriplegic, when he was in his most vulnerable, powerless state. He was a patient in a correctional hospital, yet his own mutism created the perfect storm for Stella to torture him without notice or reprimand. She had willingly cut and burned him as he lay helpless beneath her.

What had Mary told him when he first arrived—Stella had been the only one assigned to his case for weeks? The man had no one to protect him or intervene and in a twisted way, that was Edwin's own fault. He was the one who shot a man in the back as he ran away. Did it matter that Duke was a criminal when Edwin shot him? Did that justify Edwin's actions?

What would his actions be now? Alessa had suffered in more ways than should be humanly possible for months as Duke ravaged her body and decimated her psyche. Now Duke experienced the same, with Fate assigning his executioner as his own flesh and blood, the daughter he had never known he lost. There was no way Stella's face hadn't served as its own kind of torture. Her mother's features were inscrutable as she sliced Duke from his neck down for days on end. Had that damaged Duke's mind the same way as he had done to Alessa when he raped her with another man's skin on his face?

Perspiration broke out on his forehead as Edwin agonized over what to do. If Gaines were here, he would surely tell Edwin to report Stella immediately and have her arrested on the spot. His protective instincts would override any other possible decision, forever determined to capture all the monsters in existence. He would point out that Stella was only just getting started and would likely continue to torture a helpless man before moving on to other victims. Gaines wouldn't hesitate to arrest her, Edwin was certain.

Shelley, the only devil equal to Gaines' angel, would surely argue the opposite. Bastards like Avery Winslow deserved to be broken, beaten, and pissed on. Knowing Shelley, he would have offered to be the first to provide the punishment. An eye for an eye was still a viable argument in criminal laws around the United States. Edwin was justified in his desire to see Duke face true retribution. Having around the clock care in a hospital the taxpayers provided was not nearly harsh enough for what the asshole deserved. Shelley would have advocated for Edwin to walk away as if nothing had changed. Edwin felt just as sure of that as he was of Gaines' opinion.

Edwin swallowed slowly, sneaking a glance in Stella's direction. Her whole body stood tensely, waiting for Edwin's reaction. He didn't think she was so much as breathing at the moment.

Shrugging, he turned his attention back to Mary. "Someone has to pay the price," Edwin said.

Bonus Chapter

BONUS SCENE
1990

Alessa

Alessa rounded the counter with a hot pot of fresh coffee in hand and paused abruptly when she saw one of the regulars sitting at his usual table. Nobody at the coffee shop knew the man's name, but she'd been the victim of more than one joke session after everyone noticed how closely the man watched her. His eyes were always so unsettling, staring intensely as if he wanted to peel back her flesh and see what lay underneath.

The man never allowed anyone to wait on him except Alessa. At first everyone at Groundbreaking stepped up, fearing that the guy's obsession might not be quite so harmless, but after his blatant refusal to interact with any other employees, the coffee shop owner wasn't willing to risk a bad customer experience.

Alessa steeled her shoulders back, plastering a fake smile on her face, and approached his table. After a while, when her gut instincts finally calmed down, Alessa decided to befriend the man. Judging from their limited interactions, she gathered that he didn't converse with many people, and her heart sank to imagine how lonely the man must feel. If only he would stop staring at her so she didn't always feel so queasy in his presence!

"Good morning. Care to try our new brown sugar espresso?" she asked him.

Rather than reply, the man's eyes darted from her hairline all the way down to the swell of her breasts. Before Alessa had time to redirect his attention, his penetrating eyes flicked back up to hers.

"Just a black coffee, please," he requested. Although it was customary for people to order at the counter and then grab their drinks once their numbers were called, the first time he placed an order, he hadn't known what the order on the receipt meant. He sat there for hours without picking up his coffee that sat directly in front of him on the counter. All of her coworkers laughed at his mistake, but Alessa took pity on him and began taking his order right from the table.

"Coming right up," she assured him.

The man held out a five dollar bill, and she had to repress a shudder as the tips of his fingers brushed her hand. Alessa's eyes widened as she noted the way his nostrils flared at their contact, almost like it exhilarated him. She gave herself an internal shake at such a ridiculous idea.

"Oooh, how's your stalker today?" Colin teased when she returned behind the counter after refilling a couple mugs for other patrons.

Alessa flashed him a look of annoyance. "Stop that, he might hear you!" she hissed. Even with her back turned, she could feel the man's eyes watching her every move.

Colin snorted. "Maybe he should hear me. The dude certainly needs the wake up call."

Turning to the register, Alessa entered the customer's order for black coffee and got his change from the cash till. "I think he's just lonely. Maybe I remind him of a sister or cousin that he lost."

Her friend shook his head sadly. "I love that you continue to see the world through rose tinted glasses, Lessie, but let's be real here. That man is obsessed with you!"

Alessa didn't bother to reply. Setting a full coffee mug down on a tray, she returned to the dining area and set it down in front of the man, who kept his gaze trained on her face.

"You know, I might get in trouble if I keep handling your transactions from out here," Alessa said as she plopped his change down on the table next to the mug. "You're supposed to order up at the register."

"Will you be the one to take my order?" he asked. Even his voice sounded intense, like her answer determined life or death.

The inflection in his tone made her pause again. She did her best to act casually, though her stomach fluttered with anxiety. "If I'm able to."

"You should always be able to," the man countered.

The fluttering increased. She laughed it off. "Plain, black coffee is nothing special. Anybody here can do it."

After a long pause, during which the man's eyes never left hers, at last he nodded once. "I'll keep that in mind…Alessa."

It was the first time he'd ever said her name, and this time the anxious flutters in her stomach blossomed into downright panic. Goosebumps broke out along her arms. He said her name as a caress, like it was the most beautiful word in the dictionary.

Slowly she backed away, her tight smile still stretching her cheeks. As soon as she reached the counter, Alessa darted into the back room and let out a ragged exhale.

Colin popped his head in. "Everything okay?"

Of course everything was fine. Alessa was just overreacting after watching that dreadful slasher movie with Mallory last night. Fitful nightmares kept her awake half the night and now she was picturing that innocent customer as a murdering lunatic for no good reason.

She brushed her hair back from her face and offered Colin the same tight smile from the dining room. "Yep. Everything's great."

"Good," he joked, "because someone spilled their mocha everywhere and it's your turn to mop."

Alessa smiled for real this time. "Be right there."

I just have to get through this shift, she reminded herself. *Harrison comes home soon and then everything will go back to normal.*

With that comforting thought in mind, Alessa began to fill the mop bucket, images of eerie customers and sadistic killers long gone.

ACKNOWLEDGMENTS

This book has evolved so much over the past few years, and I have to thank everyone who has been there with me from the beginning. I never would have written this book without you, Kat, so thank you for being such a cheerleader in my early writing days. I love you all the more for it.

Many thanks to my family, including all my extended aunts, uncles, and cousins, who keep reading my books and supporting my work. I never realized I had so many people in my corner until I took a giant leap of faith.

My forever number one, Toni Baker, who still champions this book like it's in the running for a Pulitzer Prize, everybody should be so lucky as to have a friend like you. Meeting you was Fate and it changed the course of my literary life.

A special thank you to Andy Payne for the new cover. It fits the theme of this book so much better now. I appreciate your artistry so much!

My book club girlies, Toni, Ky, Heather, Lisa, Brooke, Renee, and Maddie, thank you for taking part in this wild ride with me. Everyday this whole "author" thing throws me another curveball, yet y'all continue to ride the waves with me. I'm sorry for all the times I made you cry, but hopefully I've made you laugh just as often.

To all the LEO's out there trying to keep us safe, a sincere thank you.

My Starlet readers who take a chance on indie authors like me make this all worth it. Every time I see a good review I'm reminded of what makes all the hard days of writer's block worth it.

And last but not least, to Jack, Tristan, and Cael, my very reasons for existence. I'm sorry how much writing this book took out of me. I know I asked for a lot when I sacrificed my old career to be a writer, but you've been right there by my side the entire time. I love all three of you so, so much, and I hope you're proud of me. The greatest gift in life is being your mom.

Even though they aren't alive to read this book and would definitely hate it if they did, I have to acknowledge that this book, and all my other books, never would have happened without the early encouragement of my grandparents. From taking me to the library every week, to buying me an infinite amount of notebooks to jot down ideas, to encouraging me to share the stories in my head…you both changed my life in funda-mental ways, and I'm sorry I never had the chance to tell you while you were alive.

-SG

ABOUT THE AUTHOR

Samantha Gail is a former Probation Parole Officer who supervised sex offenders before deciding she needed more happily ever after's and decided to write books instead. Her work falls in multiple genres, primarily thrillers, romances, and fantasies. She currently resides in Ohio with her three children and three fur babies.

ALSO BY SAMANTHA GAIL

Thrillers:

Number One Fan

Romances:

Behind My Hazel Eyes

Full Circle

Count Me In

From Santa, With Love

Romantasies:

Epoch

Era

TURN THE PAGE FOR THE FIRST CHAPTER IN SAMANTHA GAIL'S LATEST
THRILLER, NUMBER ONE FAN

NUMBER ONE FAN

a novel

SAMANTHA GAIL

CHAPTER ONE

"Dolian Crawford is set to become the world's highest grossing actor of all time at just 29 years old."
-People Magazine

Imogen Reilly did not have time for the security guard to question her press badge. Did it look a little manhandled after her brother, Austin, played with it? Absolutely. But that certainly didn't mean the guard had the right to deny her access to the press box at the red carpet premiere of Dolian Crawford's latest movie.

This was the kind of opportunity most journalists and celebrity bloggers salivated over. It was her chance to finally get up close and personal with the entertainment industry, which was exactly the kind of break she needed. Her weekly blog, *Hollywood Unmasked*, hadn't exactly "unmasked" anything yet.

The homunculus guard standing in front of her now, blocking her entry, with his black sunglasses, bulging biceps, and angry scowl prevented her from doing just that.

"Sir, is there any update?" Imogen asked him. The first security officer took her badge into some unknown "computer area" to look up her credentials and left the man-troll behind to scan in press badges as journalists and preferred paparazzi arrived.

The man's face was immovable as he turned her way before rotating back to the next guest.

Imogen already felt completely out of place because of her clothes. She had never been to a movie premiere before and assumed she needed to dress as though she herself belonged in Hollywood rather than as the broke reporter living in a tiny, five floor walk up in Compton with her mother and adult brother with Down Syndrome that she was. Everyone else who walked up so far appeared more casual and muted, wearing comfortable shoes, solid colors, and the same overcaffeinated, harried look.

People tended to write her off because she looked so much younger than her 22 years, with a waif-like figure and far below average height. Her soft brown eyes and tawny hair were unremarkable. And thanks to her nonexistent budget, Imogen shopped in the juniors' clearance section more often than not. A great choice when you're trying to stretch a dollar into five. An unforgivable choice when you're trying to blend in with the Hollywood elite as a celebrity gossip blogger.

That was why she wore the only dress she owned that made her look old enough to attend a red carpet premiere without a chaperone. However, a Barbie pink vinyl mini-dress purchased for a dollar at a dead hippie's garage sale in the Valley made her look far more appropriate on Hollywood Boulevard than anywhere else. Add that to her only decent pair of heels, large white platforms that made her tall enough to reach the top shelf at the grocery store, and Imogen stuck out like a sore thumb. She tried to pair it with diamond (aka cubic zirconia) hoops and silver bangle bracelets up both arms, but neither did much to soften the harshness of her appearance.

More than one entering press member sent her a scathing look of annoyance.

Finally, the first guard who took her badge returned. "She's good," he said incredulously to his partner.

"Thank you!" Imogen sang out, snatching the badge from his outstretched hand and shuffling as fast as she could down the makeshift hallway leading to the press box.